THE RABBI IN THE ATTIC

THE
RABBI
IN THE
ATTIC

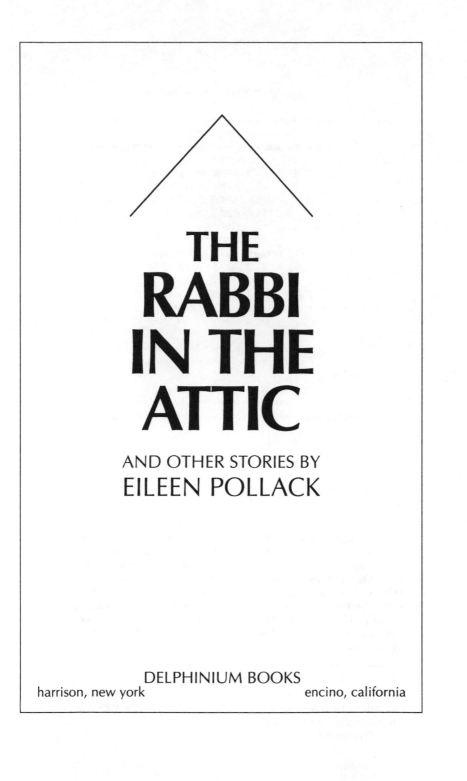

THE RABBI IN THE ATTIC

AND OTHER STORIES BY
EILEEN POLLACK

DELPHINIUM BOOKS
harrison, new york   encino, california

Library of Congress Cataloging-in-Publication Data
Pollack, Eileen, 1956–
The rabbi in the attic and other stories / by Eileen Pollack.
p. cm.
ISBN 0–671–74260–4 : $19.95
I. Title.
PS3566.04795R3   1991
813'.54—dc20   91-7507
CIP

First Edition   All rights reserved
10 9 8 7 6 5 4 3 2 1

Published by Delphinium Books, Inc.
20 Pleasant Ridge Road
Harrison, N.Y. 10528

Distributed by Simon & Schuster
Printed in the United States of America

Jacket art by Milton Charles
Text design by Milton Charles
Production services by Blaze International Productions, Inc.

These stories first appeared in slightly different form in the following magazines:

"PAST, FUTURE, ELSEWHERE," Ploughshares; "XYLEM AND PHLOEM," The Literary Review; "THE VANITY OF SMALL DIFFERENCES," Prairie Schooner (reprinted from Prairie Schooner, by permission of University of Nebraska Press. Copyright 1987 University of Nebraska Press); "THE AIR CONDITIONER" (previously titled "A WORLD WITHOUT JUDGES"), The Iowa Journal of Literary Studies; "A SENSE OF AESTHETICS," (New England Review); "THE FIFTH SEASON," Playgirl (September 1986); "HOW CAN YOU TELL ME," Sojourner (July 1986); "THE VALUE OF DIAMONDS," The Agni Review "NEVERSINK," Ploughshares.

To my parents

ACKNOWLEDGMENTS

I would like to thank James A. Michener and the Copernicus Society of America for their generous support of my work. A fellowship from the University of Iowa also helped me immeasurably in writing these stories.

I am deeply indebted to the friends, relatives and teachers whose encouragement has sustained me during the past ten years. In particular, I am grateful to Marcie Hershman, Adam Schwartz, Gary Glickman and Gish Jen for their advice on my manuscripts; to my agent, Mary Jack Wald, for her patience and faith; and, above all, to Noah and Tom, for their love.

It is the same with the act of love. To know that this man who is hungry and thirsty really exists as much as I do—that is enough, the rest follows of itself.

—Simone Weil

CONTENTS

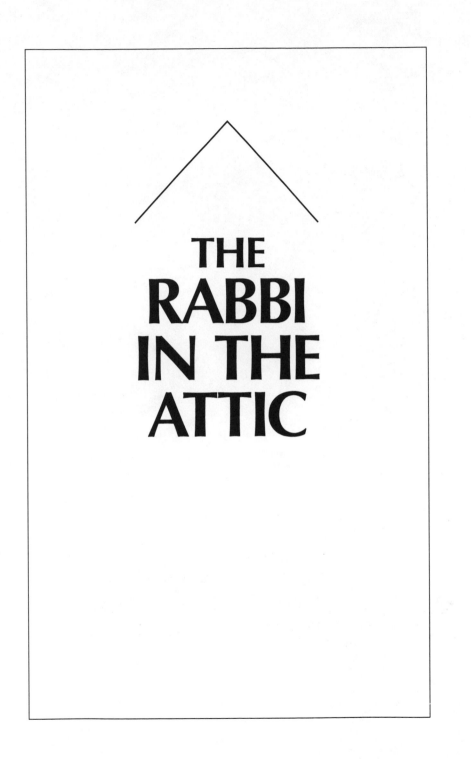

THE
RABBI
IN THE
ATTIC

PAST,
FUTURE,
ELSEWHERE

PAST,
FUTURE,
ELSEWHERE

Barbarians were churning the farms into mud, polluting our wells. I had to escape.

This was 1969. I was thirteen years old, hiding in the basement. The frayed plastic webbing of my father's green lounge chair tickled my legs, which were only half-shaped—curved here, blockish there. A photo from *Life* was taped to the window: the earth from the porthole of *Apollo 11*. The light from behind made the earth luminescent and nearly 3-D. It stared down upon me, a cloudy blue eye.

The hot-water heater kindled itself in the basement's black heart.

"We have liftoff," I said. "We have separation," and I could feel gravity slipping away.

Then the heater stopped roaring.

"We have engine malfunction"—my voice stony calm—"I repeat, engine failure." I arose from the lounge chair, swimming my arms. With my ear to the tank, which was warm as a chest, I heard: tickticktick sigh, tickticktick, slosh, like the slosh of a stomach. I rubbed the tank, soothed it. The tank purred. Then: BROOSH.

"Thank God," Houston said. "The experts were stumped. How did you fix it?"

Though I was too old to be playing such games, the lounge chair seemed to beckon as a first love might do. Other girls had crushes on Dylan, Mick Jagger, but these men seemed danger-

3

ous. I dreamed of Neil Armstrong in his white padded suit. We'd be bounding through the vacuum of an unexplored planet when a meteor would sizzle through the sky toward his head. I would push him to safety and be crushed in his place. As he carried me tenderly back to the ship I would smile at him weakly, but the pain would win out and—

"Judith, are you down there?"

My parents were standing at the top of the stairs. The door to the kitchen was open behind them so a shaft of gold light cut through the murk. This made me feel lonely, as a small fish must feel in the shadowy depths.

"I'm thinking," I said. "Can't a person find anywhere in this whole house to think?"

Ordinarily my parents would have flinched at that word. Because I was smart and obviously destined to travel much farther from Bethel than they had, they made the mistake of treating me as though I were older and braver and needed no help understanding the world. But this time my mother wanted to know: Was anything wrong? Was I feeling . . . unwell? She whispered to my father, and since both of them were small, they looked then like children daring each other to venture downstairs.

"It isn't that!" I said, and wished for a blanket to cover my body, which stretched out before me with its shadowy landscape of breasts, ribs, belly, and knees.

All week the newspaper had been lurid with photos of the naked barbarians who had overrun our town—sunbathing on car hoods, dancing to music at this "festival" of theirs—but an inky strip covered each interesting part, like a gag on a mouth. I scraped at those boxes, even turned the page over to see from the other side what was masked on the front. I felt the reporters had found out my future and printed it here, but blotted the facts I most wanted to know. At the same time I wished that every inch of those bodies had been blackened with ink. The editors were publishing my most shameful secret with only this slight disguise of my features, and the secret was this: that I wasn't destined to leap on the moon, but to grovel in mud.

I took out a book from under my chair. "I'm reading," I said.

"You'll ruin your eyes, sweetheart," my father clucked sadly. "If you'd only take that paper off the window . . ."

"That's not just some 'paper.' That's our planet. That's *Earth*. Don't you know anything?"

My father retreated, noiseless as the dust motes that chased around his head. (My father was a milkman; he woke up at three and was so schooled in silence that floorboards wouldn't whimper under his feet, doorjambs wouldn't click.)

"We're leaving the house." My mother moved down a few steps, as though the stairs were a seesaw and she had to balance her husband's retreat. "Some of us are going to try to get food to those poor hungry children."

Two days before, when the roads were still open, she'd made her weekly shopping trip to Monticello (the only stores in Bethel sold beef jerky, beer and Eskimo pies) and had found the streets jumbled with barbarians foraging for something to eat.

"I even saw people I know selling water," she said. "At a dollar a glass!"

It surprised me that anyone would think to sell water. I still regarded water, air, food and land, even gas for the car, as the barest supplies that God could hand out so all human beings could make do on Earth, the way that a teacher would supply every student with paper and books on the first day of class. But my mother's condemnation seemed far too harsh.

"Do you blame them?" I asked. "I wouldn't let those animals drink from our *hose*."

This clearly disturbed her. My mother was plump, with a plump olive face, and her moods were as easy to read as a child's. When she was disturbed everything drooped—her hair, cheeks and bosom. Even her ankle socks seemed to droop. "I know they look strange . . . but I couldn't help but think they might be my own daughter and wouldn't I want somebody else's mother to feed her?"

I was sick with the insult. "If they were too stupid to bring enough food you should let them go hungry."

"Well foolish or not," my mother admitted, "I saw this young woman . . . She was seven months pregnant. She couldn't find her husband and he had the money. . . ."

"Don't tell me you gave this woman our groceries!" I would have been embarrassed to be so naive, but my mother wore her innocence as proudly as she'd wear a suit of bright armor; if she thought well of everyone, this would deflect all ugly intentions and no one would hurt her.

"Only the bread," she told me. "And cheese. She didn't want the chicken, it was too hard to cook."

And so we had eaten our Friday-night supper without any hallah, sucking our chicken-bones to amplified shrieks—"Give me an *F!* Give me a *U!"*—as though Satan himself were holding a pep rally just down the road.

After dessert we turned on the news, and we saw on the screen not an invasion of a faraway hamlet, but our own town this night, not a mob of barbarians screaming outside the Pentagon, but outside our house. On the black-and-white set, even the film taken earlier that day was lifeless as ash so it seemed these intruders had stolen the color from the land near our home. Then the newscast went live and the cameras flew over the field near the stage, which looked like a pond writhing with newts in the beam from a flashlight, and the chop of the rotors over our roof was the same *chop-chop-chop* as from the TV. These were our roofs, our fields, the mob down the road, and my insides went cold with the helplessness of watching yourself in a dream while you drop from a cliff.

The next day my parents had walked to the synagogue, pretending they saw nothing amiss, as Lot and his wife must have tried to look casual as they picked their way through the outskirts of Sodom. And after the service they'd found out how bad the emergency was—not a few hungry kids, but a few hundred thousand. The people in charge of the festival hadn't prepared for such crowds. All the highways were choked. No food could get through. No one had wanted these young people here, but seeing they *were* here . . .

So now, Sunday morning, my father and the other delivery-men at Yasgur's were planning to carry milk to the hordes, while my mother would help the Ladies Hadassah spread tuna on white bread, which nuns from the convent would deliver on foot.

"Great," I said, "fine, go feed the enemy, only leave me alone."

"Well, if you're sure," and I heard the stairs sigh, watched the light disappear.

I was cruel to my parents and I've lived to regret this, but then I felt justified, as though *I* were the parent, yanking the arms of a daughter and son who insisted on watching a worm on the ground while a yellow-haired comet blazed through the sky. Just four weeks before, while I'd been transfixed by two men in white leaping and landing with infinite grace on the moon—on the *moon*—my mother had wandered in from the kitchen, rubbing a glass. "Judith," she said, "this is historic," but she hadn't stopped rubbing that glass with her cloth, and my father kept saying, "Such brave men these are," shaking his head in a way that implied "not brave but foolish," while to me the Messiah had announced the new kingdom. We were no longer animals whose feet had to stick in the muck of the earth. We could leap on the moon. Anything was possible. But how could I argue with people who preferred a lifetime in orbit around this small town—delivering milk, shopping and cooking and washing the pots—to a flight to the moon?

That night as I lay on my back on the lawn, plotting my course by connecting the stars, I whispered: "I'm coming." And the next day I bicycled up and down hills to Monticello and took out some books about space travel, asteroids, gravity, light. I didn't understand a word that I read but I felt their mere presence would help me become an astronaut sooner: I could stack these thick books, climb on top, brush the stars.

Then a boy I knew, Steven, informed me that astronauts had to be men, in perfect condition, with 20-20 eyesight so their glasses wouldn't float from their faces or break at critical times. After that I spent hours chinning myself from the beams in the basement until my arms grew as muscular as any boy's, though I later found out no boy would have felt that fullness and throb as he pulled himself up, thighs pressed, legs crossed. I did twenty push-ups, palms damp on the floor, jumped rope, *slap,*

slap, slap. I spun in a circle so I *would not* throw up when tested for the job in that bucket in Houston. And I strengthened my sight by taking off my glasses, lifting a corner of the photo on the window and straining to read the signs on the farm stand in the Dwyers' front yard.

"Sweet corn," I said, though I knew I was reading from common sense—what else would the Dwyers be advertising at this time of year? I was squinting to make out the next line of print—tomatoes? peas? melons?—when an ambulance pulled up and Steven jumped out. He trotted up our drive like an overwound toy. He was always so scrubbed that he appeared to be wearing a doctor's white coat even when dressed in corduroy trousers and a polo shirt for school. Now that he actually was wearing a lab coat (it hung past his knees) he was blindingly clean.

Of everyone I knew only Steven had dreams as intense as my own. This must have been why I had let him lead me one night to the Little League field behind the Jewish cemetery and why I had confided what others would have mocked, pointing to illustrate at the pulsing full moon. That's when he said that astronauts weren't allowed to wear glasses, and he lifted off mine, leaned down, kissed my cheek where it merged with my nose, and told me his dream of mapping each neuron and cell in the brain so he could determine the tangles and gaps that made people ill, as his mother was ill. Using his thumb, he traced the long nerve from my toes to my thigh, and I knew he was using his dream as a reason to touch me this way, but right then the moon seemed very far-off, a circle of ice, and his fingers were warm.

"You're cold," Steven said. "It's like you're not here."

And even as I lay there I thought this was true. I regarded my body as some sort of spaceship that workmen were building, and I wasn't yet sure I could trust their designs, things might go wrong—already I'd witnessed that leaking of blood—so I hadn't decided if I should move in. I saw myself lying on the bleachers near Steven, long, narrow, stiff, with an angular chin, eyes pale as slugs with my glasses removed.

"Even your hair is cold," Steven said as his hand fell away.

Now he bent to my window, and his face gleamed behind the earth like a bulb. "You've got to come quick. The kids at the concert are really getting hurt. They're all on bad trips. Someone called up my father and asked him to come."

Steven's father was a surgeon, a swaggering man though just five-foot-two. Dr. Rock ran the hospital as if any question of his authority would be punished by traction, so no one objected when he let his son Steven take blood from patients, give shots and stitch wounds, though Steven had only just turned fifteen.

"I'll be his assistant," Steven said now, "and you can help *me*. But you have to hurry up. It took us all morning just to get this far and we still have the hardest half-mile to go. We can't leave the ambulance, it's full of supplies."

"How could you?" I said. "They're our enemies, remember? These people think you can cure a disease by rubbing a certain part of your foot! They don't like machines. They don't like *computers*. You can't reach the moon without a computer! If they want to louse up their minds with those drugs, why don't you let them?"

His expression was blank, as though he had never heard this before, and I realized he hadn't; I'd been the one who'd done all the talking and he'd only nodded to humor this girl he wanted to kiss.

"It's a great chance to practice. Maybe I'll get to help my dad operate."

The ambulance whined.

"Sure you won't come?"

I shook my head no.

"Well, if you do, he said we'd be working in some kind of tent." And he trotted away.

With Steven's departure the cellar seemed twice as dim as before. I lay on the lounge chair. The air was so heavy I felt I was lying smothered beneath a big, musty cow. With my book on my chest I daydreamed that I'd left this planet behind—it was charred and defiled, and I was the last civilized being, in a ship so advanced that I would lack nothing, except somewhere to land, and someone to greet me when I returned.

"Guess no one's home." A voice from outside, or maybe a dream.

"Hey, trick or treat!" A reedy voice, singsong. "Give us some food or we'll give you a trick!"

"Shit, man, I'm hungry." This voice was deep, its edges were rough. "Can't you just smell that food? Bourgeois fuckin' pigs, hiding in the dark and stuffing their faces while the people are eating berries and shit. Let's liberate the food. Food for the people!"

And I charged up the stairs the way that a sleeper will bolt from her bed swinging her arms to ward off a dream before she wakes up and knows where she is, so I found myself standing with nothing but a book and a flimsy screen door protecting me from three starving barbarians.

The smallest was scraggly, with a beard like a goat's. He was shirtless, in cut-offs and small muddy sneakers. The second was a black man with a square-cut black beard in a dozen thin braids, each laced with gold. The biggest barbarian was shaggy, unkempt, but even in my fear I could sense something sweet and harmless about him, a circus bear fed on popcorn and nuts. He had on a jumpsuit; the patch on the chest was embroidered with RUFE. His feet were enormous and hair sprouted from his toe joints.

"Jesus, we scared her," the goat-boy was saying. "We didn't mean to scare you. Jesus, we'd never . . . We were kidding around. Pretending to be these tough guys, you know?"

The black one said, "Shit. We just need a phone. Fitz here, Fitzgibbon"—he pointed to the goat-boy—"was on his way home when we shanghaied him here. His poor momma must be shitless by now so we thought he could call."

"And then we smelled food," the goat-boy said, wistful. "We thought maybe your parents would give us some food."

I kept the door locked, my book poised to strike. Who'd believe that a barbarian cared if his mother knew where he was? But they did seem upset, as though the Three Stooges had realized their slapstick had really hurt someone. I hadn't had time to put on my glasses and this made them blurry, less capable of harm.

"Well, then, come on," the bearish one said. "Can't you see that we've frightened her out of her gourd?" His accent was Southern, his tongue thick and slow as a bear's tongue would be. It struck me as right that a bear should be Southern—I suppose that the bears in some Walt Disney movie had spoken like this, and bears were slow-witted and crude in a way I'd grown up thinking Southern men were. But I couldn't figure out . . . Didn't Southern men hate black men? Didn't they hang them from trees?

The bear swiped his friend's arm and I almost expected to see bloody claw marks. "Imagine just can't you if some big, ugly fella with braids in his beard showed up at *your* door? You figure your sister should welcome him in?"

"Braids? Hey, I . . . Shit." He touched his beard. "Shit. There was this girl, and she asked if she couldn't put braids in my beard, and I said why not, it would help kill the time. Just a game, man, you know? Don't you ever play games? Don't you ever dress up in your momma's high heels?"

This was too much to tolerate. "I have better things to do."

"Can see that," the bear said. He narrowed his eyes and recited the title of the book I was holding. "*Gravitational Theory.* That's awful heavy reading for someone your age."

"How would *you* know," I asked.

"Sure he knows," chimed the goat-boy. "At Princeton they call him the Astrophys Whiz."

This didn't take me in. None of the astronauts *I'd* ever seen would walk around barefoot, though I had seen Neil Armstrong wearing a jump suit.

"Don't let the hair fool you." The goat-boy was grinning. "I mean, think of Einstein. Now *he* was a mess."

"And you two?" I sneered, "I guess you're both Einsteins?"

"Jesus no," said the goat-boy. "Do you think we'd do anything as practical as that? Leon here"—he pointed—"when Leon grows up he's going to be a pure mathematician."

"Pure as the snow! Pure as the rain!" Leon crossed his white T-shirt. "And Fitz here's a classicist," though I had no idea what a classicist was. "Fitz, do your shit, man. Show her how useless a classicist is."

And the goat-boy threw back his skinny neck and recited—
no, sang—a poem in a language I didn't understand, though I
did feel the poetry, like the gallop of horses, and the goat-boy
kept singing until I was hypnotized and let down my book.

"Sorry to have troubled you." The bear turned to leave.
"We'll just go next door."

"Oh no," I said quickly, "the Dwyers have Dobermans and
old Mr. Dwyer said he'd turn the dogs loose. . . ." I stopped
there, ashamed to remember that I had once been in favor of
old Mr. Dwyer siccing his dogs on any barbarian who came
near his farm. "You can use the phone here."

"You're sure of that?" the bear said. "If you'd rather we
didn't . . ."

He thought I was scared!

"All right, if you're sure. Fitz can go in, and Leon and me,
we'll stay on the porch."

The goat-boy pawed his sneakers to scrape off the mud. If he
meant to slice me open and paint the walls red he wouldn't be
so careful to clean off his shoes. I lifted the latch.

"It's a big house," he said as we walked through the foyer. "I
grew up in the city, we just had two rooms."

We got to the kitchen and I watched him dial 0.

"Yes, thank you, ma'am, I'd like to place a call, long-
distance, collect, to Mrs. Anne Fitzgibbon from her son Timo-
thy."

When his mother got on I could tell she'd been crazy from
fright where he was.

"Yes, Mom. I'm sure, Mom. I really didn't mean to give you
such grief but this was my first chance to get to a phone." He
tried to assure her that he was all right, getting plenty to eat, so
his words made me feel like a kidnapper who had treated him
badly and forced him to lie to his mother at gunpoint.

He hung up the phone. "What a wonderful smell." He sniffed
with his mouth. "I'll bet you had chicken. I smell pickles . . .
and potatoes . . . I even smell your mother."

"*I* don't smell anything." I was horrified that anyone should
say our house smelled; most of our neighbors wore the odor of
their barnyards like ratty old coats they couldn't stand to part

with, but my family took pride in how often we bathed, how the kitchen floor shone.

The goat-boy said, "A person can't smell her own house. You need an outsider. Someone who's trained. Archaeology, see? When you dig up some ruins you have to be able to sniff out the food the people once ate there, what sort of clothes and perfume they wore, how they treated their slaves."

I knew he was lying, but believed him enough to feel sad that no one would stand here and sniff and know I had lived. And I nearly believed he could sniff out my future, as he'd sniffed out the past. I wanted to ask: Would I go to the moon? Or would the barbarians destroy the world first?

We reached the front door. Leon and the bear stood up and stretched.

"I could make you some sandwiches."

"Oh, we don't want to bother—"

"No, it's okay. You just stay here."

I ran to the kitchen. We didn't have much food, but I found a few slices of stale pumpernickel bread and a jar of peanut butter. And honey. I thought that a bear would like honey. So I spread that on too.

The barbarians stuffed their mouths with these sandwiches, then they couldn't say a word.

"W-w-w-w," moaned Leon, "w-water," and I thought of the hose, but I ran off and got them glasses of milk.

"Ahh," said the goat-boy. He lifted his glass. "Milk fit for gods." And I had to laugh because he and Leon had milky white rings encircling their mouths; they didn't look like gods but surprised little boys. The two seemed offended, but they glanced at each other and swiped at their mouths with the backs of their hands.

"I don't suppose you'd know a place we could wash at?" The bearish one stood and yanked down his jump suit where it caught in his crotch. "Some swimming hole nearby?"

"Yeah," Leon said, "I sure as shit could go for a swim."

"There's a pond," I said, happy to have the right answer, though sorry to think they would soon leave my porch.

Leon wrinkled his nose. "Not some little cow pond covered

with green shit and pissed in by about a half-million hippies like the cow pond back there?"

"No, this one's big, and the water's really clean." I flushed with the arrogance of access to places that strangers couldn't find. Then I realized these strangers wouldn't be able to find the pond without me. "I could show you," I said, then wished that I hadn't.

"That would be awful nice," the bear said, and smiled. "Then you and I can talk about gravity. That is, if you want."

"Just a minute," I said, and ran to the cellar to put on my glasses, so when I came back I saw all three clearly, their pimples and dirt, the pores where the beard hairs poked through their skin, and this made them seem less frightening, and more.

"Follow me," I said. And I led our parade down a trail through the woods; it seemed the cool air had fled the barbarians and was trembling here beneath this camouflage of leaves. The trail passed a tractor whose tires had been used for archery practice. I felt someone draw the metallic tip of one of those arrows down my neck, down my spine, but I turned and saw no one except for the goat-boy, who was sniffing the air and skipping a little, and the other two behind him.

When we got to the pond I heard Leon whistle.

"Shit, look at that. In Newark, man . . . shit."

I didn't understand. This was only the pond down the road from my house. Then I saw it as a boy from a city might see it, and if I'd accused the barbarians of stealing the color from Bethel, they gave it back doubly, once right-side up and again upside down. Every orange salamander and blue darning needle signaled me like some code from beyond.

The goat-boy and Leon stripped to their undershorts, then dove in long arcs, came up again and started to race, one heavy black arm and one scrawny pale arm rising and falling, the gold-threaded braids of Leon's beard floating out from his chin like some intricate lure.

"Hmm, I'm afraid . . ." The bearish one was fiddling with the zipper of his jump suit.

"Afraid of the water?" I asked.

"No, afraid I don't have any underwear."

"I won't look," I promised, though I found when he started to pull down his zipper I couldn't turn away. As he stepped from the jump suit I expected to see a heavy black rectangle blocking his crotch. Instead, what I saw was my first naked man, layered in fur so he seemed like an animal, a burly brown bear. Poking from the pouch that hung between his legs was a separate little animal—a baby, a pet, like a baby kangaroo peeking out shyly and waving its arm. And what I felt then wasn't love at first sight, but my first sight of love, of what it could mean to love someone else, a stranger, not family, and how risky this was, loving a pitifully weak, naked man.

He clumsily paddled out a few yards, furry bum in the air. "Don't you want to come in? Water's just right."

I shook my head no. "I don't have a suit," though this was ridiculous—neither did he. And the way that he looked at my body just then made me want to disclaim it: "That body's not mine, I haven't moved in." But I knew that I had, though I didn't feel at home yet, its corners still dark, its workings mysterious.

He was standing in the shallows up to his waist, slapping the water as a bear tries to slap a fish onto shore. This made the reflections of the trees and sky shimmer, then shatter to fragments of green, blue and white, which were fragmented further by the drops on my glasses.

The goat-boy and Leon dragged themselves, dripping, onto the rocks to warm in the sun. "Man, don't those lizards have the right idea?" And they both fell asleep.

Grumbling because the stones cut his feet, the bear hobbled through the shallows. He sprawled by my side, draping his jump suit over his middle.

"I'm lying here naked and you don't know my name." He held out a paw. "Meyer Rabinowitz, pleased to meet you."

"Not Rufe?"

"Rufe? Oh yeah, this." He plucked at the jump suit. "Guess somewheres outside Atlanta, Georgia, a fella named Rufe is pumping gas naked."

"You're Jewish. And Southern." None of our relatives lived farther south than Paramus, New Jersey.

"If your mind can't stretch over those two categories, you'll

never be a physicist. You've got to be able to imagine a thing"—
the word came out *thang*—"being two thangs at once."

"A physicist? Who said I'd want to be that? Is that what you
are? I thought they said you were some kind of astronaut."

"That's all right," he said. "Even my mother can't keep it
straight. The difference is this: An astronaut goes up there,
flying in space, but an astrophysicist only *thinks* about going,
what the trip would be like."

"You never leave Earth?"

"A fat guy like me? Besides, I got asthma."

I was very disappointed, but glad that I hadn't really believed
this was a man who could pass NASA's test. "It doesn't make
sense. I don't understand how you think about space. What do
you think about?"

"For now I just think about whatever my professors tell me to
think about. But later . . . I mean, when I'm out on my own
. . ." He leaned forward, excited, and his jump suit slipped a
little, exposing his navel; its pattern resembled the continents
and oceans dividing the earth. "What I'd really like to think
about is what it's like living in higher dimensions."

I'd been fooled after all. "You're not talking science. You're
talking the way the barbarians talk."

"Barbarians?"

I waved my hand toward the dairy.

He wagged his head, laughing. "That what you call them?
How come 'barbarians'?"

"We learned it in school. The barbarians came down and
took over Europe and except for the monks there, nobody read.
They kept science alive while the vandals outside their caves
pillaged and sacked."

"That what you think? You're really afraid of those hippies
out there? You're an awful strange kid."

I should have felt strange then. I had felt strange all my life.
I'd had the premonition I would never have allies, except false
ones like Steven. But now I could see I was part of a team, and
though our team, the monks, might be greatly outnumbered, I
wouldn't have to fight the barbarians alone.

"Guess I'd better tell you about higher dimensions, in case

it's all up to you." He slid down the rock. His toe stirred the pond. "It's this way," he said. "Suppose you had left a note for your parents: 'I went for a swim, and if you come looking here's where I'll be.' "

The example seemed ominous. Was he trying to say that I had been foolish not to leave such a note?

"Well, you'd need three dimensions to say where you were, three dimensions in *space*. And you'd have to let them know *when* you would be here or they'd miss you entirely. You and your parents would pass through each other in space-time, now wouldn't you?"

I guessed that we would and this made me feel sad, like Dorothy in Oz when she'd seen Auntie Em in the witch's glass ball and called out her name, "Auntie Em, Auntie Em," but hadn't been able to make her aunt hear.

"It's like this," he said, using a stone to draw on the rock the way little girls draw boards for hopscotch. When he finished I saw two ice cream cones with their pointy ends touching.

"See this point here?" Meyer placed his finger where the ice cream cones met. "That's us, here and now. And all this up here"—rubbing his finger on the right-side-up cone—"that's our future, okay? All the places and times we'd be able to reach moving at any speed slower than light. Because no one can ever go faster than light. You must have read that."

Although I had read this, the equations that proved it were a dense drape of lace that I could not peer through to the reasons beyond, and so, in my ignorance, I was free to believe that once I got up there I would show they were wrong, my rocket would tear that paper-thin curtain, that barrier of light.

I nodded. "I read it."

"But you think maybe somehow *you'll* find a way to go faster than light?"

I shrugged. I didn't want him to think I was boasting.

He snorted. "Okay. Everyone thinks that. But you'll find out you're wrong. This is the only future you'll have. And this cone back here, this cone's our past. And all of this other stuff, outside the cones, all this is elsewhere."

"Elsewhere?" I said.

"Sure," Meyer said. "Out here is elsewhere, the places you and I can't ever reach, can't ever have been, because even if we traveled fast as a light beam all our born days, that's far as we'd get."

I still felt defiant. "How do they know?"

"Because there are limits. Who knows, maybe angels can live out in elsewhere, but people can only live in the past, or the future, or now." He seemed to be thinking aloud for my benefit and this eased the frustration of having to travel slower than light. "Animals, I suppose, can just live in now, we're ahead of them there. People at least can imagine what it's like to live out in elsewhere. At least we have that."

I was going to ask him to help me imagine what elsewhere was like, but a cough tore the stillness. The goat-boy and Leon had awakened, I saw, and were passing a cigarette back and forth, back and forth. I was stunned by this intimacy. Then something—the smell, like some bittersweet flower, or the curve of their cheeks as they sucked at the smoke—shocked me the way that seeing a movie star in person can shock.

"But they're smart guys!" I said. "Leon knows math."

He hunched his big shoulders. "Smart guys do dumb thangs. Leon thinks it helps him visualize thangs like imaginary numbers. And Fitz, well, he likes it, he can't seem to stop."

I suddenly glimpsed the future and it had no Fitz in it. His mother was weeping, haunting this rock and weeping for a son who had killed himself smoking too much marijuana.

"Why are you here?" I asked Meyer brusquely.

"You mean, why are the three of us here at this pond?"

"No, I mean all of you. Why did you come?"

"Me? I don't know. The music, I suppose. I needed a rest before the next term. I like the outdoors. And I figure it's good to pack in as many thangs as you can before you're too old. Some of them, like Fitz, they came for the ride. And a few of them were hoping to find somethang . . . big. I guess they found that. Somethang big, somethang pure. You know what you see when you look at the moon? You think it's all right to spend your whole life trying to get there, it's so big and pure? That's how they feel. They don't even see the mud that they're sitting in. They found somethang pure."

"Does that mean they'll *stay*?"

He laughed. "I don't think so. No matter how stoned you are, you can't ignore the mud and the stink and the hunger for more than a while. Not if you're human. You can't live in elsewhere, you can't live in a vacuum, and you can't live in squalor with a smile on your face much more than a week."

My relief didn't last long. He asked me politely if I'd please turn my head, and when I looked back he was standing and dressed.

"Hey, don't y'all think we should go?" he shouted to the others. "Don't want to miss Hendrix. That's why I came." Then he turned back to me. "You've been very kind." He held out his hands and lifted me up. "Don't look so glum. World's not so big. We could meet again."

I wanted to set a place and a time, all four dimensions, so I'd know he'd be waiting and the years wouldn't feel long. But before I could say this, Leon had bowed and the goat-boy had kissed the back of my hand and all three had left.

I must have found my way back to the house, lain brooding on my lounge chair, but no events marked the passage of time so those hours are lost. I only remember when my parents returned. I heard noise in the kitchen and went up to join them.

"I've a mind to press charges!" My father was rifling the drawer by the sink. "The cowards!" he said. He took out the Band-Aids and slammed the drawer shut. This noise from my father was as shocking as speech from a mute would have been. He handed the box of Band-Aids to my mother, who was slumped on a stool, and that's when I noticed that her checked blouse was ripped. A safety pin held the pieces together, but a slice of bright pink brassiere still winked through.

"How did you do that?"

"There's no need to tell her," he cautioned my mother. "The son's in her class."

"It was someone I know?" Why would anyone I know rip my mother's checked blouse?

She applied a small Band-Aid to a scratch on her wrist. "Oh it's nothing," she said, though she never had drooped so badly—her anklets had vanished into her shoes. "We ran into old Mr. Dwyer in town, and he and a few of the neighbors are furious that we'd try to help."

My *father* was furious. "If they don't want to buy Max's milk anymore, that's their prerogative. But ripping a blouse! Scratching a woman who tries to do good!"

Since my father spent his days delivering milk and was so smooth and pale, I'd always half-thought his essence was *milk*, which I guess meant untroubled, innocent, clean, but his face was so streaked and his features so clouded that I couldn't help but think of the milk behind the dairy that was left to be dumped, it was tainted or sour.

My mother was holding her hands to her blouse, hanging her head. "It was partly my fault. When I pushed him away my arm caught his buckle."

I tried to imagine my mother wrestling with old Mr. Dwyer— he was only an inch or two taller than she was, and quite a bit plumper.

"And blaming the Jews! To say Max is a kike who rented his land to Communists because he can't resist money!" He always had assumed that since he was privileged to open the boxes on his neighbors' back stoops and decipher the notes they'd left him inside ("Judd has an ulcer . . ." "Can't pay this week . . ." ". . . miscarriage . . ." ". . . transfer . . ."), because they allowed him to see them in curlers and torn robes or long johns, he knew who they were.

"If that farmer wants a lesson in manners," he said, "he should look at those kids. Who would expect they would be so polite? Look what they gave, for a few quarts of milk." He pulled a feather from his pocket; in a crate by the door were a string of purple beads, a collection of hats of all sorts and shapes, a broken guitar, a bouquet of weeds in a ponytail wrapper, a freshly whittled flute and a cookbook whose recipes were blessed by a man whose mustache and nose made him resemble my grandfather Morris. "So maybe they don't act like people like us. The young men don't mind if their girlfriends show off their bodies in public—not to say the girls have bodies to shame them. Such big, healthy girls!" And his face made me think he was seeing them now, those big, naked girls.

"And the little ones." My mother refastened the pin so it hid the pink bra. (Why had she bought it? Her others were white.) "In town they were saying the diseases are dreadful. They can't get the pumps in to drain out the toilets."

My father joined in. "If a fire breaks out . . ."

"I guess I should open a can of soup for dinner." My mother didn't move. "But I'd feel guilty eating with those poor hungry children . . . And sleeping tonight on a bed with clean sheets . . ."

That was it! I'd invite them to sleep in our house, in cots in my room.

I left my parents sitting on the floor in the kitchen, sifting through the relics they'd acquired that day, and I almost wish I hadn't. My father was never so silent again, my mother drooped much more often, it seemed. And though their confrontation with old Mr. Dwyer only began a chain of events that made them feel less and less part of the town, I blame this beginning for their decision many years later to do what they'd said they never would do: They moved away from Bethel when my father retired. And then they kept moving, trying new places—they even bought a camper, lived in that for a year—as if once they'd been knocked from their tiny fixed orbits, they wobbled, unrestrained, all over the country. First they moved to Florida, then to Phoenix, then to Albuquerque, then to Houston near me. (I was glad when they left, afraid they'd find out that I wasn't as smart as they once might have thought, wasn't destined for greatness; the machines made my job seem more impressive than it actually was.) They still tried to see only the best in the people they met, even if this meant they had to move on before seeing the worst. And whenever I got a postcard from someplace like L.A. or Reno, I feared for their innocence as once I had scorned it, and I was impatient with their wanderings as I had once been impatient with their unchanging lives. Because even though I didn't want to go home to Bethel, I felt they should be there in case that I did. I felt I'd gone swimming and they'd stolen the shore.

It was five when I left them. The day had been clear, but now, as I walked, two thin black clouds swirled through the sky like a helicopter's rotors slicing the sun. In the shadows of a cornfield I made out two men, one holding his fly, the patter of his urine spraying the stalks, the other man squatting with his pants to his knees. When the wind came I thought it was bringing their smell, but as I walked on, the air thickened with the odor of three-day-old garbage and I had to pull the neck of my jersey over my nose to inhale the fresh breezes captured in the fabric days before on the clothesline. How could they stand it? But then I remembered what the goat-boy had said about people not being able to smell their own smell, and what Meyer had told me about people who wanted so badly to think they'd found something pure that they *wouldn't* smell its smell, at least for a while.

The sky was gray-black and the winds had picked up so they swirled bits of litter over my head. I heard human howls and grunts from the woods, saw flames here and there, and I almost turned back—the trucks wouldn't get through and we all would be burned. But then I saw faces bobbing over the flames like yellow balloons and I realized these people were cooking their dinners, what little they had, though how could they eat with so many flies? These rose from the mud with each step I took, settled on my eyelids, trapped themselves in my ears. I could hear trees and wires snapping like whips, and the throb of the music—I couldn't hear the words—and thunder, in the distance, and the helicopters grinding over our heads.

And though I brag now about having grown up there, having been in that crowd when I was thirteen, the truth is I only remember my terror, my wish to escape. I wandered those fields I'd known all my life, picking my way among feet, heads and limbs. I stepped over bodies face-down in the mud, and I knew it was hopeless, I never would find Meyer or the goat-boy or Leon.

I saw a big tent. I went in and stood. A woman in a uniform

came up and said: "Honey, are you in there? What did you take?," snapping her fingers in front of my eyes.

"No time for that, just get her a blanket." Dr. Rock, rushing by, glanced at my face without recognition. "These fucking asshole parents ought to be shot, exposing a kid to something like this."

The nurse touched my arm, but I shook her off. I saw Steven kneeling by a female barbarian, swabbing a cut. He was still shining white but the whiteness was stained, which unsettled me as much as seeing a statue spattered with blood. His eyes weren't focused, so it took him a while to realize I'd come.

"You're too late," he said. "This woman had a baby . . . and this other one, she had . . . My father said some butcher must have done a bad job but I'm not sure what he. . . . And this kid, he was sleeping, and some jerk on a tractor thought the sleeping bag was empty and ran over it with those really big wheels! And this one diabetic who didn't bring her insulin, she went into shock. What jerks! I mean, coming to someplace like this and you don't bring your medicine? And these guys on bad trips, one had this knife and he came at my father—"

"Goddamn it Steven, get your ass over here!"

Steven obeyed, leaving me at the edge of the tent. The wind ripped right through, blowing gauze pads from carts, rattling bottles. The canvas roof billowed and the center pole shook so I went back outside, out in the rain, which tore at my skin. A dozen barbarians were stomping and sliding and splashing each other, but everyone else was huddled together close to the ground, holding garbage bags, sleeping bags, parkas and blankets over their heads; in the half-light it seemed the ground itself shook.

"Hey, come on in."

Slowly I knelt and took shelter under a huge plastic tarp. It was humid and dark, body to body. Someone put an arm over my shoulder and we started to sway; people were chanting "no rain, no rain" as though this were a spell to make the rain stop. We were so many people so close together I had the sensation of losing my boundaries—the wind had stripped off the walls of the house that I had moved into only that day, and I had trouble telling where my own body ended and the others began.

This scared me so much that I said half-aloud: "I'm not far from home. I've been here before." And I pictured the field the way I had seen it thousands of times, the green and gold pasture with its intricate shading and texture of weeds, clover, alfalfa, a great green bowl rising to a rim where it met a blue sky with clouds like the blue-and-white china in my mother's glass cabinet, and the land beyond that, with its swells and depressions, so a tractor would sink and disappear a moment, then float back to view.

I tried to imagine the scent of fresh hay warmed by the sun, but the stench of the present brought me back to this place. I was stuck in this time and would never get out. We would die in this place, buried in mud, so that years in the future archaeologists would stand here and see only dirt, though they might sniff our presence under the earth and know we had lived, know we had once been huddled together under this tarp chanting "no rain, no rain" as if we believed that we could get elsewhere simply by wishing as hard as we could.

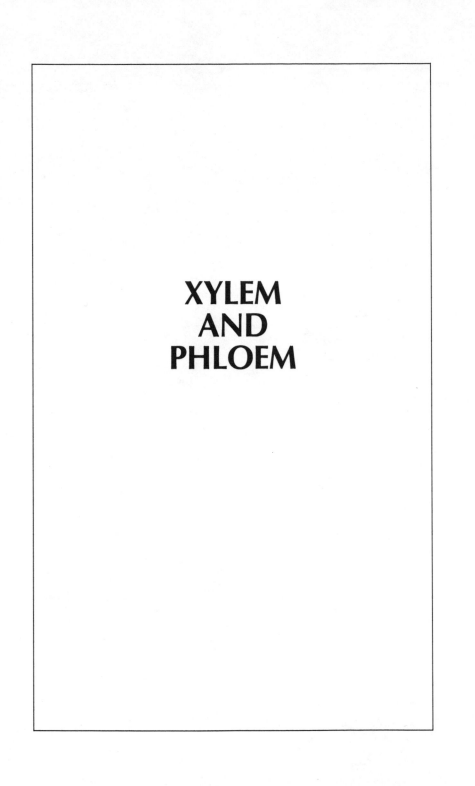

XYLEM
AND
PHLOEM

XYLEM
AND
PHLOEM

My sister was trying to examine her hair, but whenever she tilted her head toward the mirror her enormous belly bulged against the sink. For nineteen of her thirty-three years, Laura had kept the kink of the Semite shocked straight with chemicals. When flecks of age appeared, she started to dye it. Then she got pregnant, and she let her hair become as kinky and gray as it wanted to be. She had read that harsh chemicals poured on the head of an expectant mother could bring deformity on the soft, curled body of her unborn child; she imagined the fetus, delicate as a hair, straightening upon contact. In recoil from caffeine she directed her secretary to prepare only Postum. In terror of white wine she relaxed with herb tea.

"Mole, you're the expert," she pleaded with me. "What else must I avoid?"

Laura, a security analyst, is as quick with kindness as she is with her judgments of new bonds. If she had given birth to a mass of helpless flesh, she would have huddled lifelong with the child, and suffered for it. So she called me each day: Should she prohibit her fellow executives from smoking in her presence? Could fumes from the paint in her new house stupefy the fetus in her womb? "Of all people," she said, "you should understand."

I had studied the dangers of heredity in textbook after textbook. My family was certain that too many photos of grotesque babies had frightened me from motherhood, but this wasn't

27

true. I saw no horror in variation; I only wondered what might have caused it and tried to discover the amazing process by which a scrambling of the genetic code might spell the future of a child with six fingers, or a halo of copper encircling each iris, or skin and hair as softly colored as milk ice. I had invested twelve years in learning the alphabet of inherited disease. All this would be wasted if I chose to have children. My research demanded complete devotion—twelve, often sixteen hours each day, no rest on weekends. Nor was this my eccentric standard. Even at three o'clock on most Saturday mornings the lab in which I worked was brightly lit, crowded. Our experiments were timed to organisms that had little respect for the sleep cycles of humans. Essential equipment was often free only from midnight until dawn. Researchers elsewhere would be working while we slept, finding the answers that we had been seeking; they would publish their data first, leave us with nothing. Sadly I watched as other women in my profession got married, bore children, lost energy, interest, slipped farther behind until they were forgotten.

It was true that I had sacrificed what my family considered to be a normal life—a permanent, well-tended home, a husband and children—to science. But I would have been selfish to pass up my chance to help thousands of children for one child of my own. My family wouldn't grant this, kept hinting, cajoling.

My sister leaned as close the mirror as she could. "For every two weeks I've been pregnant, a dozen have turned gray"—she plucked a few hairs—"and a dozen for every day I've been past-due." That would have made more than a hundred for the latter alone. "By now my baby must be too big. He'll get stuck. They'll have to use forceps. They'll crush something in his head. I know it. I'm going to call my OB today and tell her to just cut me open."

"Laura," I said, "no doctor will perform a C-section unless you need one. The baby won't get stuck." Then, to divert her, I revealed my good news. I had been waiting for two days to find a moment when she wasn't choosing among bassinets or issuing orders over the phone to her secretary. "I've got something to show you." I took a letter from my shirt pocket. "I've been offered a position. At the Max Planck. It's an institute," I said. "In Germany."

She scowled at my reflection. "And you're going?"

"No one would turn down—"

"But what about Daniel? You've lived with Daniel for two years. We were all hoping . . . How can you be so cruel?"

"To whom?"

She turned, and her belly swung toward me. "How can you even ask? To Daniel, who's loved you for two years and who'll be miserable without you. To your parents, who each day are getting older and who would be very unhappy to see you even less than the twice a year you now visit. And to your nephew, who'll be auntless without you."

And what about me? Why did my family always interpret my achievements as cruelty? Why did they view my lack of a husband and nice home, a wardrobe and clear skin to rival Laura's, as failures—when I didn't?

I put the letter back in my pocket. Laura tilted her head over the toilet. She looked a dull green. We waited. "I don't think it's labor," she decided, "just the weather. It's so hot. I shouldn't have gone outside. I'll lie down."

She went to her bedroom and left me to wander through the house alone. With its glass walls and steel trim that curved in a tower around the staircase, the house seemed as if it were a giant food processor waiting to refine any irregularities within its walls to a uniform paste. I caught glimpses of myself in every smooth surface—a tall, bony woman whose uneven features were splattered with acne, whose blue jeans were too short, whose torn shirt was mottled with brown stains, the badges of lab work.

I escaped outdoors, where the only shade was a thin rod of black thrown by the seedling my brother-in-law, Edward, had just planted. He was holding its one branch, as he might hold a child's hand.

"You're the biologist," he said. "Do you think it will grow fast enough to be able to hold a tire swing by the time Alan is five or six?"

"Alan? Who's Alan?"

"Your nephew. Or Alice, if it's an Alice. The man at the nursery swore to me that this brand of apple would grow fast, but I don't think I believe him."

The apple tree looked as if it would topple under the weight of a sparrow. "I'm not a botanist," I said. "I have no idea how quickly trees grow."

Edward looked confused. He prided himself on being able to make conversation with any client, and his firm handled accounts as diverse as the makers of puppy chow and denture adhesives. Assuming a more confident tone, he tried again. "I'll buy a tree that's full grown. Maybe a big oak. This place could use big oaks."

The development was bare of all decoration other than scaffolds and brick heaps, ladders, cement trucks. The construction industry in most of the country was moribund that year, but on that one hill in southern Connecticut, the intricate frames of seventeen houses had grown to huge proportions. Every so often a large car would float around the unnamed streets, an owner inspecting a new house like a child circling his birthday presents. Three couples besides my sister and Edward had moved in already, but the sod on their lawns was still scored by evenly spaced lines. The drought had kept the grass as pale and nappy as an infant's hair, and the new houses stood out, exposed.

Two lots were just big holes. They reminded me of an afternoon twenty-six years before when I had followed a moving bump of earth to the edge of a deep pit in my parents' then-young neighborhood. I slipped in and couldn't climb out, but instead of crying, I held my breath, shut my eyes, burrowed and burrowed, trying to understand how any creature could survive underground. When my parents found me, I was half-buried, hungry, and so muddy that my mother had to hold me at arms' length. But I was happy. I had decided what I wanted to be when I grew up. "A mole," I told her, and even as an adult, I still had the name, "Mole."

I thought to warn Edward, who was watering his twig, that the builders should fence off the basements. But then I remembered that only one child lived on the hill as yet, and Eric was wise enough not to fall into a pit. Eric, who was two, belonged to the couple next door to my sister. His head was too large and too long—"my favorite Martian," as his mother called him, though she could make such jokes only after she had trundled him from pediatrician to pediatrician, twelve opinions in two weeks. Only after all twelve doctors had denied that water was sloshing through his cranial cavities could she enjoy her pride in a son who looked like a premature and alien genius, with huge eyes that didn't blink and a placid composure.

Laura had never been intimate with a child before meeting Eric. One day he climbed onto her lap and rubbed his palm thoughtfully over the lapel of her suit, then her cheeks and her chin, and looked into her eyes for several minutes with a deep, fixed gaze. Convinced that all babies were as quiet and contemplative as Eric, she filed her diaphragm in a metal box behind her tax records. Her obstetrician suggested testing. After a week of self-torture and six phone calls to me, my sister declined. She couldn't bear the image of the probing needle. Nor would she subject the fetus to the weakest of sound waves. Instead, for nine months, she worried, avoided, and phoned me.

When I went back inside, I found she had risen and was preparing dinner. She wasn't hungry, but didn't want to deny food to her husband, guest, fetus. She said she was sorry she had criticized me. If I insisted on accepting the new job, she would give me two suits of which she had grown tired. These, she assured me, would endow me with authority over my first graduate students and help me to attract a replacement for Daniel. I didn't want to tell her that the only people who would walk into a lab wearing three-piece suits were salesmen from biological supply houses, so I just thanked her.

We spent the evening in the glass-and-chrome living room, "waiting for Laura to pop," as Edward put it. At ten she looked weepy. "Something's wrong, I'm sure of it. I haven't felt him moving all night. He's dead inside me." But Edward soothed her, and five minutes later Laura seemed cheerful. "Tomorrow we'll go shopping. I'll treat you to a new shirt. How can you wear a shirt that has such stains?"

I thanked her again, but said I would be leaving the next

morning for our parents' home in the Berkshires. "The heat won't have reached there. I'm used to Seattle, the cool mist."

"You won't stay until you can meet your nephew? I'm sorry I didn't time it right, but you won't stay?"

"When you've delivered I'll come back, with Mother."

"You always leave as soon as you've arrived," she said. "You're not an intrusion." She tried to smooth my twisted hair, but I backed away.

My mother always insisted that I provide her with my expected arrival time so she would be able to fret if I were late. It was a game for her, the reward being relief. I had phoned that morning from my sister's and told her to expect me about three, but I missed my connection and didn't come until five.

"That terminal is so dangerous," she said in greeting, her pointed features arranged to show concern. "There have been *incidents*. I hated to picture you there." Yet she had dedicated the preceding two hours to imagining every danger that might have befallen me. "Not that I minded the excuse to stretch out here. Our porch is the coolest place in the Northeast. As I always say, the breezes here never die." She rose from the lounge chair, still and tall, held me for as long as she thought I would permit it, then asked: "Did Laura looked strained? Was her face pale? Has the baby dropped yet?"

"Dropped?"

She seemed impatient with this lack of knowledge in a female biologist of thirty-two. "Dropped lower, in her belly. From here to here." She indicated the movement of the fetus on her own stick-thin body. "It should have happened weeks ago."

"Not yet. But she seemed healthy to me. Only worried. Over nothing."

She poked her fingers into her dull hair, lifting the curls from where they had been flattened during her lounging. My mother is not lazy, but she used to work herself into dryness during the school year—she taught the slow readers of our town—and so had to wait on the porch for each summer's breezes and showers to restore her tenderness and strength for the new term.

"Your legs must be cramped," she said, reasoning from her

own varicose-blue legs. She always said she had gotten "those veins" from carrying me, as if she had sacrificed her chances to win a beauty pageant by bearing my weight, yet also had earned a distinction from this. She said it as if she carried my weight still. "We have just enough time for a walk before your father gets home."

This was our tradition: to commemorate each of my returns with a promenade around our circular block. Twelve houses ringed the cow pond at the neighborhood's center, and as we walked clockwise my mother would tell me the news of each household, as though we were clock hands ticking off the hours, tolling through the six months since I had been home. At the twelfth hour, when we reached our own house, I would tell her my news, the final tolling.

But tonight, instead of starting with news of the Fleischmanns, who lived in the first house, my mother began with the cow pond, and it seemed as though the clock were ignoring the time to tell me the problems with its own mechanism, the gears at its center. The pond, she said, had grown fetid with algae. Someone had suggested a herbicide, but this had been dismissed. "The danger," she said, though none of the children who once had lived here were now younger than thirty. My father proposed carp, but a license was needed, and the species that ate weeds had to be flown in from Arkansas, or China.

"It's a bad omen," my mother told me. "Last week, three ducks crawled up in our driveway and died. I'm not superstitious, but when I was carrying *her*," and I knew that my mother didn't mean Laura, or me, but the first child she had carried, the stillborn, "all our new bushes were dripping with tent caterpillars."

In 1948 our neighborhood had been a cow pasture, bristling with sharp yellow straw, porcupines and barbed wire. Then my parents moved onto the hill, raising white planks to the hot sun, wrapping the bare walls in scraggling arborvitae, replanting the sharp straw with soft green. Other homesteaders followed, digging, sowing and tending, until the roots and branches had woven themselves into a dense, strong fabric.

Now the neighborhood and its hedges seemed stronger than

the people who had built them. Max Fleischmann, my mother said, had been convicted of tax fraud. After two months in prison he had developed ulcers and been sent home. He lived in seclusion, doing penance on bland food, hidden from gossip by the topiary he had shaped.

Her head shaking slightly over Max's troubles, my mother led me through air so heavy and warm it was like a green fluid that muted emotion, disturbance. As we reached the next house, two on the clock dial, on a broad-chested old man in a sweatsuit opened the front door and ran in slow motion, heel-toeing past us. I heard him meow.

"According to Davey," my mother explained, "the walking prevents everything except double chins, and the meowing prevents that." She stretched her lips toward her ears and made a cat sound; this pulled her chin taut. "At first, it was all Louise could do to get him to give up smoking. She inscribed a message in lipstick across those nice cream walls—she said she would leave him unless he began to take care of himself. Now he's obsessed with it. He can go days without eating anything but lime juice and brown rice. And he's set up a trampoline in their back yard. He's so peculiar she can't talk to him. She just hopes it will pass."

In the Mandels' yard next door, a boy and a collie were chasing around a blue spruce tall enough to have served as the Christmas tree on the lawn of the White House.

"Don't hurt it, Duchess!" the boy shouted, but the collie kept jabbing her snout in the needles. "A squirrel with two tails!" the boy screeched, and we smiled indulgently, but just then the squirrel fooled the dog by running out the opposite side of the spruce tree and we saw that it did indeed have two tails.

"Maybe this omen is intended for the Mandels," I said quickly.

"I'd almost rather it was for us," she said, frowning. The Mandels' grandson was staying with them all summer while his mother, Lisa, who had grown up with Laura, underwent radiation for Hodgkin's. "At least if things don't go well for Laura, she might have another chance," my mother said, "though God forbid she should need one."

"Mother. Why do you have to see the squirrel as an omen of death? Why not a sign of possibility? An interesting surprise?" She didn't appear convinced. To prove that all deviations from everyday life didn't presage death, I told her: "I've been offered my own lab. In Germany."

There was only the ticking of somebody's sprinkler. Then she said: "He wanted children, didn't he."

I asked whom she meant.

"Daniel. He wanted children, and you said no, so you called off the engagement."

"Mother. We never were engaged. We just lived together. With the hours we both kept, we barely even saw each other. And I've always wanted to spend time in Europe."

"Your father and I liked him very much. You share common interests. Just because he wants a child, you'll leave him. You'll run off to Germany."

I had said nothing to her about our arguments over children, but I wasn't surprised that she had guessed this; between her powers of divination and her perceptiveness, she was a prophet of her family's future.

"Don't you see how inconsistent your position is?" she asked. "You spend your every waking hour trying to assure the world of peaceful births. You sacrifice your best years to the concept of happy parenthood. But you don't value the concept enough to live by it, to have a child of your own."

I told her that just because I believed in guaranteeing healthy children to people who wanted them did not mean I had to have them myself.

"Sarah," my mother said, "what would you think of a peddler who sold encyclopedias door-to-door but gave his children only comic books to read?"

I walked ahead quickly and finished the circle a few steps before her. My father had come home and I found him out back, trimming the willows. Without saying a word I stooped to gather the clippings. His pinched nerves would have made bending painful, but this wouldn't have stopped him. Let chaos swirl around his gates, it wouldn't get in until he was too weak to wield a rake and shovel. Each April he reduced a rebellion

of dandelions to six jars of sweet wine. He let no bush succumb
to summer bedragglement, allowed the autumn leaves to remain
on the ground only long enough to advertise the season. An
increase of entropy on his property would have been as much a
sign of impending death as a circling of buzzards.

We trimmed and gathered a long time, because even though
the willows had begun as cuttings, my father had invested the
fullness of his youth and compassion on them and they had
grown like deluded redwoods, so that each trunk was now as
big around as five stout men hugging. My mother went inside.
We kept on working until my father, to show he was finished,
began snapping his shears like bladed wings over my head.

"The giant clipper-bird is coming to bite off your nose," he
said, and looked down where I squatted. I told myself he meant
no harm; only by reducing me in age and size could he keep
himself from admiring his daughter more than he thought lucky.
Of all my family, only my father respected my work. He was a
podiatrist and so considered himself in the service of science,
though not as one of its generals—"just a humble foot-soldier,"
he liked to tell me. My father was proud of his position,
crouching over the corns and bunions of his patients. "When
they walk in my door," he would say, "they can think of nothing
but their tortured toes. I liberate their minds for loftier thoughts."

When I didn't respond to his clowning, he returned the
clippers to their hook in the basement and carried the hammock
up from the cellar. As he tied it between trees I told him my
news.

He paused, rubbing the bark with his fingers, then told me
slowly: "One day you'll see. This is what is important in life."

And I said, "What? What is important? A hammock? A maple?
A willow? Are trees what's important? They're just xylem and
phloem. They're just woody tissue. It's selfish to devote yourself
only to your house, to your family, your trees. It's selfish. You'll
leave nothing behind you. It's not right."

He turned away, too hurt to tell me: Yes, I am content with
this. With you and your sister, your mother, with this yard and
this house, with the razor that I keep as sharp as perfection to

ease what pain is within my ability to ease. Yes, content with this tree, and this bush. Content.

My mother brought iced tea, then carefully stretched out in the hammock. He climbed in beside her. I stood by the willow, telling them anecdotes of no importance until the novelty of my visit had worn off with the chill on the glasses, and my parents lay there, two long bodies in a narrow sling, the center of gravity balanced between them, but barely.

We were eating a cantaloupe so ripe its wedges seemed like offerings to some tropical goddess when my sister called to announce that nothing had happened.

"Remember, Laura, easy births run in our family," my mother told her. Then she put my father on the phone.

Laura could not put Edward on the phone because he was outside digging a hole for the huge oak he had just bought. Instead, Laura told us that Eric, the toddler from next door, had just said his first sentence, right there in her kitchen. "He saw the ice in his punch melt, and he looked up and asked me, 'Where go to?' Imagine!"

On the phone, my parents were cheerful and reassuring, but afterwards, as they sat in the kitchen, they strangled their tea bags until the leaves burst out.

"She shouldn't have waited this long," my father said. "The risk."

"It's only two percent greater after thirty," I told them.

"Two percent!" my mother said, and twisted a lemon rind to shreds. "Still, I suppose the real risk is a lonely old age. I'm glad she came to her senses before it was too late altogether. If women as bright as my daughters refuse to have children . . ."

I slipped onto the porch and tried to calm myself in the breezes. The spotlights hidden around our birches were shining up on the frozen white stalks. White moths dove in and out of the beams. The spray from a sprinkler rose in a slow measured arc, passed its zenith, turned white as it passed through the light from the birches, fell quickly, then rose again slowly and threw itself over again into the light, all the while clicking like a ratchet. The moths fled the light as the spray approached, and returned as the spray left, so the sprinkler appeared to be showering the birches not with water, but with white moths.

The rueful phrases that filtered out through the screen door told me that my parents were pitying Daniel. I wanted to shout that I was the one who deserved their sympathy. When Daniel and I had moved in together, he promised never to ask for children. He let me fall in love with him, let me get used to his presence in bed when I dragged in at daybreak from the lab, led me to believe that yes, I could have this much besides work. Then he betrayed me.

"Just one," he begged, though he admitted that my work would suffer greatly even from one child.

Why had he promised he wouldn't ask for children? Why? I demanded.

"Because I felt young then. I don't now. I'm sorry."

Only then had I applied for the position in Germany, only after Daniel had betrayed me. I wanted to storm in and yell this to my parents. Instead, I watched the spray rising, and falling, and the moths, and wished the world were not obsessed with fertility and time were not an arc under which living things felt trapped.

We awoke the next morning to find the white bellies of twenty dead perch shining up among the weeds in the cow pond. This upset my mother so badly she couldn't eat. I paddled the warped canoe to the center of the pond and scooped up the dead perch with a net. I had filled three trash bags with their corpses when I saw my mother on the shore, waving as frantically as a castaway.

"Edward just called," she said as I rowed in. "Laura's water broke last night, just after she hung up. They wanted to wait until it was over to tell us, but something has gone wrong. Your father is on his way home. Get rid of those awful fish and change out of that T-shirt. *Hurry.*"

On the long drive to the hospital my mother punctuated every fifteen miles with another theory as to the horror we would find when we got there: a baby with no lungs, no brain, with stub arms or clubbed feet.

"It's just a hard labor," I told her, irritated because it seemed a game: If only she could fool the Fates into thinking she expected a monster, they would give her a good child. Her anxious expression seemed too heightened to be real, and when I could bear it no longer I looked out the window. But this was no better—the endless houses, each with its neat yard and thick enclosure of hedges, trees, bushes, each with its family preoccupied with the comfort of its own members. I wanted to reach the hospital and lose myself in the communal exertion of doctors and nurses whose devotions were not bounded by lines of property or kinship. My father must have been as frustrated with the limits of movement as I was, because just as my mother was naming the final nightmare—Laura and the infant both dead on the table—he ignored a stop sign and raced in distraction through a wide intersection.

And so it happened that while my sister lay on a table on the hospital's fifth floor, writhing and sweating, my father was wheeled through the emergency entrance four stories below, as motionless as if he had been asleep in his hammock. My mother walked quickly beside the stretcher, his palm to her lips, until the orderlies rolled him behind steel doors.

Then she said loudly: "Why didn't it hit *me*?" and even then I was tempted to accuse her of melodrama, until I too saw the garden, the willows, the hedges, all weed-choked in neglect, and was sickened by this loss, and the abomination of these two people not being allowed to live out their last years untroubled, protected. Because they deserved this. My father had lessened the pain of thousands. My mother had saved more children from darkness with her drills in spelling, her games with vowels, than I could save in a lifetime with my science that brought information but no cures.

For an hour I carried lies from the first floor to the fifth floor and back down, until the two truths, safely in the past tense, had lost their power, and I could say simply: "It was a breech birth, the cord was crushed for a short while, but Laura and her son are resting well now." And: "He was cut badly, and from his supreme fright for his family and the sight of his own blood, our father passed out, and though he required twenty-six stitches, now he is sleeping, at peace in the knowledge that his wife and daughters and grandson are unharmed."

At last I left Edward, a disheveled man weeping from relief, and tried to get free from the hallways of stale air. But I took a wrong turn and found myself stranded in a ward for the most hopeless infants, the newborns no bigger than baked potatoes, kept warm in blankets of shiny metal, with tubes down their noses. A Hispanic woman who was staring through the glass at one incubator began knocking her head against the window, gently at first, then harder and harder, until the glass rattled and two nurses came running, took her by the shoulders and led her to her room.

I found the stairway and raced down the five flights, desperate to get away from this place, to return to Seattle, to my lab, to a world where mutation and decay were mysteries, puzzles, the pursuit of whose answers was an exquisite pleasure.

I did not want children. I *did not*. Even healthy children brought obligation, disorder. Despite all my pleas for respect, I had sacrificed nothing. Under the cover of altruism I delighted in my freedom, the precise joy of my work.

All evening I was restless with this thought. While my mother and Edward dozed in the new house, I walked the vacant yards of the development, back and forth, pacing, as if this would get me nearer Seattle. I didn't pause for hours, until a faint voice spread over the hill, a child's voice that chanted words I couldn't make out, though when I got closer I heard a question, over and over, in somber flat tones: "Where go to? Where go to?" I followed the chant to the deep hole that Edward had been digging the evening before when Laura must have called him to take her to the hospital. I looked down and saw Eric. He stopped chanting and raised his arms. As I bent to lift him, the letter from Germany fell from my pocket.

"Eric," I asked him, "where are your parents? How did you get here?" He only touched my hair, patted its roughness. "Were you looking for something?" He nodded, but I couldn't ask him what, because just then the rear door of his house flew open and a teenage girl ran out.

"Eric!" she screamed. Then she saw us. Breathless, she

reached us, and drew him to her, although he was filthy. She begged me to keep her secret—she had been talking on the phone to her friend for no more than a minute. "Don't tell his parents. Please. Promise." Reluctantly, I said yes, and she snatched him from me and raced back to his house.

I knelt beside the hole, still feeling the child's weight, his fingers in my hair. I noticed a muddy handprint on my shirt and tried to convince myself that it was no more a sign of disorder than the chemical stains on the fabric beside it. I tried, but I could not. I got up and rescued the letter from the hole.

But still my arms felt him. I studied the handprint. Five fingers. Perfect. I counted them again. One, two, three, four, five. And suddenly it seemed that a sixth finger would have been a sadness more terrible than I ever had imagined. I saw a new-born, his soft head swelling. My nephew with no arms, a twisted heart, no eyes. For a long time I stood there, and what had been only a justification (my devotion was noble, I had assured myself often, and assured all who questioned, because even though I didn't want children, how many millions of men and women *did* want them, and with what fearful passion!), that justification gained the heaviness of truth now.

Slowly I smoothed the mud from the letter, then watched as the red sun lowered itself through the skeleton of a half-built house, where it burned between wood ribs a moment, and vanished.

THE VANITY
OF SMALL
DIFFERENCES

THE VANITY
OF SMALL
DIFFERENCES

Massey killed the mouse mother, pinched her by the tail and dipped her into the beaker of disinfectant, as he might dip a tea bag. He laid the pink body just so on a towel and pierced the puffed belly. Even though he heard his grandson squirming behind him, rustling the paper clothes he was wearing, Massey paid no mind. A nick here, a cut there, the uterus popped free. He tweezed it out, careful not to nip the fetuses inside, then floated the sac in warm, salty water. He sealed the flask tightly and locked it inside a large tank that had two holes in one wall, with rubber sleeves and gloves reaching in from the holes.

"That thing looks like a fat farmer scratching his innards," the boy said.

"Well, it isn't a farmer," Massey told his grandson. "It's an isolator, and you can't go calling an isolator a 'fat farmer' or no one will know what in hell you're intending."

"So? Why should I care?"

His patience had eroded with each passing hour. With restraint, he told Joseph: "Suppose you were a scientist here. How could you tell us technicians what you wanted us to do with your mice if you called things by different names from what we call them?"

"If I was a scientist here, the only thing I'd tell you to do with my mice was to stop cutting their bellies open or I'd slit yours, and you'd know what that meant, I'll bet you."

Massey raised his hand, but his fingers were bloody, and this caused Joseph to shrink inside his too-big coveralls until he appeared mean and sassy no longer, just a skinny thirteen.

"I don't know what's wrong with me," he moaned. "I say bad things like that, then I wish I were dead. I'd never slit your belly, Granddad. I'd rather slit my own."

Joseph looked so frail that Massey would have tousled his hair, if not for the mouse guts defiling his fingers. "See that you call things by their right names from now on, that's all," he said, and went on to the next part of his chore, slipping his arms into the sleeves of the isolator and unsealing the flask that he had just put there.

Despite the rubber gloves, Massey moved his fingers in delicate motions, slicing the womb and plucking the mouse pups, delivering them from the germ-free uterus into the germ-free tank. Four naked pink lumps no bigger then pencil erasers, eyes covered with membrane, each pup a perfect copy of its siblings, not only at skin level, but as deep as its genes, the identical products of hundreds of generations of planned incest among brothers and sisters, sin sanctioned—no, prodded—by science. Every Albino Mouse just like every other Albino, but markedly different from the nude mice called Streakers, or from the Dwarf Mice, the Obese, the Moth-Eaten.

Then there were mice deviant not in appearance, but behavior. The Waltzer, dancing in endless circles like a belle in Satan's torment. The Bouncy, the Fidget, the Hot Foot, the Waddler, the Twitcher, the Twirler, the Trembler, the Jerker, the Lurcher, the Shaker—Massey had shown them all to his grandson. These pups were Rhinos, he told the boy now. For two weeks they'd sprout fur, then they'd go bald. Their skin would outstrip them; wrinkled and baggy, their pink hides would thicken. Their ears would grow pointed, their snouts would elongate, their black eyes would sink into furrows of horned skin.

"Rhino Mice are the ugliest, most ridiculous creatures the good Lord created," he told Joseph. Ridiculousness, he went on, was the wages of vanity. Think how conceited these mice were! They knew how much trouble had been expended to make their births immaculate, to guarantee their pedigrees, to purify their eccentric appearances. But they weren't special. Just ugly.

"I'm not ugly!" Joseph shouted, and the highstrung mice skittered in their sterile shavings. "I'm just different, and nobody has ever paid me wages to be it. And if anybody looks ridiculous, it's you, because your head isn't much different from a Rhino's, and on you it looks lots worse." Then the boy withered and ran out.

Massey didn't follow. It would be good to let the boy wander through a big, unfriendly building where he wasn't important enough to get inside a single magnetically locked room. Joseph had left his street clothes in his grandfather's locker; he couldn't leave wearing paper. Massey stopped in the men's room.

Right away, his reflection over the sink made him soften. He didn't often scrutinize his appearance—not because it was hateful to him, as it once had been, but because he had learned long ago that no one's appearance deserved much attention. Now he saw his hairless pink head, the scalp convoluted with age and fat. His face was as wrinkled as a brain, his small eyes like black nails driven in pouches, his ears made prominent by the lack of hair around them. His nose had a red tip. All I need's a tail, Massey thought, and forgave the boy easily.

Besides, he loved Joseph. If he hadn't loved him, would he have been so desperate to save him? He couldn't let someone he loved waste himself on spray-painting his hair green, getting his ear pierced at a women's jewelry store and sticking a feather through the hole, and turning his allowance into an ungodly large collection of record albums by bands whose names reminded Massey of the strains of neurologically disordered inmates at the Mouse House. He shuddered when he thought of the school concert during which Joseph had stood up to play a trumpet solo and launched instead into his own demented version of "The Brave Bugler" until the rest of the band had dropped away in confusion. Then Joseph raced off the stage; he quit the band during intermission, even before the conductor could expel him.

The boy's parents, helpless before his excesses, had sent him to his grandfather in Tennessee for a two-week corrective visit.

When the boy arrived, Massey immediately went through his valise and forbade him to wear the most outlandish garments, giving him instead the shorts, trousers and permanent-press shirts that the boy's grandmother had picked out at Penney's.

"You can either put on these new clothes, or you can go around naked and attract all the attention you seem to desire," Massey told him. "Now get ready and we'll take you out for a welcome-back-to-Tennessee dinner."

Ten minutes later, Joseph walked steel-eyed and naked from the front door to the driveway, with his grandmother watching. Then he lost his boldness and tore back to the house. The next morning, he came down to breakfast dressed half in his outcast's clothes and half in the new clothes from Penney's. Massey threatened to burn the old clothes. But Joseph's grandmother took his side. She whispered her reasons to Massey: half a normal boy was better than none, and any extreme measure might cause a relapse to total foolishness, or worse, total nudity.

So Massey just went on to the second lesson. That evening he took the boy to a field beyond the last ring of houses in Plainview Estates and showed him the overwhelming number of stars in the night sky. "I'll bet a hundred boys like you, green hair and feathers and such all, live on those planets. Isn't anything you could do to earn God's notice."

But Joseph only became obsessed with the notion that hundreds of other Josephs existed in the universe. He tried to contact them by trumpeting his theme song to the heavens, until his grandfather commanded him to stop, at which the boy played the keys without blowing.

"He won't need the music to hear me," the boy said, "just air waves. Or thought waves," and kept clicking at the stars.

After that, he never played a note in his grandfather's hearing, just clicked and sibilated, though he carried the trumpet wherever he went. Thank goodness the guard at the Mouse House had ordered Joseph to leave his trumpet in Decon, to keep him from blowing germs on the rare mice.

When Massey found the boy in the locker room at last, Joseph apologized stiffly. In silence he tore off the paper coveralls and slippers, girded his cotton-covered child's bottom in heavy layers of camouflage khaki, an armor of pockets and countless brass buckles of no use, then stamped his feet into black boots intended for paratroopers, weaving and tugging the laces for minutes. Finally, he buttoned his blue shirt up his delicate white chest, along the soft crease between the rows of his small ribs.

Massey had barely led the boy out of the scrub room, glad that none of his co-workers had seen how strange his grandson looked in his street clothes, when the boy muttered fiercely: "When I get older and have lots of money from my trumpet, I'll buy this place and set all the mice free because they're the neatest animals in the world and they deserve better than slicing."

"They wouldn't last a minute," his grandfather told him. "They've never touched a germ and wouldn't know how to get food if it wasn't mashed in a pellet and dropped by their noses. Something would eat *them*. This place is a freak house, and all freaks are weaklings."

He drove the car to the gate and jabbed his magnetic card into a sensor that looked like a cobra's head. A turnpike arm swung up. Massey looked at the boy to see if he was struck with his own insignificance at not having a magnetic card with which to tame the cobra, but the boy's eyes were burning a hole in the windshield.

"They're just mice that have airs," Massey said, and was pleased to see the building recede to an inconsequential size in the rearview mirror.

The Mouse House—really the Chatamaguchie National Breeding Laboratory—was, in Massey's opinion, a monument to the freak: six hundred thousand glorified house-pests, cared for with as much religious devotion as if they had been temple monkeys in India. When a particular strain was instrumental in a discovery of genetic importance, employees of the Mouse House would boast of "their mice." All except Massey, who knew that this job didn't make him special. Getting it had just been blind fortune. He had been born in this nowhere corner of Tennessee twenty years before the mouse labs even had existed. He had gone to war, and he had come back to Chatamaguchie because he hadn't known where else to go. As he remembered the place, no one much lived there, and the people who did just tried to get by and mind their own farm-yards.

Driving the boy home, he tried to re-create that long-vanished landscape for Joseph, tried to erase the fast-food restaurants and motels of the Pike and restore the unassuming town whose peacefulness had been his sustaining memory through the long war.

"Must have been even more boring than it is now," the boy said. "Must have been just like any other one-horse town."

Even though Joseph had grown up in Chatamaguchie, he knew nothing of its history: how the government had needed a swamp hole where scientists could work on the bomb in con-cealment, how the Army had purchased the whole place and ruined it. Massey had come home from the war and been shocked to discover a raw and sprawling village fifteen miles east of the city proper—guard towers, Quonset huts, plank walks above muddy streets, pile reactors, uranium purifiers, physicists and engineers and their families, all hidden and fenced in among the greeny vines of the backwoods.

The physicists had bred mice in a shack, to have them handy for experimental doses of radiation. After the war, biologists elsewhere began needing pedigreed mice for their research and the Mouse House was moved to a much bigger building. Over the years, the bomb labs and the Mouse House had crawled out of the woods and gobbled up the town, so that half of Chata-maguchie was now Ph.D.s and their families, and all the rest natives who were proud if they had finished high school. The two halves lived separate, but every one in Chatamaguchie, genius and unlettered alike, worked at the labs or the Mouse House.

Massey had been a medic's assistant in the war, so he was assigned to a job in the Mouse House. His nimble fingers had earned him such duties as chopping up tumors and teasing uteruses from pregnant mouse bellies, but most often he was just a caretaker. The mice might be fancy and favorites to others, but to him they were just tiny machines that turned big vats of pellets into big vats of mouse shit. Three dumpsters daily. Machines that made mouse pups. Three million yearly.

If the other caretakers wanted to pump up their egos because they served freak mice—Massey said this to Joseph as they turned into Plainview Estates—that was from the desperate need they shared with most people to distinguish themselves in some small way from other people. Take the man who lived across the street. Just because he had gone from drinking six cups of coffee a day to none at all, he thought he'd been redeemed and was determined to save the caffeinated soul of every person who was kind enough to invite him to dinner. Or the old biddy next door, who informed everybody that she just couldn't keep regular unless she started every day with a glass of cold water and ten minutes reading a book on the toilet.

"I've seen what befalls people who try to be different at all costs," Massey told Joseph. "And that's just what it costs them—everything they have."

"It doesn't cost me much," Joseph retorted, "and when I get older, I'll be rich from my trumpet and it won't matter. I'll buy a neat mansion for you and Grandma so you won't need to live in a crummy house in the middle of all these other crummy houses."

"Why, thank you," he said. "That's very generous. But your grandmother and I are very happy in this house. We have each other and such a nice family, that's enough for us." Then at last he gave in to his impulse and tousled the boy's spiky hair.

The next afternoon Massey was swabbing an operating table when he heard a command over the P.A. that he should report to the caretakers' lounge. He finished his swabbing, slid fifteen dead mothers down a chute to the furnace and obeyed the summons.

His supervisor was waiting with a dented shoe box in his small, outstretched hands. "Some hillbilly grandma left this at the front desk," he piped. "Her granddaughter passed on, and she heard we grow mice to cure cancer, so she went out and caught these. I shouldn't have even let them into the building. First thing you know and they've got loose, spread mange to the nudies, had some fun with the lady mice and mixed their bad genes in with the pure ones. I'd tell you to just let them go, but you know the order. Gets to be a habit, and pretty soon the environs are overrun and the neighbors start screaming. Every mouse they see, it's some dangerous mutant that's going to eat them. Get rid of these, okay? Thanks, Massey, old man. You're a good soldier." He set the box on the coffee table and pid-a-padded out of the lounge.

Massey lifted the box lid. The mice made him feel funny. Shocked, almost. Yet they were just barn mice, with gray coats and small ears. Not big mice. Not little. Just normal.

That was it. Normal. He touched a soft head. The mouse shook. Massey ran one thumb over the gray silk. His boss had been right. They couldn't just be let go. He lifted the smallest mouse. It peed in terror. Gently, he placed his thumb and forefinger just behind the gray head, applied a quick pressure and yanked the tail down. The mouse died with no struggle.

The other mice whispered. Of course they had been whispering all the time. He just hadn't heard them because a man never heard anything while he was killing. Still, he felt odd. He looked at the mouse that hung from his fingers. Why should a creature die because it was normal? Maybe he couldn't set the other mice free, but nothing in the rules said he couldn't take them home with him.

He took a napkin from the pile near the coffee pot, wrapped up the dead mouse, then popped the shrouded corpse through a slot to the incinerator. He carried the shoe box to Decon, where the guard made him open the lid and explain. Being singled out gave Massey discomfort, but he told himself again that no rules forbade him.

"They're a lesson for someone," he said to the guard. And when the man nodded, Massey scurried out.

When Massey drove up and saw his house, he became chilled by the possibility that his grandson was beyond saving: He would live and die ridiculous. The fence had been woven with four colors of crepe streamers. Strands of orange, pink, lilac and purple rained from the trees, poured down the front path and bled through the wet grass near the rotating sprinkler.

The boy was standing beside a clothes-drying umbrella that looked like a maypole. His trumpet was hung with crepe-paper braids. His small fingers pumped the keys with fury, but the instrument made no sounds except clicks and hisses. Colored paper encircled his thin neck and wound down a T-shirt with flamingos on it. Below his white shorts, each skinny leg was a candy cane with stripes.

When the boy saw his grandfather, he took the horn from his lips. "I haven't been able to tell your house from the others since I got here." He seemed proud and ashamed. "I thought of this today."

Massey was close to strangling the boy, but Joseph looked deeply into his horn and murmured, "I can't help it," and Massey just pitied him. He knew that he himself had never fallen victim to the vanity of small differences only because his parents had been lessons to him, as had the Army. Blessed with this wisdom, he had come home and married an unassuming woman who believed in humility. She had borne him two daughters, who always had attempted to be like their girlfriends. Both girls had married nice boys and raised nice, normal children—except for this grandson. Maybe it wasn't the boy's fault after all. Raised by humble people, Joseph had never been able to learn the dangers of pride, and when his father had been transferred to Miami the year before, Joseph had been exposed to the strangeness of that place with no defense against it.

"Just take down this nonsense," he told the boy. "If it's gone before dinner, I'll show you a surprise." On his way to the garage with the shoe box, Massey looked over his shoulder and was relieved to see the boy reaching hand-over-hand to pull down a streamer from the old oak.

He was even more relieved when the boy seemed to understand the lesson of the barn mice, understand that his grandfather was not a killer and that ordinary creatures were healthier and more lovable than freaks. The boy listened intently as his grandfather told him that mice suffered if they were handled too much. At supper, Joseph refrained from his usual antics, such as jamming corncobs in his ears to win his grandmother's laughter—Massey had told her just to ignore him, but she said she preferred Joseph's clowning to his writhing in embarrassment every time she came near him.

"Besides," she said, giggling, "he *makes* me laugh at him."

But the boy must have learned that getting laughed at was a punishment for outlandish behavior, not a reward. Encouraged, Massey took down the family album, and while his wife cleared the table he sat next to Joseph and reviewed the photos.

He turned first to a picture of an absurdly fat man, a mountain in white clothes and a helmet flowing with veils. Massey Senior's beekeeping had been eccentric, but he had never made much of a living from it. No, his vanity had been his prognostication. "Come a day when the Colored Man will eat at the same counter with us." "Come a day when pictures will enter our houses with the music." And, from the humming in his beehives, the weather.

But he hadn't predicted the heart attack that had killed him at forty and so hadn't purchased enough life insurance. That diminished the legend that he'd been a seer and sent his wife Ruth to serve doughnuts for a living. ("That's her," he told Joseph, with reverence and shame. The boy gave a low whistle.)

"I must be the only person in the county who doesn't like chocolate," Ruth Massey used to inform her customers, "or coconut, either," holding her chin up. "It's too bad, because I can eat whatever I want and get no fatter than that coffee stirrer. Some women I won't name say they've got thyroid. My little pinky! They come in and eat half a dozen Bavarian Cremes, then they cook up a thyroid!" She'd revolve herself slowly in front of the mirror and admire the ease with which she fit into the smallest size of the doughnut company's stretchy peach uniform. People in the shop would nudge each other and say, "No one keeps herself from aging like Ruth Massey."

Now she sat all day tied to a wheelchair in a lineup of old men and women who were so formless that Massey couldn't tell right off which was his mother. He decided that he'd take Joseph to the home the next afternoon.

But Joseph complained that he already had invited a couple

of the other children in the development to help him celebrate
the last day of his visit. Previously, he had said they were
boring. Massey was so pleased at Joseph's attempt to engage in
normal pastimes that he granted his approval.

For the rest of the evening the boy practiced his trumpet
silently on the living room floor. After Joseph had gone to bed,
Massey told his wife he hoped the boy's calmness would last
long enough for their daughter to see it. "He just needed a firm
hand. Not that *you* used one. How could you watch while he
papered our yard and not stop him?"

"I can't scold him," she said. "He hurts worse from scolding
than any child I've seen."

"He'll hurt himself worse if he goes on."

She picked up the album, replaced it on the shelf, then stated
slowly: "God doesn't love people just because they're different,
but He doesn't hate them either. Oh, maybe He has a few
chuckles at their expense, but He loves them, too, because
they're His children."

He smiled at his wife. She couldn't be right, but he was
moved by the simplicity of her thoughts, of her apron and dress,
and the house that she kept for him, not showy or cluttered.
Ever since Joseph had said that he looked like a Rhino, Massey
had felt vulnerable, as if he stood out. But this house and this
woman made him feel hidden. He bent down and brushed his
lips against her puff of gray hair.

Flustered, she drew back. "I saw some yarn on sale, a pastel
peach color, and I thought I might knit a shawl for Mother Ruth
with it."

He straightened. "I guess it couldn't hurt," he told her, and
led the way upstairs.

The following day, Massey brought home a cracked plastic
cage from the Mouse House. Entering the garage to replace the
shoe box, he stopped dead. A crowd of boys and girls were
gathered around the workbench. "A couple of" meant two to
Massey, not fourteen. The last thing he had wanted by saving
the mice was to make himself into the town's Pied Piper.

Joseph stood at the center of the ring. It pained Massey to

think that his grandson was setting himself up for the derision of his peers. None of the fourteen, all blue jeans and sweatshirts, stood out from the others. Joseph was a blaze of absurdity in their midst, rhinestones dangling from one earlobe, steel studs on his black vest, pants that glowed orange.

"I grew up around here," the boy was saying, and they listened as rapt as if he had been a demagogue poor-boy campaigning for Congress. "I grew up around here, so I know how boring it can get. You want to feel like someone, shake everyone up, but if you do different, people say you're queer. Down in Miami—that's where I live now—everyone does it, so no one gets called queer, and life's lots less boring, I'll tell you.

"I mean, look at these mice. The reason that most mice get their necks broke in traps is because they all look like nothing. But just you imagine if one of *these* mice ran out of its hole and into your kitchen. Your dad wouldn't stomp it. He'd try to catch it and put it on TV. If all of the world's mice looked like these here, none of them would get killed and none would get laughed at."

The boy moved to one side to open the workbench more clearly to their view. Massey stepped forward. The children turned their heads.

He couldn't believe it. One mouse was wearing a little blue suit with white stripes; tied to its head was a hat like a sailor's. A second mouse was as red and shiny as a toy fire engine. A third was wrapped in a space suit of aluminum foil. Other mice had antlers made out of tree twigs, tails plumed with feathers, fur pasted with gold stars and glitter. One mouse, in a tutu, was shoelaced to a cardboard cutout of Fred Astaire.

That did it. If their skins were painted, living things couldn't breathe. And the Lord hadn't meant for His four-legged creatures to be tied in the embrace of cardboard movie stars and forced to stand upright. Massey pushed through the circle, pulled the boy roughly to him and sat heavily with the boy across his lap. Joseph was too stunned to struggle. He didn't even try to twist around, just hung limply over his grandfather's thick knees. The boy's pants were stretchy at the waist, as were his Jockeys, and before Massey knew it, his hand was slapping naked buttocks.

After the second slap the boy jumped to his feet, grabbed his pants up to his hips, tucked the shoe box under his arm and pushed his way through the other children. "Isn't any human being deserves that!" he shrilled out, and ran down the driveway.

Massey found himself sitting awkwardly on the bench with fourteen blank-faced adolescents around him, until one by one they dropped their eyes to their sneakers and drifted away. All right, he should have punished Joseph in private. But it was high time that someone had beaten this nonsense out of the boy.

When Joseph didn't return for dinner, Massey didn't worry. The boy would no doubt brood on his spanking, and when the evening got too dark and chilly he would come home and sneak upstairs. He knew that his bus would leave for Miami at eight the next morning; he wouldn't risk getting left in Tennessee a minute longer than necessary.

Massey put on his bathrobe and started up the stairs. Good thing his wife was still at the church, cooking hot dogs for bingo—she would have insisted he call the police. He snapped the light off and lay on the blanket. He closed his eyes, dozed, and saw himself shoveling live mice from a squirming heap into an incinerator. When he opened his eyes, he was as wet as if he actually had been stoking a furnace. He heard only his breathing, heavy and rough, until the slow notes of a lonely horn mingled with his rasping.

At first he thought someone was playing a phonograph. The song was familiar, but he couldn't name it because the musician was turning it upside down and inside out, ruining the simple tune with a tortuous squealing and wailing. Then his ears trained on the source of the music. He went to the window over his yard.

Joseph was holding his trumpet to the moon. No crepe-paper braids ornamented the horn now, only the cold, molten light, burnishing the brass. The boy stood in a circle of dead branches and colored paper. A red watering can sat by his feet, and the shoe box.

As Massey listened, the improvisation untangled itself into an unadorned Taps. This made him think of the boys in the Army, each considering himself invincible because of who his daddy was or the great job or girlfriend he had waiting for him, and the next thing you knew, he was a dead boy with no face.

Massey had not realized that his grandson could play the trumpet so it gave a person the shivers. The trumpet must have been something deeper in Joseph than green hair or earrings, something he couldn't help. Maybe if Joseph were given permission for just this one difference, he would give up the others.

But the boy couldn't be allowed to show off at such a late hour in such an exposed place. The phone would start ringing any moment. Massey tied up his bathrobe, but even before he could step from the window, the boy had stopped playing. Massey watched as Joseph doused the dry wood and paper with water from the can. Then, just as Massey was seeing that the spout on the can had nothing to do with water, the flames rose in a low circle around the boy.

"Put that out this instant!" he yelled to Joseph. "Go turn the hose on it!"

The boy needed only to step over the fire to get clear, but he just resumed his playing, a more frenzied song now, notes as erratic as the spastic dancing of the flames around him.

He thumped quickly downstairs, marking his steps by "Jesus" and "damn him" until he reached bottom and raced out the door. He was halfway to the boy when the gas can exploded.

The flames whooshed up and closed around Joseph, as high as the boy's head. "Run through! Run, quick!" But Joseph was an immobile dark core in the fire; from the waist down he appeared to belong to it already.

Massey tore off his bathrobe and charged with his head down. "I'm a big tough-skinned rhino," he told himself. "I'll turn pink but won't feel it," and crashed through the flames. He hooked the boy's armpits and dragged him to safety, but he wouldn't let Joseph go for fear the boy would try to run from the fire on his back and so fan the flames there. Massey pulled off the vest, with its melting leather and its steel studs like hot brands. He threw the boy to the ground and yanked off his pants, then fell on top of Joseph and smothered his burning hair and underwear against the damp grass.

The boy's whimpering and rambling seemed to be coming from deep inside Massey's own body. He became conscious that he was lying naked on his naked grandson, and rolled off.

The boy lay for a moment as though he were dead. Then he shot up. "I left it! My trumpet! I left *them*! The shoe box!" He screamed from the pain that he probably didn't know yet was in his skin and not in his head, in what he thought he had lost. Then he collapsed.

Massey knelt by the boy and stared at the black skin, which already had blistered, and knew that his grandson would never again strive for notice, yet never escape it. As the neighbors came running across the yards of their houses, he leaned down and tried to shelter the boy.

HWANG'S
MISSING
HAND

HWANG'S
MISSING
HAND

I had lived fifteen years in Paradise, New York, without ever climbing to the offices and apartments above the shops on Main Street. The town was so tiny that it seems inconceivable I wouldn't have explored every square inch. But in small country towns, where no grid of streets maps out the status of anyone who lives at a given address, each family must chart its own forbidden neighborhoods.

When my father was young and still delivered mail on the hills above Main Street, he classified people according to whether their houses were silent or trembling with noise—not just the frenzied yapping of dogs, but the curses of a husband berating his wife for a weak cup of coffee or an imagined affair; the wails of a child being slapped for no reason; even a radio turned up too loud. If my father had to knock and ask for a signature, he hoped that nothing more threatening than a woman in a housedress would open the door. If her robe wasn't tied, if she flirted or scowled, he warned us against the family that night. When he grew older and was given the route the other men wanted—he'd have to climb stairs, but he wouldn't have to lug his bag up those hills—he cautioned my mother: "If you *have* to shop on Main Street, please, for God's sake, keep your feet on the ground!"

I came to imagine that second-floor world as an island that

floated over my head like Gulliver's Laputa, its inhabitants rich in some dangerous knowledge I needed to learn. I would look up and see the stockbroker's office where Lorna Berg had worked before she stole money and was sent off to jail (her son was the handsomest boy in our grade, kind, though aloof), or a man in an undershirt, the expression on his face not quite desire and not quite disdain. Each window seemed to illustrate an emotion whose name I couldn't yet pronounce. It was maddening to stand there like a backwards first-grader, not knowing the words to describe what I felt.

And now, at fifteen, I finally had a reason to ascend to that world: I had been granted an interview for my very first job, for a firm that insured camps and resorts throughout the Northeast.

"Over my dead body," my father said at dinner. "You don't know what's up there."

By "up there," he meant the floor above Sears.

"Don't you trust me?" I asked.

"Of course we do!" My mother wiped her hands on her apron and sat down to eat, though my father and I already were done. "It's not *you* we don't trust. You're too young to know what can go on in an office like that."

For a moment I thought she might actually tell me—if she knew it herself. But I saw her reconsider.

"All I can say is, no matter what time I walk by that building, two or three men are leaning out the windows"—she lowered her voice— *"watching women go by."*

I reminded my parents that I had to start saving money for college.

"Not like *that,*" my father said.

But the only other choice for girls in our town was waiting on tables at the local hotels, where they lost their virginity and learned to use drugs. In the end, the very name of the business calmed my parents. (*"Insurance,"* they whispered in their bedroom debates.) And how could they fear for my safety in a place where my history teacher, whom they knew and respected, earned extra money by working part-time?

My teacher, Mr. Noble, had informed me of the interview a few days before.

"Rothman," he said, "I lied to these people, I said you were competent."

I love his brusque speech, the way he called me "Rothman" instead of "Dianne." He had to disguise how much he favored me over my classmates; in the back of the room, two other students were planning the trip we would soon make to Gettysburg.

"It's a shame they won't let you be an adjustor, but the boss will never change. He'll never let a girl go out in the field. Still, in that office . . . Keep your eyes and ears open and you'll pick up a lot."

Like everyone else, I knew about the office where Mr. Noble worked. He often told cryptic stories in class about being an adjustor; their point seemed to be that the world wasn't the safe, rational place the rest of our teachers had led us to think. Like the R.O.T.C. captain who came to recruit seniors for the Army, Mr. Noble seemed to advertise a life that was more exciting and serious than the one that my parents had planned out for me. I wasn't supposed to be drawn to such stories. I was meant to pass through high school, and after that college, without being touched. This would earn me a job that would let me pass through life in much the same way. I didn't have to do anything. A's flew to me, clung. They formed a spiky armor that kept away trouble and boys my own age. I had never gotten a B. So what if I did? B's were just ink on paper.

"You'll have to take a test," Mr. Noble said. "But even a girl with your limited intelligence ought to squeak by."

He put his hand on my shoulder and walked me to the door. This display of affection, naked as it was, meant less than the insults. Dale and Andy looked up, then went back to their road maps, the gesture no more troubling than the sight of Mr. Noble, who also coached football, with his arm around a player.

We stood in the hall. Other kids passed by, but he didn't drop his hand.

"Don't blow it, okay?" He said this as if the test were a

gauntlet that I might not get through; but, if I did, he would be standing at the finish line, arms stretched out wide.

My interview was set for a quarter to four, but I got to the building a half-hour early. I killed some time inspecting the window of Ruthie's Fine Dresses. None of my friends went into Ruthie's except to make fun of the double-knit pantsuits and long-line brassieres; we never wore anything but tight straight-legged Lee's, T-shirts and workboots. For the interview I'd had to squirm my way into the only dress I owned, a stretchy blue mini I had bought in seventh grade. Earlier that day, when I had stopped by to see Mr. Noble for last-minute hints as to how to get the job, he had slammed his desk shut and looked at me hard. I thought he would tell me to go home and change. Instead, he whistled softly through the gap in his teeth.

"Well look at that," he said. "Rothman's got legs. And nice ones at that. Can't figure out why you girls go around like a bunch of stormtroopers. Especially girls who look so nice in a dress."

No one had ever bothered to comment on my body before this. Beauty and dress were not categories on which I was judged. Until then, I had existed in just two dimensions, and suddenly Mr. Noble had added a third. I examined my reflection in the window of Ruthie's, shyly, as though I were peeking at somebody else in the nude. I studied the way the elastic of my dress—the top part was gathered in puckery rows—stretched across my breasts, bunched at my waist, stretched again at my hips. I had pulled back my hair and I hadn't worn make-up so my face was a pale, featureless oval like the faces of the mannequins. My reflection was standing next to a dummy in a clingy red nightgown, hips thrust toward the glass. Only when a friend of my mother caught me staring ("You're a little too young to be shopping for a trousseau!") did I force myself to leave.

At last, at three-forty, I entered the door between Sears and the deli. The stairs rose before me like a rickety ladder. I had assumed that the office would be right at the top; instead, I found a maze of gloomy halls with warped floors. I passed DR.

HAND, PODIATRIST, a photographer's studio, a taxidermist, a door with a sign in gold script that said NOVELTIES AND JOKES, but the frosted-glass panes showed no lights inside.

I reached a dead end. A round, beveled window coated with filth looked out on Main Street. I had come several blocks, right through the walls of three or four buildings! I shivered with the thrill of finding connections where none were before.

Finally, a light behind one of the doors. COLONIAL CONNECTI-CUT INSURANCE, PLEASE ENTER.

The clock on the wall said three-fifty-two. I was seven minutes late! I almost walked out. I thought that a single mistake, like the faintest of taps on the end of a lever, would swing my whole life through a radical arc; I would never have another chance to succeed.

But the front desk was empty. Maybe they would think I had been waiting all along. . . . I sat on the bench that ran down one wall. From a room I couldn't see came high, nasal voices like strings being tuned, the rhythmic percussion of fingers on keys, syncopated by bells. I sat on that bench and listened with the same tautness in my chest and tingle in my thighs that I had felt when my music class had traveled to New York and entered a theater as immense as a universe, a galaxy of crystal over our heads, and listened to an orchestra pluck, hum and whistle, preparing for Carmen to appear on the stage.

"Can I help you? Oh, never mind. I *know* who you are. Don't tell me you've just been sitting there waiting!" The women who said this seemed less like a diva than a Kabuki performer. Her lacquered black hair was piled on her head, with a bright yellow pencil stuck in the top. A big crimson circle spotted each cheek and a heavy black eyebrow rose like a roof over each eye. She inspected me closely.

"Quite an outfit," she said. "Too bad we need a girl who has more in her favor than tits and an ass."

This woman seemed to hate me simply because I was younger than she was and had long, pretty legs! How could she think that she knew who I was? And what better sign that I had entered the life for which I had been waiting than being mistaken for somebody else?

"Jane!" she shouted. "Jane! That new girl is out here!" She turned back to me, a smirk on her red kiss-shaped lips. "You're Jack's girl," she said.

Jack? I thought. Jack? Mr. Noble's first name! This woman had the power to call Mr. Noble "Jack"!

"He sends us a different girl every few summers. They seem to come in cycles . . . a blonde, then a redhead. . . . You must be the brunette."

She made him sound like a pimp.

"He raves about them all." She glanced at me to see how I would take the news that I wasn't as special as I once might have thought. "But most of Jack's girls don't have what it takes."

What could this all-important quality be? Did I have it or not? And who in our school, the principal included, would have presumed to speak of Mr. Noble in this finger-wagging tone?

A high-pitched man's voice called from an office: "Cybil! Where'd you go? I *said* that I needed you."

"Oh, phooey," she said, flapping her hand. But the gesture didn't fool me. Her power was false; it only extended to young girls like me.

She huffed from the room. A few moments later an older woman appeared, tall and thin-boned, with sparse grayish hair. Her lipstick was white, as was the powder on her eyelids and cheeks; she seemed to be trying to cover her features as she might have used Wite-Out to erase a mistake.

"I'm Jane Givens," she said. "And *you* are Dianne. I've heard wonderful things about you, Dianne!"

Unlike the other woman, she seemed eager to believe them. She was handing me a gift: her innocence, her faith. I had been so looking forward to a dangerous adventure, and now I'd be burdened with this delicate gift.

"All right," she said cheerily. She held out a loop of brilliant blue plastic about six inches wide. "There's an easy little test. I'm sure that a girl who comes so highly recommended . . ."

I stood from the bench. The tops of my pantyhose showed beneath my hem. As I tugged down my dress I saw on her face that she had *wanted* to like me, now wondered if she should.

"You *can* use a dictaphone? I hope Jack wouldn't waste my time with a girl who has weak dictaphone skills."

For Mr. Noble's honor I would have to say yes. But this didn't seem a lie. If other girls knew how to use this machine, I could figure it out.

"I know," I said. "I can."

That's all it took to restore her good faith. "Of course you do!" she said. "I'm sure you'll do fine."

She led me through the room where the secretaries worked. All six wore earphones. The wires seemed to link them to a force that let their fingers vibrate so fast. And they talked as they typed, like an acrobatic troupe weaving scarves as they danced. I paused to watch, spellbound, but my guide hurried on; I was still an outsider, not privileged to witness this private display.

The rooms that we passed through grew smaller and darker. We picked our way between stalagmites of furniture and office machines and rusted gray file cabinets whose labels read EXPIRED, CASE CLOSED or DECEASED. I was starting to worry that I should have unravelled a thread from my purse when we reached the last room, the smallest and grimiest, with a dented metal desk and a chair with no back. On the desk was a gray, boxy machine I assumed was a dictaphone, a massive old typewriter and a Styrofoam cup with brown gum at the bottom.

"All right then." She gave me the blue plastic belt. "All you have to do is type what you hear, just the way you hear it." She patted my head. "I'll be back in half an hour. Take it easy. Don't rush."

So. There I was. The shiny blue plastic, rippling with waves, called to me like a Caribbean sea. It wasn't hard to guess how the dictaphone worked—slip the belt on the drum, slide the drum in the box. And surely the earphones belonged in my ears. My foot found the pedal. Prideful, I flicked the typewriter switch. The machine must have been the first electric model ever designed; when I opened the lid, I saw the flaked skin and fingernails, eyelashes, hair and pink eraser nubbins of the many secretaries who had used it before me.

The drawer was full of paper, yellow and creased as an old

woman's skin. I rolled a sheet in the typewriter, stepped on the pedal of the dictaphone and listened.

"Day of a curse . . . They stripped the clay man. . . ."

Instead of some sort of legal dictation, they had given me a sermon! That couldn't be right. But hadn't she told me to type what I heard? It must be a trick to test my obedience.

"Manna overcame the curse. . . . Destroyed in our sight . . . In Jews and asses . . . Ne'er goes she I shun . . ."

The man seemed to be preaching with a mouth full of sand. And the "r" on my typewriter kept getting stuck, so by the time I had finished, he was preaching in brogue: "Day of a currrrrse . . . Manna overrrrcame the currrrrse. . . . "

I tore up the paper, rolled in another, made the dictaphone back up. But when it went forward, like a recent acquaintance who regrets that he has been too confiding too soon, it skipped everything I had heard. Nothing I did helped me recover the start of the tape. I pushed on to the end, and when I looked back I saw that I had typed more gibberish in brogue.

Just as a girl with no knowledge of sex can often be seduced by the first boy who tries, so too a girl who never has failed gives in to despair at the smallest mistake. As I stared at that page of nonsense I panicked. The room had no windows, but I guessed it was dark out—I had been here forever. I couldn't face Jane Givens. I looked for a door that wouldn't take me back the way I had come and was finally expelled to the hallway outside. A small spill of light washed over the tiles at the top of a staircase. These weren't the same stairs I had come up, but once on the sidewalk I took my bearings from the Methodist church. The sky behind the steeple was blue, pink and white, as cheerful as icing.

I hated that sky, as I hated the smell of the young grass, the breezes that tickled my legs as a grown-up might tickle a grumpy little child. I climbed the hill to our house, where my mother was anxiously awaiting my arrival, staring out the window and tenderly molding salmon croquettes in the palms of her hands.

I slept little that night. In just a few hours I would have to tell Mr. Noble that he had gone to all that trouble to set up an interview for a girl who didn't have it. I almost stayed home, but what if he learned how badly I had done from somebody else?

It's easy to say that I gave Mr. Noble powers of judgment no one deserves. But at that age I needed so much to learn what it means to be human that I was grateful to any adult with the courage, or maybe the vanity, to stand up before me and reveal who he was.

Mr. Noble had lived a more dramatic life than anyone I knew. His father and uncle had died in a coal mine not far from Scranton. He lied about his age and ran off to join the Navy, reaching Korea just in time to be wounded—a gun had exploded, burning his chest. Back home at eighteen he talked his way into some little college, then took a teaching job in Paradise, where the industry—tourism—was as spotless and safe as a freshly made bed. By the time he woke up and missed the excitement of his earlier life, he was married to a woman as Catholic as he was and the father of six.

He wasn't the most popular teacher in school. He scared kids too much. But he was the most powerful. He was manly and rough, with a strong, well-lined face. Unlike Mr. Busey, whose fly was always open, or Mr. Walsh, who wore the same shapeless suit every day, Mr. Noble wore trousers that fit him the way a man's trousers should and white cotton shirts with the sleeves pushed way up. He would cock his fingers like a gun and order some kid: "Tell us everything you know about Eugene V. Debs."

He taught American History, 1850 to the Present, and something called Government. He didn't try to be objective. His vision of history was the only one he saw, so he thought it was fact. Week after week he repeated his "facts" until each of his students had absorbed by hypnosis: "Sacco and Vanzetti were martyrs to bigotry"; "The unions saved America"; "If Truman hadn't dropped the bomb on Japan, a million GI's would have died on its shores." No matter what politics his students later adopted, they would find themselves teaching their own kids these maxims at dinner some night, as they would find themselves singing Mr. Noble's favorite song, "Lips That Touch Liquor Will Never Touch Mine," when their husbands or wives asked for a drink.

His views about sex were more complicated. "All this freedom to lay anybody you want isn't going to last," he cautioned the boys. "Better get it while you can." "Ask them all," he advised. "A lot will say no, but you'll be surprised how many say yes." "The quiet girls," he said, "they're the ones who are hot."

Then he cautioned the girls: "Don't let them fool you. Men don't want women as equal partners—in bed or anywhere else. That's just a line. Be your own person. Don't give it away."

One time he asked: "I see what the guys get from all this free sex. But what do you girls get?"

"Fun," I said softly. Then, taking heart: "We get fun, Mr. Noble. Don't you think a woman enjoys having sex as much as a man?"

I spoke rarely in class—I was one of the quiet girls whom Mr. Noble teased. But nobody snickered or made a lewd joke; I had brought information that few of them had. Of course I was bluffing. I never had slept with a man. But how could I let Mr. Noble assume that girls were inferior? And I knew I was right. Just a hand on my shoulder could flood me with warmth. The *thought* of unbuttoning a man's shirt and kissing the hair on his chest could make me cry out.

"You think so?" He studied me. "I sure hope you're right." But in Mr. Noble's mind a woman was either a virgin, a wife or a good-hearted whore, and he couldn't understand where I fit in this scheme.

That morning in class, after I had failed my test for the job, I tried not to be noticed. I didn't hang around to talk about the latest Watergate news, school gossip, my future as a union organizer. As I slipped out the door I sensed his eyes on my neck, but when I glanced back he was wiping his scribbles from the board with a sponge, and with them, it seemed, any concern he had once felt for me.

I couldn't leave it that way. After dismissal I dawdled through the parking lot.

"Hey, Rothman, get over here!" He was standing by his Ford. He took off his jacket and tossed it on the seat. "Don't you owe me the courtesy of letting me know how yesterday went?"

"I fucked up," I said. (Like him, I was rude so no one would guess how deeply I cared.)

"What's that supposed to mean?"

"I fucked up the test. It was my fault. I couldn't do it."

To the side of the parking lot a boy in white flannel was batting pop balls into the outfield, where his teammates stood waiting with hands and gloves cupped, eyes lifted in prayer. Below us, on the track, girls in red gym suits scissored their legs and leapt over hurdles, threw their arched bodies over high poles. And those moments when they floated, suspended in air, made me understand why most other people preferred to be weightless, to live in the light. Maybe I would learn to prefer it as well, now that I had to.

"Ahh, you sound just like them." He motioned at the athletes. " 'Boo-hoo, Mr. Noble, I couldn't do this test. It was my fault. I'm stupid.' What a load of horseshit. You didn't try hard enough. Or maybe you got spooked. Or maybe it was *their* fault, ever think of that? Those machines you were using, ten to one they were junk. That Eicher is the tightest—"

"Watch out! Heads up!"

The ball bounced near our feet. He bent, scooped it up, then kneaded the leather as my mother would knead a salmon croquette.

"I suppose you'll give up. Just like the rest. I say to them: 'Okay, you can take the test again,' and they look scared as hell. They'd rather lay down and play dead."

He snaked back his arm and sent that ball soaring over the fence, over the heads of the guys who were waiting to catch it in the outfield, all the way to the pitcher; the ball smacked his glove. Nothing, I thought, would ever be more beautiful than the muscles in that forearm, tense against the skin, the ripple of his shoulder under his shirt, the flex of his wrist as he unfurled the ball, its arc through the air.

"It's your life," he said. He got in his car. "I'm just disappointed. I would've enjoyed having you around this summer."

He drove from the lot. For a long time I watched as the girls my own age kept running around that cindery track, kicking off, floating, legs long and taut, like thoroughbred horses being trained for a steeplechase, around and around.

Instead of going home I went back down to Main Street. It wasn't the pep talk, the obvious psychology of "I suppose you'll give up." It was just the information that I wasn't to blame. Why couldn't I have *seen* that?

I didn't get as lost finding the office as I had the day before. A dumpy, dour woman was sitting behind the receptionist's desk. "What do you want?"

"I'd like to see Miss Givens."

She regarded me as though I were up to some mischief, then turned and called: "Jane!"

Jane Givens hurried in, hugging a stack of files to her chest.

"I was nervous," I said. "I shouldn't have left without telling you. Could I please take the test again?"

"You were nervous." She nodded. "I understand," she said. She had spent her life avoiding anything that scared her. "But I have to get these finished. You know where it is. Go ahead and try it. And then, well, we'll see."

On my way to the room I forced myself to open one of the file drawers— it smelled of rotting paper—and I peeked in some folders. In each was a sheet labeled ACCIDENT REPORT. So this was the "sermon" I had heard on the tape! Not "Strip the clay man" but "Description of Claimant," not "Manna overcame the curse" but "Manner of Occurrence," and so with the rest: "Description of Site," "Injuries and Losses" and "Negotiations." The longest part was always "Manner of Occurrence," the story of whatever calamity had struck some worker or guest at a place we insured.

The blue plastic belt was just where I had left it, inside the machine. With my eyes shut I focused every brain cell on drawing that disembodied voice through staticky space. I still couldn't decipher most of the words, but I didn't let that stop me. I filled in the gaps with whatever seemed right, as you try to make sense of a dream the next morning or fill in your memories of a childhood event.

A second-cook named Lee had saved many years to bring his fiancée over from China. He got her a job washing dishes. Several months later, he found her in the pantry with the first-cook, named Hwang, who was holding her wrists and kissing her neck—or trying to kiss it, as the woman maintained. Lee seemed to accept that his wife was too frail to fight Hwang's advances. He didn't even seem to bear ill will toward Hwang; they had been very close friends, the only Chinese who had worked at this place before the wife arrived. But the next week, while the men were hacking apart an order of beef, Lee brought down his cleaver just below Hwang's wrist. According to Lee, the cleaver had slipped. Witnesses claimed that he had taken revenge. Either way, our company had to pay for Hwang's hand.

I typed very slowly and made few mistakes, though the "r's" still repeated.

"The typewriter's broken," I complained to Miss Givens when I gave her the sheets.

"Isn't it *dreadful?*" She smiled at me knowingly, as some women smile when deriding men's flaws. "All of them have something! We've been asking for new ones for the past twenty years."

I looked around the room at the other secretaries, who were still typing busily and tossing conversation at each other's heads. But I saw something else now. Every so often one of the women would smack her IBM, throw open its lid and poke at its guts. The women grimaced and swore, but this seemed an act in which they found pleasure. They had martyred themselves to these faulty machines and the men who gave dictation.

Over in the corner a small black-haired woman shook a fist at her dictaphone, a tiny Ralph Cramden. "Oooh, I'm gonna kill you. Straight to the moon." She switched on the intercom, which shrieked like a cat. "Alphie, come out here. I can't understand a damn thing you're saying."

A few moments later, a rumpled, sad-eyed man slouched toward her desk.

"Alphie," she said, "I've warned you and warned you, if you're going to dictate you gotta put that thing down."

"Aw, Agnes, get your ears cleaned."

From just this one sentence, which he mumbled around his enormous cigar, I recognized the garbled voice on my belt. He leaned down toward Agnes, transferred her earphones to his own ears and listened.

"*I* don't know," he groused. "It's something about the claimant getting kicked in the *tuches* by a horse."

"I'll kick *you* in the *tuches*!"

It upset me to learn that the world of adults—outside our house—was broken, disordered, anything went, a big unwatched playground: "I'm going to kill you! I'll chop off your hand!" But this also allowed the mystery and passion that my parents' planned universe seemed to preclude. In the spaces between the words you heard clearly, possibility dwelled; you were free to invent whatever meaning you chose.

Miss Givens asked some questions about how I did at school, my father's occupation, was I able to operate an adding machine, and from just these few hints she constructed a story about who I was. Because of this story, she decided to hire me. She decided to *like* me.

"Wait here, Dianne. I have to find the forms you're supposed to fill out."

As I stood by her desk the telephone rang. After a game that might have been called "It's Not *My* Turn to Get It," the Kabuki-secretary punched a button and answered. After she'd hung up, she announced to the rest of us: "This kid in the Poconos was chasing a girl and he ran through a door. A *glass* door. He got two hundred stitches." She said this as if the stitches had been a well-deserved punishment. "Good thing it wasn't the girl," she went on. "With a boy, scars don't matter." Her voice didn't allow a chance in the world that it wasn't his fault. He was young, he was male, so he must have been a hooligan.

Maybe this was true. But wasn't it possible that he and the girl had been playing the sort of game adolescents play with each other because it lets them touch, then run off again, pretending the brush of hand against breast or muscular thigh was only an accident? Maybe, as a joke, the girl had stepped lightly out of the way, while the boy, running faster, unable to slow his clumsy momentum, had crashed through the glass.

"Save it for Jack Noble. It's his territory. He's stopping by later to pick up his cases." This came from a woman veiled in blue smoke. She held her cigarette in a hand that was cocked like the hands of the mannequins in Ruthie's display. "Jack's always glad to go to the Poconos. Gives him the chance to stop off and see his tootsie in Scranton."

"Tootsie!" sniffed the woman who had taken the call. "That's a nice way to put it."

How could they know that Mr. Noble liked to visit a prostitute in Scranton? Not that I doubted for a moment he did. Not that I cared. Paying a prostitute, like joining the Navy, fighting for a union or digging for coal, seemed to me then to be one of the great transactions that made an ordinary man a part of something larger, something with weight. Besides, they sounded so cruel that I had to defend him. I imagined the prostitute sprawled on her bed, fleshy and white against red velvet sheets. "Jackie, don't go. When will you visit your Tootsie again?" And his wife at home, waiting. All these women, waiting, tied to their dictaphones, their kitchens, their beds. I would never be a woman who sat around, waiting. I would take what I wanted and leave, just like Jack.

Miss Givens returned with my application. I hadn't yet memorized my number from the government so I copied it from the card in my purse. As I filled in the blanks, I felt I had registered as a grown-up at last.

I met Mr. Noble as he came up the stairs. We seemed to be standing in the chute to a mine. I could even smell coal, though that must have been cigarette smoke clinging to his skin.

"Dianne," he said. "So?" His eyebrows went up.

His using my first name gave me a jolt. "So I got it," I said.

"You got it." He smiled. The gap between his teeth made him look young. "I guess we'll be seeing a lot of each other."

Silence choked the stairway like heavy black dust.

"There's a case in the Poconos," I said to him finally. "A kid ran through some glass."

"Damn it," he said. "There goes my weekend. That's a four-hour drive each way."

"You can always stop and visit your girlfriend in Scranton." I said this in a voice that I didn't know I had—husky, a woman's voice, wounded and coy. Nothing would have followed that summer if I hadn't said those words in that tone.

He drew back, surprised. "I thought I'd have an ally! You haven't worked there a day and . . . Ahh, they're just jealous."

I believed this was true.

"They don't understand how a man . . . Never mind. The fact is I don't know anyone in Scranton. Not anymore. And it gets lonely driving. How'd you like to come along? I can teach you the ropes."

I saw all those women tied to their dictaphones. I saw Mr. Noble holding a rope, the reins to a horse. These seemed to be the only options I had.

"So, how about it?" He pulled out his Pall Malls ("Wherever Particular People Congregate" it said on the pack) and lit a cigarette as casually as though such an invitation were an everyday thing. I pretended the same. We were planning a trip like the one our class was taking to Gettysburg next month. As we drove through the Poconos he would *teach me the ropes*.

"Sure. I don't mind."

"Good," he said, flicking the match to the floor. "Is there somewhere I can meet you on my way out of town in the morning?"

It surprised me how little thought this required. "How about the spillway out by the reservoir?" I would have to get there early, so he wouldn't catch me riding my bike, like a child.

He nodded. "That's fine. Be there at seven. And after we're done I'll treat you to dinner. I know a great little roadhouse."

I must have looked nervous.

"Don't worry," he said, "I'll get you back before bedtime." He held out his hand. "So, welcome aboard."

The touch of his palm—warm, dry, the flesh hardened beneath—made me understand, finally, the force that my parents so feared because it could swipe away order, make a mockery of plans. I was dizzy, and hot. My knees felt too spongy to hold up my legs.

"See you bright and early." He jogged up the steps, whistling "Lips That Touch Liquor Will Never Touch Mine."

I tried to walk home, but I only got as far as the bench near the bank. I watched people park their cars, feed coins to the meters. The men bought their papers and ducked in for haircuts, the women picked up their newly heeled shoes, came out of the bakery with waxed-paper bags of rye bread and rolls. Most of these people were as solemn as though completing such chores had been their whole purpose in reaching this age. But a few men and women, among them a close friend of my father, seemed skittish, distracted, kept glancing around and stopping to remember what to do next, and it struck me these errands might only be a cover for their real, secret lives.

I went with Jack Noble to the Poconos that Saturday. We didn't sleep together that night, or that summer, but eventually we did.

One afternoon the following August we were lying in a cabin on a lake in the Poconos and Jack swore he remembered every word I had said, every caress. He seemed to regard our affair as a great historical event he was proud to live through. He said that he hadn't felt this alive since his time in the Navy, as humble as though I had done him a kindness, like the major who had stopped by his bed in the hospital and asked how he felt. As he said this, he slipped his hand down my breast and cradled my waist with a gratitude and tenderness I couldn't have predicted a grown man would show.

"What I'm doing is wrong. Don't you think I know that?" he said. "It's like in the Navy. You get all caught up in . . . You don't think how serious . . . And then you get hurt, or you hurt someone else. I *have* to stop," he said. "You can't understand. . . . I'm just the first man you'll be with. Already you're thinking how I'll compare to the boys you'll meet in college, the professors you'll have. For me, you're the last. After you, I'll spend thirty, forty years remembering back."

To make him feel better I stroked his scarred chest, the skin there as puckered as the elastic on the dress I had worn to my interview. I envied how Jack had gotten those scars. That's how little I loved him. That's how young I still was.

Both of us knew our affair couldn't go on. But we thought we could end it whenever we chose. That wasn't the case. Toward the end of the second summer I worked at Colonial Conn, the secretary with the lacquered black hair told Jack that she had punched the wrong button on her telephone and heard what he'd said to me earlier that day. Jane Givens wouldn't believe her, but finally she had to. Jane had worked in that office for twenty-eight years, but she never had suspected that people really did the terrible things that she heard through her earphones. The revelation that they did made her even more sparse and pale than before. (A few summers later, on a visit to my parents, I saw her on the street and I ducked in a store. Why had I been so eager to squander the gifts she had given me, her faith and good will? Did I think that I'd always have so much of these to spare?)

Jack, being so much older than I was, had much more to lose. His wife wouldn't divorce him, but their twins, Matt and Erin, ran away from home. They came back, of course—they were only thirteen—but they never forgave him for their mother's shame, or their own. Mr. Seiken, the principal, let him go quietly, but Jack was afraid to apply for a job in some other school. He eventually became the assistant claims manager for an office in Pittsburgh. The one time he wrote, he said he missed teaching more than he ever could have guessed that he would.

The scandal took a terrible toll on my parents, but they never blamed me. They acted as though I had been injured, the victim of an accident beyond my control. It took me many years to convince them that such "accidents" befell me too often to be random bad luck.

I got to go to college, and, as Jack had predicted, to love other men. Because I was young, my actions barely mattered. A terrible mistake could still be atoned for, a wrong path retraced. Only later in my life did my errors bring sorrow that couldn't be recalled: when I slept with the friend of a man that I loved and he called off our wedding; when I screamed at my father what I had been wanting to scream for so many years— that I really was no better than the slatternly wives who tried to convince him to steal a few minutes from his route in their beds—then wished that I hadn't, he would never forgive me.

Maybe it was right that I wasn't held responsible for anything that happened. I was only fifteen. Jack was my teacher. He should have known better. But the facts of the incident, like the words on a dictaphone or the documents I studied for my history degree—can be construed many ways. And sometimes I think that I used Jack to learn what I wanted to know, and then I moved on. Jack loved me much more than I ever loved him. He lost everything he had.

All this came later. The first week I worked at Colonial Conn I was asked to type the settlement in the case the other women had taken to calling "Hwang's Missing Hand." An accident that serious could have dragged on for years. But, for some reason, Hwang accepted a sum far below what the company might have paid if he had claimed that he could no longer cook. Lee and his wife ran away suddenly. As I typed this, I wondered if she had ever loved Hwang, or if she had only gone in that pantry to learn what she'd missed those long years in China, so pure and alone.

With his check from our company Hwang bought a restaurant on the outskirts of town. Last week I was driving to a history conference in Upstate New York and I detoured through Paradise. I had no one to eat with—my father is dead and my mother in a nursing home, where she stares out a window, kneading thin air. I stopped in Hwang's restaurant, and I had to fight the impulse to go in the kitchen and watch him chop vegetables or bone a fish with one hand. I wanted to ask if he still kept his other hand—I imagined it mummified, soft as a glove—in a velvet-lined box, a memento of his passion, all he had risked and lost.

THE RABBI
IN THE
ATTIC

THE RABBI
IN THE
ATTIC

I.

The rabbi wouldn't move out. The house he wouldn't leave was for the use only of the spiritual leader of Emess Yisroel, which he was no longer. But how could we ask the burly police to break in with axes, to browbeat and handcuff a tiny old man, to cart off our rabbi to a black paddy wagon under the gaze of the town's gentle Christians?

Crushed in dilemma, our synagogue's leaders couldn't help but think what a delight the coming Holidays would be if only the rabbi had retained all his marbles. Such a throat—made of gold! And the cords in that throat—as sweet as the strings of King David's harp. His voice carried forward all for which we Jews were most nostalgic. To hear it, our hearts leapt. This was a voice that usually would bless only the wealthiest Reform congregations, not Jews in the Borscht Belt who kept alive serving the few old-age resorts that hadn't yet died.

And, at first, Rabbi Heckler had seemed sane, though intense. He scuttled through the synagogue and the streets of our town with his bloodshot eyes blinking, a fossil crustacean whose invisible feelers were taking in details, which he wrote in a book, licking the pen. Everyone assumed he was getting acquainted, keeping straight the names of important people. His sermons were harsh, but the tottering deaf men and chattering widows who made up attendance on most Sabbaths didn't hear

85

what he said. Even when he addressed the younger members at the *bar mitsve* of Natty Cook's eldest, his voice was so soothing, so resonant, so moving—especially after the *boytshik* screeching of Natty Cook's eldest—that few of us realized he had issued a warning that if we kept sinning, he would "whip us in shipshape."

He began with the children. In their after-school classes he drilled them in prayers, grammar, laws, these children who had only been asked until then to color with crayons or gamble with *dreydels*. Now, he clicked in his black shoes up and down the aisles. Holding a pen cocked in his hand, he would stop by a desk. "Okay, you will please to recite the *Alenu*. No looking, no stopping, and please, no mistaking."

The unlucky student gripped the sides of his desk and tried to remember even the first word of the *Alenu*. Though this was "*alenu*," the student couldn't think with the rabbi's black shoe rat-tat-tatting the floor.

"So? You have finished?"

When the student said nothing, the pen thwacked his head so loudly that his classmates jerked in their seats. Then the rabbi stepped forward to stand by the next chair.

"Rabbi, I'm sorry, I didn't have the time. My basketball team—"

"So! Time for bouncing, but not for study? How! Are we Greeks? You memorize—or else!"

All of them wriggled, anxious to escape, but the rabbi pulled out his notebook and barked: "Schwartz, tell your father he must come to *shul* on *shabbes*, he does this—or else!" And: "Rosen, your mother buys *treyf* meat from A & P when Rachlis, who is kosher, is next door. Tell her she must buy kosher—or else!"

This went on until the children lived in such terror of "Rabbi Or Else," his drills and his pen, his recruitment of spies, that they pleaded with their parents to let them stay home, feigned stomachache or headache, and if this failed, played hooky.

He turned next on their mothers. Interrupting a session of the Board of Trustees, he told the twelve men: "I must speak of your wives."

The Board heard his shoes click on the floor as he circled their backs.

"Our wives?" The men twisted, trying to see.

"Too visible," he said.

"I don't understand," said Herman Zlotkin, the Board's long-time Treasurer and the largest man on it, though smaller than his wife, a woman who was prone to wearing bright colors. "Too visible, Rabbi? You don't mean to say—"

"Hidden. They must not be seen."

"Are you insinuating we must lock up our wives?"

"No, no, not locking. A balcony will do. With a tall screen around."

"A balcony? Tall screen? It isn't enough the women sit apart, they must also be hidden? Even if we thought our wives were so beautiful that they might distract us, are you suggesting we completely rebuild the sanctuary, spend thousands of dollars, money we don't have . . ." Zlotkin waved his enormous ledger, then started to push himself up from his chair.

The rabbi, half his size, put a hand on his shoulder and kept him from rising. "Rebuilding is ideal, but no one will say I am not reasonable person. For cheaper money, we build a wall down the aisle between us."

The meeting, which had been intended to last only a short time so the Trustees could finalize plans for a Monte Carlo fundraiser, kept the men from their wives until early that morning. The rabbi kept circling, didn't weaken or sweat, shot Scripture at their backs while they drew together like settlers in a wagon train with no ammunition. They suffered besiegement until they were able to convince Rabbi Heckler that his motion be tabled to give them a chance to look into the cost of partitions and walls.

At this he decided that the Trustees were worthless. He must try his own method: He would harry the few old ladies who still worshipped at the synagogue in the hope they would eventually stay home altogether. In the midst of a service he would say from the pulpit: "Mrs. So-and-so, quiet, no gossip or leave." And Mrs. So-and-so left, as fast as she could on legs that were feathers. Even Miss Abel, who prepared the *kiddush* that followed the service, was reprimanded for rattling her trays in the next room while prayers were in progress.

At the beginning, since the rabbi lived alone, his wife having passed on from lumps in the breast, the women took pity and asked him to supper. Miss Abel, who had waited fifty years for a man of rigorous principle—iron in his bones, a Jewish crusader—to come to her town, invited the rabbi to dinner in her tiny apartment, then spent the weekend soaking a brisket in brine and squinting at labels in frozen-food cases in search of "Ⓤ's" and "*Pareve's*" that would have been too small for eyes that were younger and aided by much cleaner spectacles. When she finally set the table, the linen was new, the silver just-boiled and the sweet wine and soda sealed with the approval of convocations of rabbis.

Promptly at seven Rabbi Heckler buzzed and entered, bypassed the table without even glancing, made straight for the kitchen and cited infractions she never had heard of—the wrong brand marshmallow, wrong washing arrangement. He nibbled a few grapes, swallowed a mouthful of raspberry soda, then excused himself early, at which Miss Abel declared to her empty apartment: "Let him eat his so-very-kosher meals alone!"

Even at weddings he often would not eat. Many times he refused even to perform the service. He would tie up an engagement in such knots of Talmudic objection that no one was able to untangle his logic. Not only wouldn't he marry a couple if each child and parent were not one-hundred-percent Jewish by his specifications, he would visit those couples united by previous rabbis or judges and harangue and harass them until they were crying.

One afternoon he confronted the McCoys (Adele née Rabinowitz and Frank Patrick Randall) in front of Woolworth's and accused them of completing the project that had been started by Hitler.

"And this? What is this?" He grabbed Frank Junior's arm. "Is fowl? Is fish? Is circumcised? Is not?"

While Frank Junior wailed and tried to get free, Adele's mother, Eva, happened by in her car. She parked, gaped, got out, and grew so incensed that although she had not spoken to her mix-marriaged daughter in five years, she reconciled herself to a situation that seemed less sinful the longer the rabbi ranted. By the end of his tirade Eva was shouting: "Frank McCoy is a good and kind man who cares for my daughter. He does not scream on Main Street or make innocent boys cry. And if you, Rabbi Heckler, continue to represent the Jewish religion in my town, I just might convert to Catholicism." At which Eva embraced her son-in-law Frank with a passion that made all three McCoys gasp.

A separatist rabbi: No mixing! No *goyim*! He shamed us in front of our liberal neighbors—a Jew had to look down in front of liberals! He would not even take part in the yearly meeting of the town's clergy, a discussion of projects of mutual concern, merely because he wouldn't enter a church—as if a Unitarian Social Hall could be mistaken for a church!

Our embarrassment mounted as he began to wage holy war on us men. If an office or store remained open on the Sabbath, he would burst through the door, disregard patrons, lecture and threaten. So incensed was he when he discovered that Isidore Pipchuck, the town chiropractor and synagogue *shammes*, the man who on weekdays manipulated the affairs of the congregation with such dexterity that the very building might have crumbled without his efforts to hold it together, on Saturday afternoons, not more than an hour after the service, this same Izzy Pipchuck was back in his office manipulating the strained muscles of patients, writing bills for them, handling their money.

The rabbi steamed across Pipchuck's waiting room with such speed that three *Reader's Digests* were sucked in his wake. From the threshold of Pipchuck's inner office the rabbi issued this ultimatum, right across the shirtless back of a patient: "You must abide by the *shabbes* rule of no labor—or else you must step down as *shammes*."

"These hands heal suffering!" hissed Pipchuck, a man made of wires with a fine skin stretched over them, his entire being an organ of such refined sensitivity to slight that he registered every mis-said word as an insult to his name, faith, profession. This triggered revenge, whether real or imagined. He would grab in his hands the flesh of the slighter and pull it and twist it until he heard moaning: "Thank you, oh, thanks Doc, I owe you my life."

Pipchuck faced the rabbi. "This man was in pain! Could God object to the art of healing? And who else would perform the duties of the *shammes* for no pay? Just try to manage without Izzy Pipchuck!"

"We manage," he said. "We manage without a pagan who spends *shabbes* rubbing naked bodies."

The patient who had been stretched on the table in Pipchuck's office struggled to sit up, uncertain whether he had been insulted, or only Pipchuck. Since this patient also happened to be Hyman Abromovitz, the synagogue president, Pipchuck availed himself of the chance to express his anger by taking leave from the sexton's duties—*let* the building crumble!—and to declare that he would not attend another service if the rabbi ran it.

Attendance fell further when the rabbi nosed out the secret parking lot where the old men who judged themselves too feeble to walk to *shul* on the Sabbath parked their cars. He crouched by the dumpsters of Sy's Hotel Plumbing. When a car would sneak in, the rabbi pounced. *Ambush!* His sharp shoes kicked tires, his small fists beat windshields. Even Herman Zlotkin he kept imprisoned inside his black Buick, though Zlotkin howled: "I must ride! A heavyset man with emphysema cannot be expected to walk up a steep hill. How would it look if the Treasurer, who is an elected official, was found dead in the weeds!" Because this Herman Zlotkin did indeed live in terror that he would drop dead the next instant. He frequently pictured his collapse among the corroded remains of hotels in his junkyard, and, as bulky as he was, he feared he might lie unnoticed and rusting among the old stoves and bedsprings for weeks.

"So lose weight!" the rabbi shouted at Zlotkin, who even now was sitting in tears at the image of his own oxidation. "Lose weight, but don't drive!"

The ten of us men who walked to the *shul* he covered with shame. "How dare arrive late! Come at beginning or don't come at all." He saw into our pockets: "How dare carry money on God's holy day!" And: "Abromovitz, get up!" (Yes, he called even the curve-backed president to account.) "If you can't stand up quicker don't sit on the stage, a bad example to all." (Or maybe, we murmured, this rabbi thinks that he is the only person who belongs on the stage.)

Finally, he expelled Lazarus Schmuckler, the retired *shoychet,* little old mushroom Lazarus Schmuckler, because he made noise. This wispy nothing who *davened* so only the white hairs in his nose got the pleasure of hearing, he made too much noise? No, he prayed softly. But after each *aw-mayn* he added a coda, put all his tiny soul of a mushroom into chanting: da-DAI-dai-dai-ai-ai-DAI-ai-ai. And the rabbi couldn't stand this donkey tail being pinned on his voice, so out Schmuckler went.

The very next night Rabbi Heckler revealed just how badly he was infatuated with his own voice, so we realized that he was not just a stickler, but a lunatic also. He commanded a taxi to drive to the fanciest hotel in the Mountains, and when the gatekeeper inquired whether the man in the back seat was a paying guest or not—the hotel, after all, was not for town riffraff who sought free amusement—the rabbi informed him: "I play the piano!" and the gatekeeper nodded and let him pass through, thinking this must be tonight's entertainment.

When Rabbi Heckler appeared in the dining room he was noticed with amazement and alarm by Pipchuck and Schmuckler, neither man riffraff, each had a purpose: Pipchuck rubbed the limbs of guests who had contorted themselves in Simon Sez and shuffleboard, while Schmuckler, who had once been the chief inspector of the hotel's kitchens—an inspector who kindly averted his eyes when a beef cut or saucepan wasn't quite kosher—had been given permission to eat here for free whenever he pleased, which was often, it seemed.

Pipchuck and Schmuckler watched as the rabbi wiped off the keys of the piano in front of the room and began serenading the guests as they dined. And did Rabbi Heckler enlighten this crowd with melodies or folk songs from Hebrew culture? No. Broadway show tunes. *South Pacific. Oklahoma!* A medley of love songs from Gershwin and Berlin.

Between soup and fish, the guests clapped their hands.

"Such a wonderful voice! What timbre! What range!"

"But there's something peculiar . . ."

"So cute, though. Old-fashioned."

"Once, he was someone. Now he's a has-been. A *shikker,* may be."

Pipchuck jumped up. Already he was tying the straitjacket behind Rabbi Heckler. Schmuckler, in whom the flavor of revenge would have revolted as strongly as oysters, tugged at Pipchuck's sleeve. "Perhaps if we ask very nicely he'll go."

"And perhaps the owners will call the asylum and have him hauled off!" At this Pipchuck skipped to the manager's office. He returned with two bellhops, who casually approached the mystery pianist and asked him to stop. Once more. A third time. They lifted him by an armpit, an arm.

He started to rave: "A rabbi! How dare!"

The young bellhops paused, but what could they do? Holy man or not, he was still a disruption. Egged on by Pipchuck ("Don't trust him! He's crazy! Look at his eyes!"), they dragged him outside.

But the rabbi kept screaming from beyond the locked door. Everyone heard him over dessert: "Philistines! Cossacks! Let me in—or else!"

This straw was the last. The Trustees appointed their most tactful threesome to visit, advise. Over tea Zlotkin scolded: The time was approaching to vote on his contract (two sugars, stirring), and if Rabbi Heckler didn't change his behavior . . . a reprimand only, and thanks for the tea.

For a week Rabbi Heckler lessened his fervor . . . until the next Sabbath, when he delivered a sermon whose theme was forgiveness. Those few of us who heard it assumed he was asking a second chance, mercy, and we thanked the Almighty that his madness had gone. Several eyes were moist, and Miss Abel's arms lifted as if to welcome her errant crusader back to the bosom of his congregation. Then came the end of the sermon, its moral: "And so you must find in your hearts to forgive, show your enemy kindness, give him a contract—or else he will sue!"

The Board of Trustees gathered around their table, as grim as twelve hangmen. They would let Rabbi Heckler present his defense. He still had supporters, for what was his crime except for devotion, and wasn't his voice as rare as a lark's?

But when he was summoned, he taunted the men: "You'll regret! I won't go!"

"Is that a threat, Rabbi?"

"Yes," he said simply, and lost his supporters.

His contract expired. The Board didn't renew it. But the rabbi wouldn't leave the house to which his right also had expired. Pipchuck (self-banished no longer, his value now proved) shared surveillance of the house with Abromovitz and Zlotkin. As far as they knew, the rabbi never went out, and when the three men peered through the shutters, they saw bare floors and walls. The rabbi had lived there with only a suitcase, a few books, a cot, all of which he must have moved to the attic to gain a better perspective, one room to defend. The only light shimmered from the third-story window.

To pass the dark evenings they imagined him spooning cold food from tin cans, pissing in the empties and pouring the contents from his window at dawn. Secretly, each of the sentinels was glad the rabbi didn't come down to breathe the night air. Who knew but they might appear in the next morning's paper, rolling across a lawn while choking a rabbi?

"Time is on our side," said Pipchuck one night as the three men kept watch. "Also, the law."

"The law, eh? The law—feh!" Thus spoke Herman Zlotkin, with the contempt of a man who has just been told by the Town Council to put up a high fence to conceal his big house and the scrap yard around it. ("To him all that rusty metal looks green," the synagogue wags said, though not to his face.) "Not only won't the law solve our problem," Zlotkin went on, "if no law existed, our problem wouldn't either." He hacked and growled harshly, as if he had installed in his throat a crane such as he employed to hoist scrap in his yard, and when the phlegm came up, he wrapped it in cotton and made a deposit in his trouser pockets. His companions ignored this. They told themselves mucus was not mucus in the pockets of Herman Zlotkin, it congealed to silver and fell from the cloth in thick coins, which he donated to the synagogue and the public library with such generosity that even the Town Council had taken four decades to politely request that he put up the fence.

"No Christian could comprehend how a congregation could dismiss a reverend for too-strict observance," said Hyman Abromovitz, who not only presided over our synagogue, but also taught science at the junior high school in town. He was missing one eye, but, even so, his discernment was keen; he dissected the world into microscopic divisions. "The Catholics," he went on, "have many laws also, but a church cannot dismiss. The Pope has that power, but he too is zealous. Complaints of this nature would only be taken in the priest's favor. And Protestants? Their idea of a zealot is a minister who asks them politely on Sunday to help with the bake sale that's coming on Wednesday. No Christian could conceive that our laws number six-hundred-thirty."

"Excuse me, Hyman, but the laws number only six hundred," said Pipchuck.

Abromovitz pawed his cane through the dirt, one stroke, another, tallying the laws as they came to his head. As a man of science he placed chiropractors in the same category as faith healers and dispensers of hoodoo, but his bent back responded better to Pipchuck's hoodoo than science, a dependence so irksome that Abromovitz always looked out through his good eye for any chance to catch Pipchuck in error. "It is six-hundred-thirty, not one more or less!"

"Please, please," said Zlotkin. "You'll both agree, I'm sure, that all but a few of these laws are worthless—rusty bits, spare parts that should have been scrapped in the days of King Solomon. I suggest that we tackle our immediate trouble. In four days, Rosh Hashanah, and we have no rabbi."

Each of the wise men now stood in silence, entertaining this notion: They would lure Rabbi Heckler from the house with flattery, and, after the last prayer on Yom Kippur, they would nab him and drive him to New York, where they would leave him with a few dollars to tide him over. But sadly they each reached this conclusion: The madman was too smart. He would never come out of the house unless the congregation promised to renew his contract, binding for one year, perhaps forever. This was his design. He knew we would get frantic as the New Year approached and we had no rabbi to sing on our behalf, apologize for us in tones that were pleasing, deliver a honeyed petition to insure our inclusion in the Book of Life, which now lay open on the Almighty's lap. So many people always attended the service on Rosh Hashanah that the secretary had to sell reservations. Such a mob and no rabbi . . . there might be a riot. And who could be hired on such a short notice? What rabbi would come to this impoverished nowhere for the *pishochs* we offered, especially if he had to rent his own lodgings— the congregation had no money for an apartment when a perfectly good house (with expensive upkeep) adjoined it already.

"Gentlemen," said Zlotkin, who had been meditating in just this manner, "the answer has come to me at last." While he hacked they waited, as if his insides were fertile not only for mucus and money, but also ideas. "We obviously must seek out a rabbi who is desperate for a post. Perhaps he is—you'll excuse me, Hyman—a cripple in some way that makes him undesirable for a less tolerant congregation than ourselves. Perhaps he has a new wife, who is pregnant, he's fresh from the Yeshiva, he's in debt, whatever. Now, when he gets here, we tell him: 'This house is your house, but you must get out the current occupant. He will listen to you. A rabbi knows what arguments to use on a rabbi. If you do not succeed, we're very sorry, but you must find your own lodgings.' And, if he's desperate, he will make the attempt."

No need to relate in Talmudic detail the objections of Pipchuck, Abromovitz' rejoinders. These were for show. In their hearts all three men acknowledged that such an understanding of human behavior lay at the base of Zlotkin's riches. And the next day, when they were driving in Zlotkin's Buick to New York to ask the Director of the Yeshiva if he could assign an Orthodox rabbi who was desperate for a post, the only dissension among them was as to the best way to phrase the request.

Now, you might well ask: Why should a congregation that

prefers free living to rigid obedience look for a rabbi of the Orthodox persuasion instead of the newer, more liberal traditions—Conservative, Reform? The answer is simple: Orthodox comes cheapest.

But the dispenser of Orthodox rabbis was tired of seeing his graduates abused. "Ten rabbis in twelve years! You treat them like sawdust. And now you want my help in order so you can treat *two* rabbis bad at the same time."

"Begging your pardon, Honored Rabbi Doctor," said Pipchuck, "but we have none at all. If you will remember, our previous rabbi now has no contract."

"And you have no compassion! I can guess your plan. You would subject a fresh-new rabbi to kicking his elder into the street. You would treat an old man who is unwell in the head to this disgrace."

"Begging your pardon, Honored Rabbi Doctor," said Pipchuck, "but if you knew he was unwell in the head, you might have warned us before we hired—"

The rabbi lifted a fist. "You say this to me? When you needed a rabbi, did you dare come and say: 'Assign us a rabbi, this is your job'? No! And why not? Because you are ashamed. Because you pay less and treat worse than any congregation in New York—in United States, perhaps! No, you cannot face me, so what do you do? You get a rabbi from a newspaper. Does it never occur to you that a rabbi who is trying to sell himself in an advertisement under the notice for old refrigerators, is something wrong with him? That if something is not fishy, he would get his job through me? No, you are perfect matches for each other. You have him, you keep him. You will not drive crazy a young man who has a future before him. And God help the poor old rabbi you have driven to seek refuge in that house."

"Perhaps true," said Abromovitz, "but if you will not help us, we must seek a rabbi from one of the other seminaries. This will mean one less Orthodox congregation in the world, and it will be your fault."

"My fault? Is my fault? One less of your kind, good rubbish! Go hire a bishop, a Buddhist for all I care!"

Subdued, the three left, conferred among themselves, de-

scended by car from the Bronx to Manhattan, parked the Buick
in what they hoped was a safe spot not far from the Conservative
college and stepped onto the sidewalk, where all three, even
Zlotkin, were jostled by strangers with faces as indifferent and
battered as the bottoms of old kettles and taunted by hoodlums
who carried on their shoulders demon-filled boxes. Pipchuck
healed cripples, but here were so many deformed human
beings, people in pain that lay beyond even his knowledge of
vertebrae to cure, that his own legs grew heavy from despair.
Abromovitz, whose single joy in life was the bringing of order,
especially to youngsters, saw that the larger world was so
powerful and ruthless that it would never let itself be stuffed into
the compartments he so cherished. In the minds of all three
men was one thought: Abandon this mission, get back to the
Catskills. But how could they do this if they didn't bring a rabbi?

"Gentlemen," said Zlotkin, "let us gird up our courage.
Because we have no choice. We must ask directions." Which
Zlotkin himself did, thinking he would rather die from a knife
wound, a martyr for his friends, than collapse to no use among
toilets and tubs.

With Zlotkin in front, the three men at last scaled Morningside
Heights. They found the right office, gained an appointment,
waited and waited, and ten minutes later were back on the
sidewalk, daunted not only by the price they had heard quoted,
but also by the black name our town had acquired even among
the Conservative rabbis.

"Unfairly! Unfairly!" said Pipchuck.

"If the price is so much for Conservative, should we even
bother with Reform, for whom the richest congregations must
compete for the few that exist?" Abromovitz forgot his hopeless-
ness of a minute before to revel in this analysis according to the
laws of supply and demand. "And what will the Board say if we
should return with a young Reform rabbi who wears blue jeans,
strums a guitar and eats roast pork in public, a man who goes
farther than even we are willing to go?"

"Gentlemen," said Zlotkin, "we must recall," and he hitched
up his trousers, "that we have no choice."

But even the well-insulated stomach deep in Zlotkin's belly

grew cold when the Director of Placements at the Reform seminary mentioned the salary that would purchase the least-outstanding rabbi among his recent graduates.

Pipchuck was the first to recover, reassured slightly because the Director had not heard of the town's reputation or the rabbi who wouldn't leave the attic. "But isn't there one new graduate who is, how might I put this, so unfortunate in some respect, so eager for employment, that he would be glad to receive any position, even at the meager salary which is, regrettably, all we can afford?"

The Director pursed his lips. He shook his head no. Then he said: Well, he did have one rabbi . . . a good heart, not brainless, but, well, this one graduate had been lacking in . . . discipline. No, not immoral, but no head for study. Not igno-rant, just . . . fuzzy. And yes, to be frank, the singing was atrocious. But then again, she . . .

In chorus, with no disharmony from the grudges among them, there issued a wailing that sounded as if it had reached the present after a long and tear-stained journey from the Middle Ages, a prolonged lamentation of a three-letter pronoun.

But when the lament had died from their lips, they nodded, accepted, for as Zlotkin put it on the drive home: "Gentlemen, we must face up, this world is changing." He hacked, then smiled slightly. "And let us consider . . . When opposing parties are set in conflict, when the struggle is over and the dust has settled, there may be no victor, only two vanquished, and the field is left open for the appearance of a new leader, a man whom the Lord sends from only-He-knows-where to care for His people."

And with this faint comfort the men took advantage of the ten exits left them to think of the words to explain to the Board why they had hired a Reform woman rabbi with no mind or voice, even for two weeks, on a trial basis.

II.

Marion Bloomgarten had achieved ordination through the force of a good heart, then watched as her classmates were one by one chosen, even the other women, who, because they had been doubted, worked twice as hard and earned highest honors. Left on the sidelines, alone in New York, she waited for winter with no hope for work. So when Marion was summoned by the Director of Placements and told she had been given a trial position, no application or interview needed, then handed a ticket for a bus to the Catskills, she was ecstatic. True, the congregation to which she was going had been led until now by Orthodox rabbis. But this gave her visions of blowing the shofar and causing the wall between the sexes to crumble. She saw Jew and gentile sharing grapes beneath the viney roof of the *succah;* began to plan outings on which the children would open themselves to I-Thou encounters with deer, sparrows, bushes; saw a temple where the blessed could gather, a center from which a renewal could ripple outward until it encompassed a town so small that one congregation of good Jews could effect decency, clean streets, parks, playgrounds and visits to elderly shut-ins. Under her guidance, Emess Yisroel would become a synonym in the minds of people of all faiths for justice, peace, caring.

The bus terminal was a flimsy gray shack at the more decayed end of Main Street. Three men were waiting. One was so sloppy, always spitting in a rag, that she barely could look at him. The second man was nervous, with the hands of a strangler clawing the air. Behind these two creatures skulked a humpback old pirate with a patch on one eye.

She stepped from the bus.

"Miss . . . Madam . . . Rabbi . . ."

The ride in the Buick to the three-story house that stood by the synagogue was mercifully short. The house was as crooked and unkempt as the members of the greeting committee. But, to a woman who had grown up in a borough where half a duplex was considered spacious, it presented a prospect so expansive that her heart swelled to fill it. She imagined the orphans and unwed mothers, the emigrées from Russia and boat people from Asia who soon would share it with her.

She jumped from the car. A storm of tin cans ricocheted from the sidewalk. Marion ducked.

"Please, Rabbi Heckler," the strangler shouted toward the roof, "this is also a rabbi. Don't you think you should give her the same treatment as you yourself would want? Take pity on a poor struggling scholar. Take pity on . . . a woman of Torah."

This brought a bald ghost to the third-story dormer. "A woman rabbi is an a-bom-in-a-tion!" Another can flew. It bounced on the slate and rolled to her feet. She had just read the label—Rokeach Stuffed Cabbage—when the strangler pulled her back into the car.

"You will understand, I'm sure"—Zlotkin sounded offhand—"that we can neither afford to pay for a second rabbinical lodging, nor go to the courts." Cans struck the roof and windows like hail. "For two weeks, until Yom Kippur is finished, we will pay for a room at a motel. If you haven't persuaded your predecessor to vacate by then, you will have to make do as best as you're able."

When Marion heard this, comprehended their intrigue, she felt as if each word from Zlotkin had been a worm she had been forced to swallow. Angry and fearful, she started to demand that he drive her back to the station, but was stopped by the realization that she had no money for a return ticket, and that even if she did get back to New York, nothing was there—no apartment, no job. Before she knew it, she had let them drive her to the Motel on the Cliff, the only lodging within walking distance of the synagogue.

The Cliff was not a cliff at all, just a few feet of rock overlooking the town. The door of each unit once had been painted a different bright color, but these had now faded, so the motel stretched across the hill like a lurid slattern who reclined on one arm and mocked the town below.

Marion refused to let the committee carry her suitcase, less from conviction than distrust. They would meet her at the synagogue the next day, they said. Then they drove off. Marion looked up. A few of the letters of the neon were dark. MOTEL ON THE IF . "I don't mind if you test me," she muttered to God. "But cut out the wisecracks!" Suitcase in hand, she limped to her room and threw herself down on the worn chenille bedspread, where she lay the whole night searching for solace in the trials of Queen Esther, Deborah and Ruth.

III.

Prophet of the Bronx. Redeemer of New York. Marion Bloomgarten always had known that she would lead the Jews of her borough, state, country to liberation. No longer would they be slaves to their small stores, drones with no spirit, no culture except for a paper menorah taped to the window in December and a few words of Yiddish that even black actors on TV now used. But Marion would not bring the Law to redeem them, injunctions as weightless as the dandruff that sifted from the round shoulders of her Hebrew school teacher, Pathetic Pearlie, who, like Rabbi Heckler, also belonged to the cheapest of orders. Because this congregation was also not well off, and even less faithful than we Jews in the Catskills. Marion's parents and their neighbors were concerned only that they and their children not be taken for Christians, whose beliefs in religion they considered even sillier than their own. For this purpose they hired an obsolete rabbi who whispered his lessons and scratched at his crotch while his students pitched pennies into a *yarmulke* at the back of the room.

In the midst of this chaos, Marion would try composing a speech. Across a clean sheet of paper she would laboriously inscribe: THE PROPHESY OF MARION BLOOMGARTEN. Then she'd wait for God, who often spoke to her, to confide the right words. But the right words wouldn't come, no stirring phrases, and with the excuse of an asthmatic's need for water she escaped from the uproar and sat in the ladies' room until she could go home.

When Marion was twelve, Rabbi Pearl was found in the supply closet slumped over a box of paper towels, his face as blue as the numbers on his wrist. The man who replaced him was Orthodox also, but slightly progressive. To show this, he announced that he would allow the confirmation not only of males, but females as well. Though Orthodox law didn't permit a young woman to read from the Torah, she might lead a special

Friday night songfest to welcome the Sabbath. Hearing this, Marion jumped from her seat and begged to be first.

As the new rabbi tutored her in the tunes and inflections of the psalms she would sing, Marion told herself that leading her people in song was preferable to reading them a portion of Torah. Songs wouldn't enchain them the way the Law would, might even pipe the way to a new life. She would not give a speech. Instead, she would make up a song on the spot and lead all of them, singing, up and down the Bronx.

Except she couldn't sing.

"Your voice sounds like fishbones," her mother had told her. "When you sing, it's like your throat is full of fish, and the notes that you spit out, like fishbones."

This certainly was true. Between the note that she wanted and the note she could reach, whole cities might slip through, whole cultures, the entire system of Western music. Even the rabbi shrank from her singing, as if her voice were as onion-and-garlic as his breath. Marion's mother, not wanting to witness her daughter's shame, threatened to boycott the service. (Her father, she knew, would beam with approval even if she squealed like the vermin that were his business to rid from houses.)

"Mother," she said, "you're forgetting one thing: I'll be inspired."

"Never mind inspiration, you'll still spit out fishbones."

But Marion was sure that God would tune her voice, enrich it with feeling. She would wear a white dress, and with her cascades of rippling black hair she would look like a prophet. The vibrations from her throat would tickle the thin brass flames of the Pillar of Fire above the pulpit until the sculpture hummed. The mouths of the goblets inside the display case of the Hadassah gift shop would trill hymns of praise. In the room where the *kiddush* would eventually take place, the Dixie cups full of heavy dark wine and the bowls of red gelatin would oscillate, tremble, and the dainty egg *kichel* would rise in the air, sweetness borne on sweetness.

None of this happened. But hours of practice, intense concentration, and yes, inspiration, softened the fishbones, exalted the pitch so that only a few times did the abyss gape between the real and ideal. Marion saw her mother lift her head, look timidly, proudly, sit straight by her husband—who had been beaming for hours—and arrange the folds of her new dress, preparing for the admiring glances of her friends, which did indeed follow.

"The voice of the Lord is mighty; the voice of the Lord is majestic," Marion bellowed, trying to match Him.

"The voice of the Lord breaks the cedars; the Lord shatters the cedars of Lebanon," her listeners mumbled in response, so she knew they were feeling His power, and hers.

When Marion at last threw back her hair and sang out a greeting to the Bride of the Sabbath, she thought she saw the Bride enter the room, though this turned out to be a dirty white curtain tossed this way and that by the wind from a truck.

The rabbi came toward her, holding out gifts—a prayerbook with her name in gold on the cover, and collapsible candlesticks designed for a girl who would one day leave home. As her parents' friends clapped, she heard the Lord's voice sing a psalm in her ear. She waited for her chance to sing it out loud.

The rabbi was saying: "I think it is obvious to us all that Marion has performed a magnificent service this evening, and that she certainly would make a wonderful rabbi."

A rabbi, she thought, and suddenly was filled with heaven's contentment. Rabbi Bloomgarten! A life's work, a mission.

The whole room was chuckling. What was the joke? A rabbi—why not? Hadn't her voice been inspired tonight? Yes, she thought, yes, but the voice of a woman, no matter how inspired, was good for one thing: lulling babies to sleep. And the woman herself—a woman rabbi, at least—was good for a laugh.

Blindly, she felt the weight of the prayer book, the cold metal of the candlesticks, and wanted to hurl them. She walked in a daze through the *kiddush*, the handshakes. As she and her parents were saying good-bye, the rabbi told her that since she couldn't carry her gifts on the Sabbath, he would lock them in his office. Marion nodded, but she knew she would never come back to retrieve them.

And so, when she finally did leave home for college, Marion packed no candlesticks, collapsible or otherwise. Though she still thought of herself as a potential prophet, she lacked a focus of inspiration. No sooner would a philosophy or exotic religion engage her attention than she would rebel against its outlines, the very bones that held up its skin. She raised her banner against the tyranny of footnotes, the detachment of scholarship. All but the most radical instructor on campus scrawled disapproval across her essays, and when this one instructor went mad and left town, Marion felt abandoned.

She turned to causes—these required no essays—but nothing in her demeanor incited the enthusiasm of converts. Her eyes seemed a bit crossed, as though she were looking in two directions at once. And she spoke through her nose, which she frequently rubbed to help clear her asthma. Her fellow reformers mistook this as a sign of her wish to rub her nose from her face and therefore doubted her ethnic self-respect—her seriousness also, for she rarely took part in dangerous protests, because if she were to suffer an asthma attack locked in a cell, she could suffocate to death.

One Friday night in her last term at school, Marion wandered the campus alone. From the open window of the student union, over the ringing of pinball machines, old melodies reached her—an octave too high. Even God's voice was high above middle C as it urged her to enter and turn, turn full circle. . . .

Marion obeyed, and discovered that women at last had been embraced, if not in the folded-tight arms of Orthodox Judaism, than in the reluctant arms of Reform.

Judaism had changed, eyes, but Marion had not. In seminary her teachers charged that her concern for the freedom of homosexuals and the full expression of the artistic potential of people on Welfare sapped her attention from Liturgy, Midrash and Homiletics. They cringed at her singing and practice sermons. When she spoke up in class to question even the weak rituals and watered traditions the Reform had not shed, her classmates demanded: Why did she stay at the seminary if she despised its teachings? Although she didn't answer, she did know the reason: She had been called twice by God, called as a rabbi to re-instill ideals in the Jews of America. Being a rabbi satisfied something deep and inherent in Marion, and this was a good thing, because she was nearing age twenty-seven, having rejected all other paths and choices in life.

For this same reason Marion kept her appointment with the greeting committee of our congregation, allowed Zlotkin, Abromovitz and Pipchuck to guide her through the synagogue, a cinderblock bunker painted sharp green. The sanctuary had a dirty gray carpet and a holy ark that seemed more fit for a dustpan and broom than a Torah. In the entire building Marion saw no niche where a thirsty soul might find refreshment (even the fountain by the bathrooms emitted a trickle of rust).

The classroom had no windows, and when the walls started to close in on Marion, she imagined the cinderblocks covered with fronds, buds and lilies gathered by Jewish children who were at home in nature and photos of the African foster child her class would adopt by mailing a check for $15 each month. This helped her restrain herself from denouncing the treachery of her three guides or correcting them when they spoke to her as if she were block-deaf and hadn't a clue what a Jew was ("These are *siddurim,* the PRAYER BOOKS, which, you know, we PRAY FROM"), as if she were ignorant even of English ("This is where the children play PING PONG," they told her. "PADDLE, NET, BALL"). Just when she thought she could bear it no longer, her guides halted in front of a closet and told her, "This is your office," then hurried away, relief sighing from the soles of their shoes.

Marion entered the closet and sagged into the only piece of furniture inside. She had rested just long enough to discover that two of the chair's legs were broken when the door of the closet swung open again and admitted a sour woman with neck growths like grapes, which she kept squeezing with purple fingers. She thrust a purple palm forward and introduced herself as Masha Stonehammer. For two hours daily she typed, took dictation, answered the phone, and once a month dittoed the synagogue news on the mimeograph machine, which, she told Marion, had just sprung a leak.

"I am also the Sabbath *goy,*" she announced in a husky Slav accent.

Marion shook her head. What was that?

Scornful, Stonehammer informed the new rabbi: "I do for the Jews what the Jews will not do for themselves. On the Sabbath I light lights. If the furnace breaks on a day when the use of a phone is not permitted, I call the oil man. I check reservations at the door on Yom Kippur, and I write the amount each person contributes in memory of the dead."

Marion wanted to tell her that in a Reform temple these tasks would no longer be prohibited to Jews, so a non-Jew wouldn't be needed to act as a servant. But she sensed that the secretary was proud of her duties and would be disappointed to have them stripped from her, as if flicking switches when others feared God proved her courage.

"Sometimes I think I am the only person in town who celebrates every Jewish holiday," the secretary went on. "Except that I follow my own ritual for each. For me, the Sabbath is a festival of lights, Passover is a time to buy breadstuffs. I know the laws because I am called on to break them. I know the Jews better than the Jews know themselves."

Not only did she know the Jews in general, she knew them in particular, every tic and betrayal and charitable gesture of Emess Yisroel as it had passed through the previous twelve years and ten rabbis. Much of this knowledge she now imparted to Rabbi Eleven, especially the history of the lately deposed Tenth. Marion until then had been so repulsed by the greeting committee that she had felt sorry for Rabbi Heckler. Yes, he had thrown cans at her, but she had, after all, been in the company of three horrible persons. Now she was disillusioned to learn that he represented the most fanatic blindness of the Orthodoxy she hated. She also realized that Masha Stonehammer was still loyal to his regime.

"What would America be if its citizens thought all its laws were jokes?" the secretary demanded.

Marion would have tried to explain that the Reform movement was based on the principle that many Jewish laws no longer had meaning. Revelation was ongoing. Jews could decide which laws to preserve according to which strengthened their spirits, could design new forms of worship that held beauty for them, abide by a faith whose practices did not separate them from their fellow human beings but drew them closer to all creatures on Earth and to the God who still lived, not in a law book or a cloud on Mt. Sinai, but in all hearts and heads, Lord God of Ideals. But Masha Stonehammer already had left. Marion could hear the regular whumping of the mimeograph drum, the whipping of paper, as if a prisoner in some secret chamber were being flayed, his skin sifting to the floor in great sheets.

She sat in her closet and tried not to listen. She desperately needed a sermon for Rosh Hashanah. The title came easily: "New Ways for a New Year: The Essence of Reform." Then, rocking in her chair, she waited for God to write the rest of the speech. Two little boys peeked in, shot giggles at her and ran away shrieking. Then, shuffle, shuffle, a small man with white hairs that curled like frost from his nose asked permission to enter. "Missus, have you maybe seen the new rabbi?"

She stood, introduced herself and stretched out her hand. She expected rejection, but held her smile bravely.

He examined her palm as if it might conceal a buzzer, then touched two damp fingers to it. A fleeting smile, shyly: "I am Schmuckler, the exile, a leper for singing." He had come to inquire if he would be welcome on Rosh Hashanah. He would try to refrain from his dai-dai-ing, but this was a habit and he could not be sure. . . .

"Mr. Schmuckler," she told him, "sing as loud as you want. Because, to be honest, I'll need all the backup on vocals I can get."

His mushroom eyes brightened. "Really? Your singing, it's not so . . . impressive?" He bobbed on worn heels. "Oh, I must tell you, so happy to meet you!"

He began bobbing backwards. She plunged with a question. "You don't mind, Mr. Schmuckler? That I'm a woman, I mean?"

"Mind? Mind? Of course not!" Humming and smiling. "Of course, all the others . . . but good luck, Rabbi Missus, I see you tomorrow."

A spark, optimism—too soon extinguished by the appearance

of a stiff, startled woman who muttered that she had come to ask the new rabbi if the menu for the *kiddush*—lime gelatin, Mogen David, egg *kichel* and fish bits—was to his liking. But Miss Abel didn't bother to wait for an answer. What good was the opinion of a woman, a *girl,* how better than her own?

When Marion at last gave up on her sermon, a wine-colored sun was dripping its light through heavy gray clouds. Reluctant to confront the Slattern On the Cliff, she wandered toward the house that should have been hers. The lawn looked alluring. She thrust out a sandal and brushed her toes on the grass. Why had she conceded this house to the rabbi after only one skirmish? But then, what methods would have prevailed against such a fanatic? Oh, why had she come here? Where would she go next? Where was God's voice, giving direction?

Marion looked up. The tall tree was red. Its leaves were like flame licks in the last slant of sunlight.

A voice told her: Climb it. Perhaps the rabbi lay half-dead on the floor. She would carry him down, as one carried a child.

Again the voice: Climb it.

She put a sandal on each rung, climbed higher through the flames. Dark windows on the first floor. Dark on the second. But there, in the attic, a white shirt, a man bending over a trunk. Then, two white candles. At first she assumed he was lighting the candles because he had no lamps in the attic, but all his preparations made her suspicious that, although this was Wednesday, he was lighting a welcome for the Sabbath. Why give a welcome two evenings early? Or had he decreed that each day was a Sabbath, each eve a welcome? Marion felt chilled. Such devout overdoing was the stuff only of Talmudic folklore, tales of *tsadikim.*

Suddenly he was singing, blessing the candles. His voice was so mighty that she had to hold tight so she wouldn't lose her perch. He kept his eyes shut. His palms cupped the gold light he had kindled and splashed it upward, bathing his neck, face and eyelids, painting the ceiling with gold while he sang a prayer so richly drawn out it might have lasted forever, and Marion had to whisper the same prayer in English, over and over, "Blessed art thou, O Lord our God, King of the universe, who hast sanctified us with thy commandments . . . ," ten prayers to his one, so as not to lose sense of the common world's time.

By the end of his blessings dark clouds were shoving each other across the shadowy sky. A wind had blown up. Then, in the distance, a great yellow slash. The rabbi lifted his head and walked to the window, pushed it up, open. Marion crouched in a crook of the tree not two yards before him, but the rabbi was looking beyond to the lightning, singing the blessing, not drawn out this time, but searing and sharp: Blessed art thou, Lord our God, King of the universe, whose might and power fill the world.

He saw her. She didn't move. His nose twitched. She thought: There's no screen between us, I could surprise him. But to grapple with a saint . . . Yes, Jacob had tried it, but even he was left wounded.

The rabbi stepped closer and lifted one hand. To reach out and strike her? Or to pull down the window? She had to forestall him.

"Isn't there also a benediction that's supposed to be said upon seeing a beautiful woman?" She smiled weakly.

His voice was even. "A fish who lives on land is not a fish. A woman who lives in a tree is not a woman. And a woman who acts like a man is not beautiful. She is an a-bom-in-a-tion." He clawed at the window, but the humidity kept it from closing.

In an instant she thought this: Since he loves the Talmud, he must love a good debate. She leaned forward and brushed the leaves from her face. "God hates a hermit," Marion proclaimed. "And you, Rabbi Heckler, have become a hermit. Doesn't Genesis itself declare that life is good? And haven't the rabbis decreed that a person should live to the fullest, enjoy God's creation, go down in the world among men, among women?"

"Maybe, to enjoy myself, I should sit in a tree? When I am in Sodom, I should do as in Sodom?"

"If you think this is Sodom, maybe you should leave here and save yourself before God destroys the town."

"*Adoshem,* blessed be He, always gives the people of Sodom

a last chance, sends one to warn them. If they listen He saves them."

"So you think you're a prophet, Rabbi Heckler?" She had meant to imply this was *chutzpah*. But when she heard her words, Marion realized she had asked a plain question.

"I am a Jew, and these days that is enough. These candles— you see them? For thousands of years a light has been carried, preserved from any who would spit on the flame or drown it in the mud. And what would you do? Scoff at this candle, it must be useless because it is not modern. So blow it out, *pfft,* replace with electric, a flashlight, or nothing. Come, contradict me. Swear that each *shabbes* you light the candles, so the torch doesn't go out that has been burning since Year One." Brow raised, shoe tapping. "So, Mrs. 'Rabbi,' I am waiting."

It was futile to explain that each time she tried to light the candles, each time she saw a candlestick even, she was stabbed by cruel laughter.

"Aha, I am right then. You would let the torch fall. Yet you call yourself a Jew? Tomorrow I show Sodom a real Jew, real rabbi, against a monkey, chimpanzee in a tree. And they will decide among us, and be saved."

"Haven't they decided already, Rabbi Heckler?"

"For a monkey in a tree? Shoo, monkey. Shoo, chimpanzee. Shoo, shoo, go away." He flicked his hands at her, then struggled with the sash until the window slammed shut.

The wind lifted her skirt. The rain would come soon. She would lose her footing, dangle from a branch by her hair. "O Absalom," she whispered, and started down the tree. A silver flash lit up the clouds that raced overheard. "Blessed art thou, Lord our God, King of the universe. . . ." She recited the prayer to fend off her fear of the infinite night. Then she dropped from the tree and trudged to her room to finish the sermon she would give the next day.

IV.

At the bomb shelter's entrance the ogre Stonehammer was checking names against a list of the members who had made reservations. "The biggest crowd in years," she informed the new rabbi. "Curiosity, no doubt."

Marion sneaked downstairs to wait in her office and inhale a few last times before the service. The weather was muggy and her asthma had returned. How could she hope to lead the day's prayers, off-key or on, if she couldn't breathe?

At last she went upstairs to the sanctuary and stood at the back of the aisle that divided the women and men. In the chairs to her left sat the young mothers with their squirming little girls in stretchy white tights and colorful dresses that barely covered their bottoms. To her right, the young husbands, on their laps their small sons, who wore white short-sleeve shirts, tiny bow-ties and hand-crocheted *yarmulkes* bobby-pinned to their fine curly hair. In the middle of each aisle sat the middle-aged parents: short grocers who slouched humbly beside the hand-some young men who soon would be doctors; dumpy mothers who envied the thin girls they had nursed, now teachers and lawyers in elegant suits. And, in the front pews, nodding already, the elderly ladies in ragged black veils and the gray-stubbled men in misbuttoned jackets and age-yellowed prayer shawls.

She started down the aisle. No one turned or stopped talking. How could this girl in a flowing white garment that appeared to be a nightgown, her wild hair tied back like a beast on a leash, be the new rabbi?

Walking between the women and men, Marion felt an accom-plice to the caste system, segregation of sexes because a woman might distract a man from prayer or contaminate him. "For three transgressions do women die in childbirth," she recited to herself in memorized contempt of the Orthodox prayerbook, "for being careless in the observance of the laws of menstrua-tion, for not performing the ritual of *hallah,* and for not lighting the Sabbath lamp." Soon she would free the women from this degradation, free the men also from empty proscription. But slowly, don't rush. . . .

She mounted the dais. Behind her, by the ark, Abromovitz sat hunched on the president's cushions. By the men's door at the rear of the sanctuary stood Zlotkin; by the women's door,

Pipchuck. As ushers? Or had the rabbi made known his threat? Other than these three no face was familiar, except for the mushroom, Lazarus Schmuckler, who bobbed in his seat and winked his encouragement.

She rasped twice and started, not singing fully, but using the technique of dramatic actors who find themselves cast in musical movies. She sensed all eyes on her, then heard the room buzz: "A woman, a woman, look at that, a woman." Air-starved, she barely could project above it. No one sang with her, but Marion persisted, fearing the moment when the order of service would require that she blow the ram's horn. At best she would be able to sputter a poor imitation of God's call on Sinai. She felt so dizzy merely from chanting that when a white cloak floated into the sanctuary, she nearly cried out: The Bride of the Sabbath! But from the moment the white cloak opened its mouth, she knew who it was.

With a rustling of shawls, dresses, prayer books, the whole congregation turned to watch the renegade lead his own service. He swayed in the aisle beneath his white cloak as he sang a passionate aria of repentance, his voice an exquisite weapon with which he was able to puncture Marion's puny defenses. And though she continued chanting in English, everyone else began singing with Rabbi Heckler in Hebrew.

She walked to the pulpit, her heart like thunder, a sandstorm in her mouth. Then she saw him sit down in a pew at the back. He intended to let her deliver her speech! The thunder diminished to a low rumble and the words of the sermon she had written the night before came back to her, words that brought news of religion with meaning, justice and beauty, no laws except as they revealed themselves worthy.

Restless disapproval. Bewildered stirring. She had read out a declaration of independence and the ex-slaves were worried about the decisions they might have to make.

"No! This is not true!" Rabbi Heckler jumped up. All turned to face him. "One Revelation! It happened at Sinai!"

Marion wheezed. "Of course it happened. A great trumpet sounded and a deep voice boomed from the whirlwind of clouds at the summit. . . ." She had no more breath.

He took his advantage. "If nobody spoke, why did so many people at Mt. Sinai that day agree they heard God?"

"Oh, yes." All necks twisted (like PING PONG, she thought). "It must have been God and not men who told us: 'You may keep servants, may even beat them, as long as they don't die, for they are your money.' And: 'Wipe out those nations who live in the lands you would like to inhabit. Disembowel and light fire to innocent lambs and goats to satisfy Me.' Isn't it just possible, Rabbi Heckler, that God spoke more clearly to some prophets than others? Isn't it possible that each generation must listen to God with its own ears?"

"And who are you that God should speak to you? Your ears are as holy as the ears of Moses?"

"It doesn't take Moses to realize that the commandment to give charity is still worth obeying, while the commandment not to mix wool and linen in one cloth is trivial, silly, it means nothing to me."

"This is because nothing means anything to you! God gives commandments to sanctify our lives. No commandment is silly if it comes from Him. This is the entire faith of our people: We heard at Sinai, therefore we obey. God's laws bring freedom. But man as his own judge, revelation in each ear—your way lies danger, self-righteous people, or people who can't move." He gave her a chance to make her reply, but her throat had now closed. "Look, look," he shouted, "I have got her god stumped!"

Swallowing gravel, as angry at herself as if she had been drawn into arguing with a spoiled child, she stood tall and croaked: "Everyone rise!" She wheeled around to the ark, pulled open the doors and lifted out the Torah, the heavy calfskin on its massive wood spindles, all of it wrapped in satin embroidered with scepters and crowns. She hugged it to her chest and prepared to march down from the dais. The people would respond to the Torah from habit. The women would reach out, touch two fingers to the scroll, then kiss these fingers. The men would do likewise with the fringes of their shawls. All of them would sing as she marched among them holding the Torah. Then she would return the scroll to the dais, unroll it and read the Torah selection for Rosh Hashanah. Not even Rabbi Heckler would dare interrupt the reading of the Torah.

She took her first steps, her vision obscured by the wood handles of the scrolls, though she caught a flash of white just a second before she felt someone tug at the scroll in her arms. "The Torah might rip," she whispered. "It might drop to the floor." And so she let go.

Rabbi Heckler ran down the aisle with the Torah, a crab with a bundle as big as itself. We in the audience were too stunned to give chase. Abromovitz still was getting to his feet in honor of the ark's opening five minutes before. But just as the rabbi reached the door, Zlotkin stepped in his path, his arms stretched out wide. Then Pipchuck caught up. With wiry hands he lifted the Torah above the kidnapper's head. Zlotkin spun him around, clamped his arms behind him and started to drag him out through the door, though the rabbi was screaming: "A rabbi! How dare! Cossack! Anti-Semite!"

"Stop! Let him go!"

Not a head turned. Zlotkin kept dragging. Marion went for the shofar, lifted the heavy pearled horn to her lips. With a harsh breath she blasted, or rather, let out a Bronx cheer, but even this startled, brought order, stopped Zlotkin.

"Release him!" she commanded.

The rabbi crumpled, shrank into himself, a little crab creature who skittered past Zlotkin. But before he slipped out, he massed his strength once more and in a prophet's voice shouted: "Ashes and salt! That is what I leave you, ashes and salt!"

Marion shook. She was weak at the knees. She studied first Zlotkin, then each of the other three hundred faces raised toward her own. This was her congregation. Not evil people. Among them were surely good women and men. But which of them knew God? Which loved God, loved the world? For whom was existence more than ashes and salt? What in her power was vital enough to bring light and breathe life into ashes and salt? If Herman Zlotkin could somehow be forced to bless bolts of lightning, first sights of beauty and each bite he chewed, could he possibly remain the same Herman Zlotkin?

The murmuring returned. Still frightened, she retrieved the

big scroll from Pipchuck, carried the Torah back to the dais, continued the service, and each word she sang from then on was a cry, a question to God.

The congregation was silent for the rest of the prayers, but few of us stayed to partake of the *kiddush*. Miss Abel, who had been in the kitchen and so missed the showdown, was visibly upset about the leftovers. The handful of people who did stay to eat carefully kept the table between themselves and the new rabbi. Marion hadn't the heart to pursue them. Inside she was crying over the images of the crumpled rabbi, Herman Zlotkin as a mound of ashes, and Isidore Pipchuck as a pillar of salt. How to revive them? How breathe life and shine light?

Only Lazarus Schmuckler came to shake her hand and praise her singing, as if all were normal. Surely, he said, she would lead them in *tashlikh,* bring them to a stream so they could cast their bread on the water and allow it to carry their sins to the sea.

Marion worried that if she consented to this tradition, Schmuckler would have her waving a chicken over her head three times on Yom Kippur. She gave in, however, solely for his sake, and as it turned out he was the only member to take part. Joyfully he led her to the town's outskirts, where the creek that flowed in a tube beneath Main Street escaped from its prison and wandered across a field in the vague direction of the Hudson River, and therefore the sea.

Despite her skepticism that tossing bread crumbs could make her soul clean, Marion gained pleasure from her companion and their ceremony. When Schmuckler had finished sprinkling his fragments of Miss Abel's *hallah* into the stream, he and Marion returned to the synagogue for the evening service. Her mind was elsewhere and she made several errors, but only a few of us were there to hear anyway. The rabbi was exhausted, desiring only to return to the motel, but Pipchuck detained her next to the cloakroom.

"*Gut yontef, gut yontef,*" hands twisting, grin tense. "Not a bad service, Miss Rabbi Bloomgarten. A regrettable disturbance earlier today, but you handled it . . . not badly. And you were quite right that we should release poor Rabbi Heckler. He was already a beaten man, no longer a threat. We had suspected, and therefore were ready, with the result that, I am happy to announce, tonight you will sleep in the house that will be *your* house—for as long as you're with us."

Too weary to question, she scuffed across the street. The ogre was waiting; in her purple hand, a key. Stonehammer related how she had been instructed to keep watch in case the rabbi left the house to attend the service, and, if this happened, to summon a locksmith and have the bolts changed.

Marion said softly: "I thought you were on his side."

Stonehammer's head was high. "For a Jew, calling a locksmith on Rosh Hashanah is not permitted. I am the Sabbath *goy*. It was my duty."

Marion took the key and locked out Stonehammer. Wandering through the house she saw splintered floors, flaked paint and yellow wallpaper with fingernail scratch marks as high as a man's arms. No chair to sit on, no curtain or dish. She climbed to the attic, half-expecting to see him. She found only an old trunk, its lid spattered with white wax, a pyramid of canned kosher meatballs, three black-bound volumes of religious writings, a raincoat, a cot. She lay down in her clothes and soon was asleep.

A nasty buzzing. No clue where she was. The doorbell insisted. Yes, she remembered, this attic, this cot . . . Who was buzzing the bell? A congregant in need?

She found Rabbi Heckler shivering in his shirtsleeves. Rain was falling. His complexion was white and his features compliant. "The hour, I am sorry, but I have been walking. I have not been right. I could go nowhere, and now it is raining. I must have left my coat here. Please, I will get it. Then I will leave."

"Rabbi Heckler, you'll understand if I ask you to wait here while I get the raincoat."

"You do not trust me even to wait in your hallway, inside from the rain, to get warm? An old man, half your strength? If I won't get out, you throw me."

"I don't want to have to wrestle with you, Rabbi. Stand under the eaves until I get back. You'll excuse me if I don't trust a person who would steal a Torah."

"Wait. This reminds me. I have come also to say I have been wrong. This is Rosh Hashanah. I must ask forgiveness of the people I have wronged before I can ask God. Please, let me inside."

It had cost her a great deal to deny him before. Now he looked so shriveled and contrite that she let him enter, though she did block the hall.

"This morning," he said, "when I find myself running away with the Torah, I realize I am not well. Later, in the street, I think of how, when I am trying to pry it from your arms, you whisper, 'It will rip' and let go. From this I realize that you have earned the right to keep it. Little by little from then on, I understand my sins of these past months." Water dripped from his trouser legs onto the floor. "You say that I am now a hermit, but until my wife died I truly lived apart. She was my shelter, God rest her soul, so I could study in peace. Always happy, she is singing, but I say *shaa, shaa,* these songs disturb me, these songs are not meant for God's ears. So my Hattie goes to sing in the bathroom, to sing with the door closed so I can study. Anyone who sought counsel asked my wife. She was wise in the problems of this world, and I could not be bothered, I had to study. The only reason anyone kept me was the voice I have.

"Then she passed on. Then, *then* I no longer can live without knowing how food is purchased, how people act. I go out, I see. The people with 'problems' come now to ask *me.* Adulterers! Idolaters! Sodomites! I abhor! It is no wonder, I think, my wife died. I become angry. I lecture. I visit. I overdo perhaps, and despite my singing, they say I am fired, again and again, until I come here. And the rest you know."

"Rabbi Heckler." She was thoughtful. "The songs that your wife sang . . . were they Broadway show tunes?"

"Yes, yes. How did you know?"

She smiled a small smile.

"Please, I will just go for my coat."

Still smiling, she stepped aside, though she knew what would happen. Perhaps a small part of his story was true, but what part she didn't know.

She heard a devilish screech, a satisfied laugh, though the

screech might have been the hinge of the door that led to the attic, and the laughter her own.

V.

That first night Rabbi Bloomgarten slept on the floor downstairs. After Yom Kippur, she bought a mattress on credit from Sears. She didn't see Rabbi Heckler, but she constantly heard him praying and singing; the ceiling creaked loudly as he swayed overhead. At dawn he thanked God for having been spared the life of a woman. He prayed at mid-day, and a third time at dusk. In between, she guessed, he studied or napped. At six every night she heated a kosher TV dinner and set it outside the door to the attic, with plastic utensils. For his other two meals she left food that even the most observant Jew wouldn't refuse. In this she was aided by Miss Sarah Abel, who was just as happy to feed her crusader from this safe distance as to have him crusading in her apartment.

Though Miss Abel harbored suspicions about the two rabbis' living arrangement and so treated Marion as a rival always, the rest of us were tacitly grateful for what she had done. As a result of her good deed, Rabbi Bloomgarten soon was accepted by our congregation as thoroughly as had been her predecessors, which meant she was ignored almost completely. To help pass the hours when no one called on her, the rabbi took singing lessons—eventually she could reach seven or eight notes of every ten she sang—and sent for the books that she once had studied at seminary, or rather, the books she had been ordered to study, but had deemed too confining and out-of-date to open. Having despaired that her own knowledge would allow her to convert ashes and salt to roses and sunlight, she thought she could do worse than consult the writings of scholars and prophets who had spent their lives in the deepest searching for a way to God.

Neither singing nor study on the part of the rabbi brought much change in Pipchuck. But a few members of our congregation did visit some evenings—Schmuckler, Abromovitz, and often myself. Even Herman Zlotkin, on the nights when his premonitions of rust and decay were so frightening that he could not bear them alone, appeared at the door. All of us feared death—our own, our religion's—and we felt safer in the presence of this rabbi whose very sex and youth seemed an indication that our hopes were still fertile and might yet give birth to a new generation. On these evenings our rabbi, from loneliness, no doubt, talked more than was proper. She talked of her childhood, her dreams, thoughts, frustrations—among which her visitors most likely were numbered.

Because even though we listened, drank herb tea and nodded, we refused to relinquish our weak devotion to Orthodoxy. We were like students who had discovered an art book that was filled with beautiful paintings of nude men and women, and though we desired to study each picture, perhaps even try to sketch these ourselves, we were too frightened of the puritanical tyrant who still ruled our class. Because when Rabbi Bloomgarten was her most ardent and tried to convince her visitors too loudly, Rabbi Heckler would bellow his protests from his home on high, and Rabbi Bloomgarten would shout her shrill rejoinders up the stairs, all with such fervor that none of us wanted to enter the battle and risk a drubbing in front of his fellows.

Rabbi Bloomgarten did enjoy several triumphs. Instead of lime gelatin and stale *kichel* for *kiddush,* worshippers could now enjoy *hallah* baked by the children of the after-school classes under the tutelage of Miss Sarah Abel. Several communions of an I-and-Thou nature were also reported between these same students and various objects. And a boy of sixteen, because of her counseling, decided that his admiration for his lithe teammates in basketball was not sufficient cause to swallow the poison he had bought for the purpose of closing his eyes to their beauty forever.

Still, she wasn't able to relax the laws of the temple as much as she once had hoped. And though she herself was no more Orthodox than before, she found herself feeling guiltier and guiltier with each meal she didn't bless, each candle she didn't light, each bite of *treyfe* she ate, until one morning she caught herself checking the label of a shirt to see if the fabric combined linen and wool. Because wherever she was—in the house, *shul,* out walking—she thought she heard floorboards creaking above her, complaining each time that she failed to observe one of the 613 commandments so carefully inscribed on the scroll she had saved.

THE
AIR
CONDITIONER

THE
AIR
CONDITIONER

The day of the accident was not hot, but a sullen heaviness in the air warned of the coming discomforts of summer. Jessica knew that she soon would grow pale, her palms would turn clammy, her head start to ache. Even as a child her symptoms had been severe enough to force her parents to buy one of the first air conditioners in Idaho. Her father, a public defender, used it as an inducement to gain her assistance; he placed her at a table with the cold beam at her throat and a pile of envelopes to be stuffed for one of his many campaigns against racism, poverty and anti-Semitism.

Later, when she needed money to attend college, she sought summer jobs with philanthropic firms, signing on with the few that were wealthy enough to keep their offices cool. She was proud of the generous nature of her work, but soon came to realize that she never would be hardy enough to go out into the world crusading like her father, or like Herbie.

Herbie was a union organizer, forever raising an angry fist to an even angrier sun, inciting picketers to shout up at office windows, behind which the management conferred in civilized tones about other matters, their air conditioners humming loudly. Jessica met Herbie the summer he was organizing a nurses' union at one of Chicago's many hospitals. She was on her way to visit an alcoholic who once had been a welfare recipient on her caseload. Walking from the bus to the entrance

123

of the hospital, Jessica fainted. Herbie brought her around by dashing cold beer on her face.

"Where are you taking her?" he demanded of the nurses who were attempting to carry her into the lobby. "That's enemy territory."

Feebly, Jessica said that she needed to go inside anyway.

"What business do you have crossing a picket line?" he said. "You look official."

After she told him, Herbie became more pleasant, going so far as to invite her to a chili supper that evening in support of striking migrants. But later, in the crowded basement of a city rec center, eating her chili one bean at a time, Jessica passed out again. Herbie helped her to the bus stop, then, at the last moment, decided that he had better see her all the way home. In her apartment, he turned down her sheets and sat beside her for hours, brushing the damp hair from her forehead and scowling.

The next spring, a few days before they were to be married, Jessica mentioned that they would have to buy an air conditioner; they were moving to an apartment in a shabby section of the city, where the buildings did not come so equipped.

Herbie lectured her on the evils of decadent capitalist luxuries. "Who wants to live in a closed-in cubicle with no contact to the outside? If you keep your windows sealed shut, can you hear the kids shouting in the streets? The neighbors calling to each other across the alley ways?"

She wanted to tell him about the poor families she had seen standing for hours in the frozen food section at the supermarket, but she merely nodded, and so consigned herself to nine summers of affliction. As she lay awake each night, she fought spasms of sickness and tried not to envy his cool communion with sheet and pillow.

When their son Lemuel was born they put his crib in the stuffy living room. Jessica would wander into the room to make sure that the boy had not inherited her susceptibility to heat. Lemuel squirmed and frowned in his sleep, but he rarely woke up, and so she assumed that he must have grown accustomed to the humidity through early exposure. Relieved, she returned to the bed that she shared with her husband, there to lie sleepless until dawn.

After Herbie left her for a fellow organizer, Jessica choked and shuddered through one summer more, the hottest in nearly a century, trying not to hate the half of the bed beside her for being empty. She did not buy an air conditioner, afraid that Herbie would come back to her one night, see the new purchase, grow disgusted and leave again. Not until May of the second year after his departure did she waver before the prospect of yet another struggle against the season. When Lemuel came into the kitchen with sweat stains blossoming for the first time beneath the sleeves of his shirt, she put an English muffin before him and asked whether he had any opinions about air conditioners.

Staring at the peaks and valleys of his muffin, Lemuel admitted that sometimes he did hang out at a certain arcade after school, dreading his return to the overheated apartment. He assured her that he never played the games, only stood in front of a vent of cool air near the popcorn machine. "And one of my friends told me," he said, dragging his finger over the rough surface of his breakfast, "this place is strictly off-limits in the summertime."

After cleaning the table, Jessica drove to a catalogue store that was advertising a preseason discount on the previous year's stock of air conditioners. Only the demonstration model from the showroom floor remained, however. It had a scratch, but the clerk insisted the nick would not impair its function.

Herbie, she knew, would have bargained with the clerk anyway, delivering a harangue about the acquiescence of the proletariat to their own slow death by overpricing. She would have stood behind him, chewing her lip. During her entire married life, her lower lip had been scarred by a vertical purple welt. When Herbie stood up in movie theaters and shouted humorous rejoinders to bad dialogue, Jessica told herself that poorly written films with artistic pretensions deserved to be deflated, then bit her lip until the movie had faded from the screen. At night, after parties, Herbie would demand that she let him make love to her with the curtains open. She allowed him to do this because she, too, believed prudery to be a bourgeois sin, but when he bent his head to nibble at her breasts, she bit her lip and closed her eyes.

Jessica considered writing down the rules by which Herbie wanted her to live, but she knew that he would have chided her for the compulsiveness of such an act. She already had one list of do's and don't's inscribed on the back of a card she had received on her fourteenth birthday. On that day, over cake and hot chocolate, her girlfriends had told her how much they disliked her. These were their reasons: she embarrassed them in front of their teachers by knowing the dates of each piece of New Deal legislation while they barely recognized the name Franklin Roosevelt; she frowned at them for squandering their money on record albums while Biafrans went hungry; at parties, when they began to twist themselves around boys in the dim corners of downstairs dens, she would sit for a moment, straight-backed on the sofa, look around the room with an expression of disapproval, then get up and leave.

As her friends went on, Jessica began to recognize other sins that her friends didn't even know she had committed. She often had mocked Michael Emmerich's spastic movements in square dancing class. She had told Earl Kramer that she would not sit next to him in assemblies unless he brushed his teeth more often. Worst of all, she was rich, or at least middle-class, while so many other people in the world had little to eat and nowhere to sleep, and, unless her father forced her, she did nothing to lessen the pain in their lives.

Jessica decided that she had a strong propensity to do evil and so must be watchful to avoid unleashing her true nature on the world. She drew up a list of rules according to which she would condition her behavior from then on. In time, she was able to convince most people that she was a caring human being, but she knew that she was only a careful one, a master of self-discipline.

Just once did that discipline fail her. In the summer of her twenty-first year, Jessica worked as an assistant to her father's former protégé, Myles Aronson, a married lawyer more than twice her age who specialized in cases in which a client's civil liberties had been abused. Jessica became infatuated with Aronson, and he with her. He told her that she was alluring in a way that was not obvious to most men, and that she probably was capable of great and spontaneous love. Aronson himself was not handsome, but he had a thin body and long, rough fingers that Jessica found attractive.

One night she stayed late to help him prepare for a hearing. He came up behind her at the Xerox machine and held her. She did not pull away from him, and it was not until several weeks later that Jessica found a reason to tell Aronson that she could not meet him again in their motel room.

"I looked at my father this morning," she said, "and I realized that if he knew what I was doing, he would never speak to me again."

Aronson told her that he had reached a similar conclusion the day before. They parted with no bitterness, but Jessica retained a terrible anxiety that her father would find out about her affair with a man whom he considered to be his adoptive son. She retreated into slavish devotion to the rules outlined on the back of her birthday card.

Not until she met Herbie did she tuck away her list, giving precedence instead to his caustic commands. And when he left her, she was at a loss. For example: She might, through weakness, splurge on a capitalist luxury such as an air conditioner, but shouldn't she at least bargain with the clerk to make sure that she paid a reasonable price for it? Still, if she argued with the clerk, she might ruin his day, or get him in trouble with his manager. But was that any worse than hurting the millions of poor but spineless people who never would overthrow their exploiters unless she spearheaded the attack?

Wearily, she allowed the clerk to ring up the full price. He insisted on carrying the box to her car. Like most men, he could see only her frailty—she was five-feet-nine-inches, but weighed slightly less than 120 pounds.

"Will your husband be home to take it up to your apartment?" the clerk asked.

"No." She smiled sadly.

"A son, perhaps?"

The same smile. Lemuel would be at Junior Congregation, sipping Sabbath grape juice. Moreover, he was only eleven and small for his age. Not that he suffered from any physical disorders. He was simply short and slight. He recently had come through his parents' divorce and now had no father—Herbie had disappeared to California with his mistress—but Jessica did not see that the lack of a father had left Lemuel weaker than other boys. She could never understand why people tended to drop their voices when speaking of him, as the clerk did now, saying, "The cool air should make him more comfortable." And why had Lemuel been so afraid to tell her that he could not breathe in the apartment? As she drove, the rushing air stirred her thoughts. What was she doing wrong? Whom could she ask? No rules on her birthday card governed the raising of children. All she had to go on was Herbie's farewell note. "Try not to ruin Lemmie," he had written. "Try not to turn him into a tight-ass."

And Jessica had tried. Whatever Lemuel did, she never rebuked him. She never would tell him what he had done to upset her, no matter how much he begged to be told. She left him to guess, and he seemed to believe that everything he did upset her. Poor Lemuel, faded and sorry. He moved through his many worlds with one eye always upon her—even, she suspected, when she was nowhere to be seen. She decided to ask him what she could do to help ease his worries.

She parked her car in the lot behind her apartment building, lifted the heavy box from the trunk and slammed the lid shut with her elbow. Robbie, the doorman, held the front door for her, looking apprehensive that he might be obliged to help her and so corrupt his uniform with perspiration. But before he could offer his assistance, she had brushed by him and entered the elevator.

Once in her apartment on the fourteenth floor she did not even pause for a glass of iced coffee, so strong was her resolve to clear the apartment of Herbie's lingering influence. She pushed up the window and removed the screen. A breeze ruffled the thin white cotton of her blouse, and the touch of the cloth reminded her of her loneliness.

Quickly, she removed the machine from its packing and set it on the sill of the open window. Three inches of empty space gaped on either side. How could she have mismeasured the dimensions of her window so radically? Maybe the machine was missing a bracket, or a frame. She stooped to search among the pellets of foam in the box. Finding an instruction booklet, she straightened to read it, and in so doing nudged the air conditioner with her hip. It fell backwards out the window.

For several seconds she couldn't move. Then she looked down. The air conditioner was a flat gray speck near the curb. Beside it lay a bag of scattered groceries. Beyond the bag, a woman's body hugged the sidewalk.

The elevator took so long coming that Jessica used the stairwell instead, running down flight after flight of raw concrete steps. Ancient odors of fried onions, chicken fat and regurgitated milk found their last refuge here, but she did not smell their ghosts until she neared the final landing and could no longer hold her breathing or thinking in abeyance.

By the time she reached the street a crowd hid the woman from view. Jessica did not try to force through the crowd, but watched as Robbie, the doorman, backed his way out. The front of his uniform was bloody, but he took no notice of the mess on his clothes, only walked to his post beside the entrance and sat dully on his wooden stool.

An ambulance came. Paramedics broke through the circle of on-lookers with a stretcher and brought out the woman's body. Jessica could see by the swaddle of blankets that the body was the same length and width as her own.

After the paramedics had slid the stretcher into the ambulance and driven away, Jessica told a policeman that she was the person who had pushed the air conditioner out the window. She said that she would be home all day in case it was inconvenient for them to take her to the station right then. She walked back to the building, opened the door herself—Robbie did not move from his stool—and went up to her apartment.

The police saw no need to take Jessica anywhere. Two officers questioned her intently, but with courtesy and consideration. When a reporter and photographer knocked at her door, the policemen volunteered to send them away, but she said that she did not see why a woman in her position deserved the privilege of privacy. She told the reporter at length of her carelessness in leaving the air conditioner on the sill. She did not wait for him to ask how she felt about the accident, but said quite frankly that she would never be able to live with the pain of her guilt.

The photographer stopped maneuvering around her chair, snapped a final shot and motioned to the reporter that they should leave. Then the policemen went away. She walked into her bathroom and threw up. Picturing the most gruesome possibilities of metallic momentum on skin, soft tissue and organs, she threw up again. Then she started to sob. She knew that she would not be able to stop crying until she, too, was dead. She looked in her medicine cabinet and through her tears could see the bottles quivering, melting. Tweezers and emery boards lost their rigidity and wavered like snakes. Only the handle of her shaving razor retained the straight lines of its reality.

She reached for her toothbrush, clenched her fingers around a tube of toothpaste and cleaned the vomit from her mouth. When Lemuel came home a few minutes later, his mother's breath was sweet, although her eyes were still wet and ugly. The boy had never seen his mother cry, but he did not ask the reason for her grief. He sat quietly as she toasted two slices of oatmeal bread, spread the toast with peanut butter and poured him a glass of skim milk. As she was returning the jar to the cupboard, she dropped it. The jar cracked and the brown paste began oozing onto the floor. She retched. Then, in a broken voice, she told him that she had just killed a woman, that she did not think she could ever face another soul on Earth, and that he should pack his pajamas and school clothes and move in with his Aunt Dottie until provisions could be made for his future.

He ate his toast in small bites. "If you send me away," he said in the flat tones of a tired psychoanalyst, "you might not ask for me back." He finished the first slice of toast and wiped two fingers on a napkin. "I killed a cat once, on purpose," he said. "I never told you. It was too *bad* to tell you. But I never killed a person." He drank his milk, dabbed at his white mustache with the napkin, got up and placed the napkin in the trash bin. "I think I should stay."

She nodded, then ran into her bedroom, locked the door and cried until long past midnight. She did not sleep that night, nor leave her room the next day.

On the Monday after the accident, Jessica called the director of the social services agency where she worked to ask for an indefinite leave of absence. He said that he would grant the request if she insisted, but really, it would be best if she came in as though nothing had happened. Work, he said, made one's troubles disappear.

"I'm sorry," she said. "I don't see how I could continue."

He pleaded again for her return, and she remembered that Paul Fields, the man with whom she shared the duties of supervising the agency's caseworkers, had gone on vacation the Friday before, backpacking in the Rockies. The director, she realized, must be wondering how he could get along without either of them. She did not care about her boss, whom she left listening to silence on the telephone, but she did feel an obligation to Paul. It wouldn't be fair if he returned to a simmering volcano of confused bureaucracy.

Most weeks of the year, Jessica and Paul kept the agency— and each other—calm. She would peek around his partition, and if she saw him staring at the wall, she would touch his narrow shoulders and whisper something, anything, it never mattered what, because no logic could apply, it was simply the light touch of her fingers that made him swivel around to face his job again.

Paul rarely touched Jessica, but he frequently teased her. He refused to let her take the remarks of their clients too seriously; she understood Spanish, and so caught the meanings of the mumbles and curses of the men and women who saw her only as the arbiter of their humiliation. Nor would he let her completely fulfill her duties to authority. Whenever she held up a rule with which to reproach him, he chucked bits of sarcasm at it until it shattered. She would turn her head away, as if to keep the fragments from flying in her eyes. Then she would look at Paul in shy terror, waiting for him to laugh and reassure her that his missiles had been aimed at the rule and not at her.

Twice a day she brought him coffee—condensed milk, two sugars—and with every cup wondered why a highly competent man in his thirties should be no more than a supervisor at a social services agency, unmarried, living with his parents and seemingly unconcerned about his want of prestige, wife or independence. She often had considered inviting him home so she could get his opinion about Lemuel. If she didn't, it had nothing to do with the rumors of his homosexuality. She was just afraid that people would think she was so desperate for male companionship that she would become involved with a man of no ambition.

"Jessica!" she heard her boss saying into the phone. "Jessica, are you there? Please don't take offense. I am not denying that you need some time to yourself. But Jessica, remember, time heals all—"

"It wouldn't work," she said.

"No one here will accuse you of anything," he said. "If the rest of the staff had known I would be talking to you, they would have sent their condolences."

"Condolences!" she said, and hung up. "*Condolences,*" she repeated to the empty apartment.

The phone rang. It was her mother, calling to say that she would be flying in from Boise that afternoon. Jessica remembered the scolding her mother had given her years before for breaking a Hummel figurine. She expected the same scolding now, its intensity increased a thousandfold, and so awaited her mother's arrival with gratitude.

Jessica's father was unable to get away from an important trial, but he sent a letter via his wife in which he described his revulsion at having killed four Japanese soldiers during the war. He said that he had learned afterward, in talking to other men with soldiers' consciences, that some murders deserved to be ignored. This was the only way that society had found, he said, for those with subtle hearts to survive.

Jessica had never heard about her father's experiences in the army. His letter did not comfort her; it upset her more.

"There's nothing I can do for you," her mother said at last. "I've had patients like you." She was an occupational therapist at a rehabilitation center for amputees and paraplegics. "They just wanted to keep on pressing their bruises. I may as well leave."

Jessica nodded her assent and helped her mother pack. She called a taxi, but would not leave the apartment to see her mother to the airport.

Within five minutes after Jessica's mother had left, her friend Dottie, who once had been her sister-in-law Dottie, arrived. She brought Jessica a tall, thin cactus, just as she had done after Herbie's departure. Dottie was Herbie's sister, but she could not understand what Jessica ever had seen in him. Nor could she understand how her brother could have been so blind to Jessica's strengths. How many people had the unfailing will and focus of attention to forebear from doing any significant harm in the world? How many had the humility to exclude malice and jealousy from their emotions?

"We don't blame you a bit," Dottie had told Jessica after the divorce. "Herbie has been a pain in the ass since he spit at the *mohel* who circumcised him." And again, after the death of Isabella Borges, Dottie told Jessica, "We don't blame you at all."

Jessica thanked Dottie and asked her to leave. Unable to offend her by throwing away the cactus, she tucked it behind the wooden blinds over the sink, next to the first cactus. The plants remained out of sight, but she sensed the two prickly fingers pointing out her guilt at having caused two families to grow up with one parent apiece.

When Lemuel came home from school, she asked if the other children were giving him a hard time over what she had done.

"Are you kidding?" he said. "They're being nicer to me than when Whimpy died." Whimpy had been a cocker spaniel. "Some kid got up on a table in the cafeteria and yelled out, 'Hey, Lemmie, your mom flatten any more spics lately?' and the other kids jumped him." He frowned. "They shoved his face into a plate of tuna-noodle casserole."

One week after the accident Jessica baked a cornbread, wrapped it in foil and began walking south. Several blocks down the street, she started to fear that a Mexican-American family might regard a gift of cornbread as a sign of condescension. Cornbread was a specialty of hers, but she doubted that her recipe would be to their liking. She was tempted to leave the bread on a bench but was afraid that the elements might ruin it before someone could eat it.

The newspapers had gotten the Borges's address wrong and it took Jessica forty minutes of knocking at slow-to-open doors before she found the right duplex. All three Borges children were sitting on the front stoop. They were neatly dressed, their dark eyes clear. They said nothing to her, only stared. She asked if their father was home. The eldest, a slim boy with fine features, showed her in.

The long table in the living room was laden with food in an assortment of dishes and baskets, many covered with bright cloths. It was impossible to tell whether any contained cornbread. Geraldo Borges sat in an armchair, staring at a newspaper printed in Spanish. He was short and squarely built, with broad, unshaven cheeks and a flat nose. None of the children resembled their father.

"Yo soy la mujer que mató su esposa," Jessica said. I am the woman who murdered your wife.

He appeared not to have understood. "You are welcome," he said, motioning toward the other armchair. She handed him the cornbread. He accepted it with a deep nod.

"Lo siento," she said. I am sorry.

Instead of sitting, she wept. Geraldo Borges also began to weep. His children—the two younger girls, who were peering in through the screen door, and the eldest, the boy, who was so close that Jessica could see the mole on his neck—giggled in terror.

Geraldo Borges embraced Jessica. "Lo siento también," he said. I, too, am sorry.

He told her, in a mixture of Spanish and English, that a lawyer had been to the house earlier that week. Despite the lawyer's advice, he was going to sue neither the manufacturer of the fatal air conditioner nor Jessica.

"*La culpa . . .*" she said. "*La culpa es mía.*"

"*Lo siento,*" he said softly.

Jessica fled.

Always, the silent opinions of her family, friends and acquaintances had resounded in Jessica's ears like the pronouncements of incorporeal judges. In the days following the accident, these voices stopped speaking sense to her. She heard their opinions as so much soft babble. It was as if the Allied tribunal at Nuremberg had started singing Broadway show tunes into the world's waiting microphones.

Eventually, her confusion resolved itself into indifference. Even she could not govern her life by the judgments of tender idiots. Finally, on the second Sunday after the accident, she awoke to a world without judges. She lay in bed for hours, as motionless as Isabella Borges had lain on the stretcher.

Lemuel entered her room, timidly carrying a plate of caramels. "I thought you'd be hungry," he said.

"Are you?"

"I had a few bananas. But we ran out."

She was too blank to wonder how best to treat him. Only her instincts were left her, and these said to lead him to the kitchen, crack two eggs into a bowl, grate some cheese and make him an omelet. From the way he ate, she decided that her instincts had not betrayed her.

"If I were to commit suicide," she thought, "Lemuel would be an orphan." Herbie, she knew, would always be too busy to care for him properly. And to keep her son in omelets and tennis shoes, she would have to continue working.

She phoned the director of her agency at his home to say that she would be coming in to the office the next day. Before either of them had hung up, she heard her boss shouting the news to his wife.

On her first day back at work Jessica was still too numb to register the stares and whispers of her co-workers. She also was too numb to deny habit. At eleven she brought Paul Fields his first cup of coffee of the day.

"I hear you've been on vacation, too," he said. Beneath his beard and tinted glasses, his face was tanned. "You look relaxed."

"Relaxed?" Did he really not know about the accident, or was he only pretending?

"I've read that martyrs often die peacefully," he said. "And men who are reprieved after the rifles already have been pointed at their chests return to a world whose laws can't touch them." He smiled at her, and she was not offended, although she had made sure that everything about her demeanor had warned that a smile would be taken as the bitterest of insults. "It's just a shame that martyrdom and murder can't be prescribed as therapy," he said. Then he asked her out to dinner.

"No," she said, "but thank you."

"Don't you want to eat with me?"

"Yes," she said.

"Then why don't you?"

She shrugged. "All right," she said. She did not, however, bring him his second cup of coffee at three, hoping to derail her customary doubts about him by derailing her customary behavior toward him. Instead, she phoned Lemuel and told him to call his favorite sitter, then call her back and confirm that the sitter could come.

Dinner lasted three hours, the walk another two. It was not that Jessica and Paul had much to discuss. Neither wanted to talk about the office. Paul made no revelations about his living arrangements, although he laughed when they passed a violinist who was playing on the sidewalk and said that as a teenager he had threatened his parents with practicing on El platforms if they didn't let him play his saxophone in the basement at night. Since then they had learned to sleep through his subterranean blues sessions. His mother, he said, had a wonderful sense of humor, and he greatly enjoyed the company of both his parents.

At no time during the evening did either of them mention the

accident. Their silences were many, but comfortable. Just before midnight they returned to Jessica's apartment, where they
found Lemuel asleep in his bedroom and the sitter asleep on
the sofa. Jessica roused the sitter and sent him down to his
apartment on the second floor. Then, after much the same
discussion as the one about their going to dinner, Jessica let
Paul make love to her. Her blouse and undergarments worked
their way into the crevices between the cushions of the sofa, but
she felt more private than she had since her fourteenth birthday.
Paul usually kept his eyes camouflaged behind the blue lenses
of his glasses, but even now, as he inspected every inch of her
body, she did not feel watched. Surprised at her freedom, she
said, "Oh."

Lemuel, hearing their noises, wandered into the living room.
He saw his mother and went as white as moonlight. Jessica
stiffened in Paul's arms.

"Haven't you ever seen your mother naked?" Paul asked.

"No," Lemuel said.

"Well?" he asked.

The boy moved to the window. It was open, although the
curtains were drawn. There was no breeze, and Jessica's skin
burned. She felt as if someone were holding hot irons above
her, preparing to brand her. Still, she made no attempt to cover
herself. She closed her eyes for a moment, but she opened them
again.

"I think she's perfect," Lemuel said, then turned his back on
them, parted the curtains, leaned out the window and hooted
once, twice, happily into the night.

A SENSE
OF
AESTHETICS

A SENSE
OF
AESTHETICS

Most of us had to wait in the schoolyard until the first bell, but five or six girls were allowed in each morning to shower in the locker room and dry their hair under the blowers for hands. They rinsed out their panties with gritty yellow soap pumped from dispensers over the sinks, and put these back on, the cloth damp but clean next to their skin. Then they shuffled through the halls to the Home Ec department, where the nurse doled out oatmeal along with advice about avoiding V.D.

I hated those girls—for looking both ways before slipping into school through the door by the gym, for bowing their heads even when their hair was shiny and fresh. If I'd seen a classmate mouthing "B.O.," I'd have punched that boy's nose.

But I lived in town, where everyone had sinks and toilets indoors, and it wouldn't be my smell that revealed I was poor. It would be Clara Stark and her Photographic Essay of the History and Resources of Lenape County.

Miss Stark was a Scot (" 'Scotch' is a beverage, an *inebriant*," she said). The pattern on her skirts was the tartan of the Stark clan. "I'm the last living Stark," she announced the first day. "No one can wear it after I'm dead."

The topic that year was New York State history, with an emphasis on the county we lived in, and she used this excuse to tell us how her family had stripped bark from hemlocks and boiled it with boots, which they sold to Abe Lincoln to help free the slaves. The Starks used their profits to set up a bank, the

Paradise Dime, and to build a block of stores in the middle of town. The word STARK was carved in stone above the windows of my teacher's apartment. You almost could see the same letters traced on her dusty white forehead.

The assignment always started on the first day of fall, so we knew what was coming. While Miss Stark took attendance, the room buzzed with words that sounded like weapons—"telescopic lens," "light meter," "tripod." Harry Hooper said "f-stop" and "aperture" in the same lustful tone that I'd once heard him use to describe a French kiss.

"Juancito!" I whispered to the boy on my left. "Remember, you promised."

He folded his hands and shook his head no. Then he looked toward the front with a beatific smile on his delicate face.

"You coward," I said.

He turned in his seat. "You watch what you say, girl."

Miss Stark rapped her desk. "Let's have some de-cor-um!"

"It was her fault," he said. "She crazy. She don't—"

"It *was* me," I told her. "Why do you always right away blame—"

"Never mind whose fault it was. If you don't quiet down, I'll bring out the muzzles."

This was the story: Her Scotties had died and she kept their old muzzles in a drawer in her desk. She would fit a mangy muzzle that still smelled of dog drool over my face so I couldn't talk or bite.

"All right then," she said. "Shall I continue?"

No one said no, though the rules of the essay were something you knew by this point in life. You couldn't just go out and snap pictures of anything. You needed a *theme*. You had to write *captions* to explain how each photo showed a part of your theme. Finally, you had to narrate your essay in front of the class; this would give you a chance to practice your *poise*.

Before she was done explaining about arranging your photos on a piece of white oaktag with those sticky little corners from the five-and-dime store, the kids in the front were waving their hands. She pulled back her face. "If I wanted to see waving palms," she said, "I would go to *Miami*."

Only Lisa Chernov kept her hand in the air. "Miss Stark?" Lisa asked. "Could I please do my essay on the old tanning business in Lenape County?"

I turned to Juancito and gagged in my hand, but he'd changed into stone.

"Why, of course," Miss Stark said. "Come see me after class and I'll give you some hints as to where you might explore."

"Miss Stark! Oh, Miss Stark!"

I waited until all the questions were asked. They I held up my hand, straight as a spear. I didn't call her name.

"Marianne?" she said.

I stood by my seat. This wasn't required, so everyone looked. "We can't afford a car. Besides, my mother can't drive."

"Well," she said, stroking the lace at her throat, "the town is a part of the county, now isn't it? I'm sure you could find many an interesting theme without leaving Paradise."

I was ready for this. "I don't have a camera. And I don't want to ask my mother to buy one. A camera is a *lux-u-ry*." I drew out the word as Miss Stark liked to linger on words like de-cor-um. "And she works hard enough to buy our *ne-ces-si-ties*."

At this point Juancito had promised to say: "My mother does too. The essay isn't fair to poor kids like us." But he seemed to be staring out the window at the lawn, where one of the janitors was down on his knees, scraping mud from a mower.

"Your mother can't afford a camera?" she said. She looked for advice to Franklin D. Roosevelt, who hung by her desk. "You could borrow one, couldn't you? If not from a friend, then from Mr. Deeds, in art? And if those options fail, I myself have a Brownie that I would be pleased—"

"I don't accept charity." I had practiced these words. "Besides, there's the film."

"Oh dear," Miss Stark sighed. "The quality of your pictures matters, of course. A sense of aesthetics certainly counts. But not nearly so much as the content of the essay. Perhaps you could draw? Your mother is something of an artist, I've heard?" Her eyes, which were usually harsh as two tacks, shone with new warmth. "Doesn't your mother teach art at the church?"

Years later I read a novel whose heroine was called "genteel poor" and I realized Miss Stark had thought that my mother fit this description, a well-bred young woman forced to clerk in a store and teach ladies art. But I didn't know that then, and my plans were thrown off by her tender regard for my mother's hard work. I sat in my seat, despite having vowed to stand there until Miss Stark had promised that she'd never assign her essay again.

Every morning, when my mother walked to the store, people from town would offer her rides.

She would pump her arms. "Heart! Lungs!" she would shout, as though peddling these organs from the rucksack she wore. "It helps move the bowel! You should try it yourself!"

On days when it snowed, she wore a blue parka with fur on the hood. She loved that word, "parka," and sang out its syllables, as foreign as Eskimo in our town at the time, to the people who tried to convince her to ride. At the store she would trade her parka for a smock. But she wouldn't wear a red plastic badge with her name. Instead, she embroidered JEANNE on the pocket in graceful red loops. My mother was short and the counter where she worked cut her off at the chest. In the cold fluorescent light of that colorless store, only her lined, earth-colored face and braid of brown hair seemed living and warm.

The counter enclosed her, the long panes of glass held together by chrome that would give you a shock on a dry afternoon. In her spare time she polished bracelets and rings that were locked in the case like flowers too finicky to grow in the wild.

I considered real jewelry an immoral waste of money. But buying the fake stuff, which hung from steel gallows on top of the glass, showed that a person had no sense of . . . aesthetics. Under the merciless lights of the store, the heavy chains and earrings glinted like handcuffs, dog collars, bolts.

For the young girls, to whom beauty and love weren't yet weighty things, the jewelry counter offered filigree hoops and ceramic blue pansies to wear in their ears, and paper-thin charms with BEST FRIENDS engraved on a heart cut in half, so that each friend could wear half the heart on her wrist. The girls who bought this jewelry treated my mother with enormous respect. They said: "Mrs. Augustine, if you have the time, please . . ." But I didn't like the way they asked her for help in running their lives. Some girl would be watching the waterfall of watches in the Timex display, and the next thing you knew she'd be asking my mother: "What should you do if your boyfriend won't love you unless you put out?"

Even I knew the answers to the questions they asked. But more than her answers they wanted her voice.

When I think of that voice I see the big landscape she was painting that fall—a river that flowed around big mossy rocks, the foam flying up. She had lived in America since she was ten, but she still couldn't pronounce three-syllable words; her low, fluid voice would break into eddies as it passed by those words, though some other part of her voice would break free of language and rise like that bright foamy spray.

"I never could talk to my mother like this!" The girl would lean over the counter and give my mother a hug.

Why did she waste her time on these girls? I knew them from school. They were flighty, I said. I saw them as birds that had flown in a window and were flapping around, primping and screeching and making a mess. Their mothers had women who came in to clean, their fathers earned tens of thousands a year. How dare they ask for sympathy from a woman who'd been working since she was thirteen?

That day after fighting with Miss Stark in class, I walked to the store and found her advising her boss, Mr. Gipps. For most of his life Solly Gipps had sold eggs. Then egg prices fell and he'd been obliged to take a job here. He would stop by each counter and coo to the salesgirl, "Come, come, you can sell more merchandise than that." His wife had run off and he'd gotten in the habit of asking my mother: Should he let his daughters date non-Jewish boys? Should he pay the school nurse to teach them "the facts"? In return for this help, Mr. Gipps brought my mother boxes of candy that could not be sold because they'd gone stale, expired cosmetics, wilting bouquets and slightly soiled clothes. He was pleasant enough, with a square, kindly face and shiny black hair combed back from his brow. But I hated him because he had asked why she'd never gotten divorced.

"In Jewish law," he said, "if a man leaves his wife, a posse of rabbis goes to track him down. They twist the bum's arm until he comes back, or at least says she's free to marry again."

I was glad when she told him that, rabbis or not, she'd promised to wait for my father's return. He'd left her a note that said he'd come home when he learned not to drink. He was careful with words, my mother explained—he had, after all, worked many years taking down telegrams over the phone— and he wouldn't have said "when" if he'd really meant "if." (This gave me great comfort. I imagined he'd been sent to deliver a telegram, then drunk too much beer. Even now he was wobbling around some city on his bicycle, peering at street signs and asking strangers the way.)

When I got to the store, Mr. Gipps clucked: "How can you frown on such a fine afternoon? A pretty girl like you . . . If you were my daughter, I'd see you had something to smile about. Wouldn't I now, Jeanne?"

If only she would tell him: My daughter is frowning because you are here.

Instead, she said: "Hints! What Mr. Gipps is meaning is now is the time I should give you his gift." She took a white box from under the counter.

His face had that overly vulnerable look of a grown-up who hopes that his present will buy the love of some child.

"Marianne," she said, "why didn't you tell me that you needed a camera for this class that you take?"

I was afraid that you'd buy one, I thought.

"I didn't need to be told," Mr. Gipps said. "I saw Jeanne this morning and something just clicked. I said, 'Marianne is in seventh grade this year.' Then I went up to Cameras. And as it turned out, a man had returned a little Instamatic whose flash-bulbs wouldn't flash. He browbeat Miss Dowd into taking it back, which she oughtn't have done. So what could we do except give it away?"

He seemed pained at my silence, my refusal to smile.

"My daughters did their essays on the Egg and Poultry Business in Lenape County. What do *you* mean to do?"

I meant to do nothing. I couldn't draw worth beans. The other kids would have their photos of forts and I would have pages of squiggles and blots. I had come here to ask my mother for a note forbidding Miss Stark to cause me this shame. But now I couldn't ask. She nudged the box closer. Her face said: I promised that you wouldn't have to suffer for how I have lived.

The Styrofoam squeaked as the halves came apart. The foam had been hollowed so the sleek metal camera, black with gray trim, fit neatly inside. In separate compartments were the strap, plastic case, and the useless plastic cube with its four tiny bulbs.

Until then I'd never imagined that an object could call out your name.

I'm yours, it said. Yours. I have special powers. Don't give me back.

I cradled it in the palm of my hand. I couldn't help but run my finger around the rim of the lens.

"There! Didn't I tell you! Solly Gipps knows how to make a pretty girl smile!"

My fingers took joy in winding the film so the next number showed through the small yellow hole. My chest loved the weight of the camera; my neck, the bite of the strap. But no matter how much I polished the lens and tried to invoke the genie inside, my camera wouldn't give me a picture that showed how sinful it was that some human beings were miserably poor while others were rich.

This theme wasn't quite original. Browsing through *Life*, I'd come upon photos of babies with bellies as swollen as lunch bags you blow up and pop. They were stretching their hands through the gate of a mansion, curled up to sleep by a temple wall, crowding a gold limousine. I knew right away that I'd steal this idea, but I wasn't sure how. Maybe the kids who lived in the trailer parks on the outskirts of town had bellies that swollen, but here in the village poverty hid. Except for the drunk who slept in front of Town Hall—snapping his picture, I assured myself my father would sleep in a tent—the most likely candidates were the Puerto Rican families who lived in the big gray-shingle building not far from my own.

When I walked by the building, the ugliest toddler I'd ever seen was pressing her face to a window. She saw me and shrieked, then disappeared inside. I got up the courage to go down the alley and poke around back. I focused my camera on a trashcan, then a wall with the paint peeling off, but the fact was the building didn't look that bad. I was sure the apartments were furry with rats; holes in the ceilings let in the rain; toilets flooded the halls with vile-smelling slop. But I didn't have a flash, and even if I'd had one I couldn't have explained my reason for using it to the people who lived there.

I tried to persuade Juancito to help. We were sitting in his kitchen, upstairs from my own.

"Girl, I'm from Mexico." He nibbled a fritter, then wiped his fingers on a pink paper napkin. "What I got to do with them dirty P.R.'s?"

His mother was scraping the skin from a chicken foot. "*Nada!* You got *nada* to do with those pig. I hear you got somethin' I make sure you don'!" Snorting, she pitched the foot in a kettle.

Anita regarded her cooking as magic. The aromas from her stewpots and her cave of a stove made you feel famished. You would promise her anything just for a taste.

"You know Spanish, don't you?" I said to Juancito.

"Yeah. Maybe. So what?" Did I mean he had anything in common with the kids who sat in our classes chewing their thumbs? Didn't he always get A's in science and math?

"So couldn't you explain that I'm doing my essay on how they shouldn't have to live in that dump?"

He rolled his eyes. "Girl, you don't know a *thing*. Those dirty P.R.'s, they think a dump's better than where they been living on that island of theirs."

"Um-mm, that so, *la verdad, la verdad.*" She accompanied this chant by shaking more pepper into the pot.

My eyes filled with tears. Imprisoned in that building were babies with pussy sores on their cheeks and bugs in their hair. "I don't understand why you're not on my side. You don't have a car and your father is dead. What kind of essay can you do with no car?"

His mother turned to face us, her waves of fat whooshing a moment behind. "*Mi hijo* gonna do A-double-plus essay! His *tío*, he drive him around so he look . . . so he take picture of . . . What you say, *hijo*?"

"The railroad." He lifted his nose in the air. "The title of my photographic essay will be: 'All Aboard, All Aboard!: The History of the Railroad in Lenape County.' "

"Jesus," I said.

"No swear in this house!" Anita had said this hundreds of times, but I could not remember that "Jesus" was as bad as "hell," "damn" and "shit."

"Juancito," I said, "that's what everyone does." He wouldn't even have to narrate his captions; Miss Stark would take over and tell us about her great-great-grandfather buying the land that the railroad would need and selling it back at three times the price. At the end she would say: "I am *so* pleased the memory of this transportation link, so vital to our county's economic development, is being preserved in this photographic essay," and she'd give him an A.

I was deeply ashamed of my best friend. And jealous. I would have loved to take pictures of the trestles that hid in the hills around the county like shy, skinny dinosaurs, and the tracks that went nowhere, lost in the vines.

"Brown-noser, brown-noser, Juan's nose is brown." I flicked the tip of his nose, which really was brown.

"You call my boy name I sendin' you home!" She was waving a carrot; the greens brushed my face. "And don' you go gettin' my boy in no mess. *You* make a mess, one thing. But a boy, he ain' white, *he* make a mess, that it, that his chance, bye-bye, *adiós*." She tugged at her girdle through her polka-dot dress. "Why you so rile' 'bout bein' poor? You ain' never live in no box at the dump. Ain' never been hungry you chew up some leave. Ain' never been poor so the worm get inside and whatever little thing you scrape in your mouth just feed those worm."

Juancito said, "Mama! When you say things like that it makes me have to throw up!"

"*Mi hijo* got stomach made outta paper." She was shaking her head, but she seemed to be proud. "So who gonna taste this stew here and tell me, is it too hot, or ain' hot enough?" She wafted a ladleful under my nose. I couldn't help but open my mouth and lean forward. "Okay now, you promise you ain' gonna mess with this lady no more. You promise Anita you gonna be *good*."

Imagine our town as a saggy old mattress with all the poor people jumbled together in the trough down the middle. On the lump to the west the rich Christians lived in Victorian houses three stories tall; on the eastern lump, Jews, in vinyl-sided ranches with brick and stone trim. In the yards on both hills were rose gardens, willows, swing sets and pools. The cars in the driveways looked like beached whales.

I shot a whole roll of film. But several days later, when the pictures came back, I was so disappointed that I tore them in half. To save my mother's money I'd used black-and-white film; to avoid being caught I'd shot from the road. What would anyone think of these tiny gray houses, with their tiny gray trees and tiny gray pools, except that the people who lived in those houses were tiny and gray?

I punished my camera by leaving it in my underwear drawer. I sniped at Juancito for crowing about some field that he'd found where a train had blown up; he and his uncle had poked around for hours looking for bones. When my mother asked to see how my essay was going, I said: "It's not done yet," afraid she'd find out that I'd wasted her film.

But the next afternoon, as I walked by the synagogue on my way home from school, I saw the word TEMPLE on the billboard out front. I'd thought there were only temples in India, but we had them right here. "Temple" meant "church," and the churches in Paradise were the biggest, and fanciest, and therefore most sinful buildings in town.

I'd once asked my mother what religion I was and she'd said that I'd have to decide for myself.

"Well, what are *you*?"

She showed her gold tooth. "When I married your father, he was a Catholic and I was a Jew. We decided to change to be the same thing. But the only religion we could agree on was pagan."

I wasn't sure then what a pagan might be, but now I can see that my mother was right. Each apple she painted, each root, tree and rock glowed with a life that was more than its own, the life of some idol, or maybe a god, trying to escape its flat canvas world.

"You must keep this a secret." My mother turned serious; her gold tooth disappeared. "If the Reverend finds out that a pagan teaches art in the basement of his church . . . He already has suspicions"—the word had three syllables, it came out a blur—"that I bring naked people when he is not there."

I didn't want to be a Christian like the ladies in pink pantsuits in her class at the church. But I couldn't see the point of being a pagan. I had better things to do than paint pictures of fruit, or even naked men. *If* God existed, He must be the principle that Life Should Be Fair. Spending money on churches was a theft from the mouths of babies in rags. So many thieves . . . and no one but me to bring them to trial! What truth have I since seen as clearly as that, what purpose in life so pure and profound?

I scrounged enough money for a roll of color film. The churches in Paradise stood along Main Street. I started at the south end and worked my way north. I took a picture of the star tacked to the synagogue; I didn't know for sure what metal it was, so I said it was gold. The Methodist church had a slender white steeple with a silver-faced clock and a weather vane angel whose puffy cheeks blew the wind from a horn. Paradise Baptist was shaped like a castle, and First Congregational had pink marble arches, a four-headed gargoyle and a tower so high, with the clouds rushing past, that the stones seemed about to fall on my head.

It was Indian summer. Everything—the sky, the marigolds in pots near the Lutheran church, the pears on a tree on the library lawn—seemed to be made of the same fruity gems as the rings in the store. I got carried away and took photos just because I liked how things looked. By the time I reached Our Lady of Consolation, I had only one picture left on the roll. This was too bad. The Catholic church was bigger than the others combined. Two gigantic evergreens had stood by the steps, one on each side, until they'd gotten so bushy that they'd smothered the saints perched on the roof. The trees were chopped down, but their outlines still showed, and in my mind these shadows had something to do with the words Holy Ghost.

I circled the church. Enormous white underpants hung from a line—for the nuns? for the priest? I tried not to look. At the rear was St. Mary's, grades K through 6, squat and unadorned except for a statue of Christ near the playground. He looked like a misfit who'd been teased by the kids and left behind to mope.

A window shade snapped up. A woman in a head cloth peered from the glass. Before she could see me and ask what I wanted, I ran back to the church. I was tired and hot. I walked up the steps to the huge blood-red doors. Every other church I'd tried had been locked. Not that I minded. I didn't have a flash, and I wanted to say that they kept the doors locked so that no one could steal the treasures inside.

But Our Lady was open. I found myself standing in a room of blue light so quiet and cool that I felt I was floating in a very still lake. The pews were rich brown. Scattered on the seats were mossy-smelling prayer books and mimeographed pamphlets with a faint purple drawing of a mother and child. "Blessed are you among women," it said.

The blues, greens and purples from the windows played across the white plaster walls. The first window showed Jesus Christ as a baby. A plaque underneath said GRACIOUSLY GIVEN BY THE MISSES STARK. The next several windows showed Christ growing up. He got caught by the soldiers, mocked and lashed by the crowd, then nailed to a cross. This upset me so much that I turned counterclockwise and made time go backwards: He unfastened the nails and explained to the soldiers he was leaving their town, rode backwards on his donkey and returned to his home, then got younger and younger until he was a baby in the stable again, with his parents and lambs.

On the altar stood a table covered in white. There were

candles on the cloth, and peach-colored blossoms on slender green stems. Above, on the wall, was a large wooden cross with a yellow-skinned Christ. The cloth around his waist had fallen away to lay bare his ribs and the hole in his side. He had holes in his feet and the palms of his hands.

Poor tortured soul. My mother had described my father this way. "That a poor tortured soul could capture such joy with a few strokes and dabs . . . No one could paint a nude like your father, so luscious with life."

Now, in the church, I knew that my father would never come back, no more than the man asleep on that cross would pull out those nails and climb down and save the poor from the rich.

I took refuge in an alcove off to one side. A beautiful woman stood on a globe; her head was a little higher than mine. She wore an apricot gown, and a blue-and-gold cape covered her hair—like the hood of my mother's parka, I thought. Someone had hung a wreath of yellow flowers around her thin neck. She was stretching her arms from the folds of her gown, hands turned palms up, asking for something I didn't know I had.

Maybe she asked other people for things like believing in God or helping the poor. But she asked *me* for gratitude—for the blue starry globe under her feet, her beautiful face, the fine yellow flowers laced around her neck.

In front of the globe were three rows of candles with red bulbs like flames. DONATE $1 AND PUSH BUTTON, the sign said. I didn't have a dollar, but I pushed all the buttons and each one lit up until Mary was bathed in a ruby-red glow.

I lifted my camera. I thought it might work. I twisted the lens, but her face was still blurred, so I stepped back a little, and a little bit farther, and I knocked against something—a coat rack, I thought—and it fell to the floor.

Remember how you felt as a child when you broke some wine glass or vase—the queasiness, the chill so violent you shook. Then let the crash echo in a cavernous church. Picture Christ at your feet, the thorns of his crown like so many teeth strewn on the floor, two fingers snapped from his right hand and lying in a pool of red light.

Did I think of admitting what I had done? The priest lived next door. I'd seen him on the street, a jittery man with bristling red hair. I knew he would rage and tell me that I owed some awful amount. I couldn't even guess how much a statue of Jesus might cost. Maybe if he'd let me spend my whole life repaying the debt . . . But I knew what would happen. My mother would take the debt on herself, and how could she pay for a statue of God?

I righted the crucifix. How ugly it was! The cross was too small for such a large Christ, and his face was a blob, as though being divine meant you were above needing a chin. The artist had taken no care with the fingers; they were plain as two chalk sticks.

I stole a last look at Mary. She was reaching toward her son, the distance between them still glowing red. *Please let me hold him. Please let me put him together again.*

"I'm sorry," I told her. I hid the fingers in an urn. This reminded me to wipe my prints from the statue and the pew where I'd sat. A block down the street, I removed the film from my camera and buried it under some trash in a can.

My hunger for justice had grown to be ravenous, feeding as it did on the sins of the world, but now it turned inward and satisfied its appetite on my sin alone. I had destroyed not only a statue, but also my sense of myself as invulnerable, the blue starry globe under my feet.

My mother was worried. "What is it, Marianne? Has some boy upset you? Maybe you have gotten in trouble at school?"

I'd never kept a secret from my mother before.

"It couldn't be that essay with the camera?" she asked.

I still had some photos of the Puerto Ricans' building and the carcass of a cat I'd found on the sidewalk near my own house, but I needed a contrast, some photos of the rich to round out my theme.

When I started to explain this, my mother looked puzzled. She tugged at her braid. "You think we are poor? You feel that your schoolmates have something you lack?"

"No, that's not it. I don't think we're poor." And suddenly, I didn't. What I lacked was a father. He had gone away and left us. That's why my mother needed to work. How could I do an essay on my father being a drunk?

I might have come up with another idea, but I was afraid that my mother would ask Solly Gipps to drive me around the county in his Pontiac. "Smile!" he'd keep saying. "A pretty girl shouldn't frown!"

What was the use? The nun who'd seen me lurking in back of the church was even now studying the pictures in the yearbook, trying to fit my name to my face. Any moment the cops would knock down our door. My life would be over, and my mother's would too.

Miss Stark's was the last class of the day. A big roll of oaktag or a yellow box of slides sat on each desk. Miss Stark stood in front in her heavy plaid dress, pleased as a goddess who knows that her acolytes are ready to lay their best at her feet. Since "Augustine" came second after "Appelbaum," I practiced what I would tell her. "I didn't do the assignment. I can't explain why. I accept the consequences." At least I wouldn't have to suffer through another five days.

"All right people," she said. "Just to be fair, why don't we start with the end of the alphabet and go backwards this time?"

Every day that week we gathered around small blurry photos tacked to a poster or squinted from our seats at big blurry slides smeared on a screen. I tried not to care that the exposures were wrong, tried not to think what I could have done if given the chance to focus my lens on the rusted red caboose in Juancito's green field, or the old bluestone quarry so deep that the bodies of drowned little boys could never be found (or so said Brick Davies, whose essay this was, and Miss Stark confirmed it—the quarry had belonged to an uncle of hers).

I found myself hoping that some other poor kid would put up the fight I'd intended to make. But even Donna Mott, who came in each morning to shower in the locker room and rinse out her clothes, had pictures of the dairy where she worked after school.

Only the three oversized boys in back of the room mumbled

"Don't got one" when Miss Stark called their names. But they didn't stand and fight. And Miss Stark didn't scold them. She just marked an F next to each of their names. Three years from now, none of the kids who got F's on their essays would be sitting in school. None except me. *I* could get an F and it didn't mean I'd fail for the rest of my life. What it meant was Miss Stark looked at me, startled, and said, "Really, Marianne? Is something wrong at home? Come in and see me after school, we'll discuss this."

A half-hour later I walked through the empty school to her room. I paused at the threshold to gather my courage. The chairs behind the desks faced every which way, and this made me realize that each class escaped as soon as it could, leaving Miss Stark behind. The time-line that ran from the Prehistoric Era to the Modern Age never added a year while the woman who sat beneath it got old.

The light from the windows was cloudy with dust, and Miss Stark herself, her white hair and powdered face, seemed little more substantial than the motes in the air. It took her a moment to recall why I'd come, but she seemed glad to see me. She teaches because she's lonely, I thought. Talking about all her dead relatives makes her feel they're alive.

She motioned me over. "You don't have to tell me what is bothering you," she said. "Unless you think that talking will make you feel better."

She took me around. I didn't pull away. I remembered her saying, "It's the content that matters" and I pitied her because her wool dress seemed hollow, except for some ribs.

"I certainly understand your wanting your privacy." She opened her drawer. "But I wonder if this might have something to do with . . . At any rate, I always keep an extra roll of film in my desk. If you need to start over . . . Perhaps you had trouble finding a theme? You might let me suggest one. I have always thought that someone ought to do an essay . . . This used to be quite a prosperous town. The churches reflect that. Some of their artifacts, well, they're true gifts. The Catholic church, in particular, has some of the finest stained glass in the East. The windows were executed by Wendell Hunt James. Your mother would know all about him, I'm sure."

I jerked away. Tricked! Why else would she lure me to her room after school, mention the church and the word "executed" in the same breath?

"As it happens," she said, "those magnificent windows were given to the church by some great-aunts of mine. They scandalized everyone by turning Roman Catholic. Oh my, what a tempest! The family was terrified they might become nuns!"

The windows! I'd forgotten. A coincidence, that was all.

She placed the film in my hand and curled my fingers around it.

"Thank you," I said.

She patted my hair. "You're a well-bred young lady. Tell your mother I said that."

Well-bred? Did she think I was one of her Scotties? But oh, she was right. I'd even raised my hand and stood by my desk!

I ran to the door. I wanted to shout: "Keep your damn charity!" But I couldn't form the words. The look on her face . . . where had I seen it? Her expression was the same as Solomon Gipps' when he'd given me the camera. Why, Miss Stark was scared that I'd give back her gift! Miss Stark scared of me! She wanted my gratitude, maybe even my love, and if I withheld it . . . I let myself imagine hurling the film, spitting out hateful words, watching her face crumble to chalk. But the scene was so ugly that it gave me no pleasure.

"I've got to be going," I said very politely. "Thank you again."

I saw her relax. She smiled at me, and waved. "Good-bye, Marianne. Do be sure to give my regards to your mother."

"I'll *do* that," I said. Then I turned and made my exit, as poised as a queen.

I didn't want to go home to our empty apartment, so I walked to the store. The light was gold-red and the leaves like stained glass, millions of fragments, solid, yet transparent when the sun hit just so. I passed the Catholic church, and the Stark Block, and the building where the Puerto Ricans lived. I would never be caught. Someone could break a statue of Christ and still other people would talk to her kindly, even give her a hug. The rich could be rich and the poor could be poor, the guilty unpunished, yet these sins would be covered by a tapestry of light.

Several days later the Puerto Ricans' building somehow caught fire. My mother and I saw flames from our kitchen and ran down the street. I would have grabbed my camera, but I'd used up the film taking pictures of churches for my new essay.

Standing at the barricade was a woman in a nightgown, its fabric so thin the bumps around her nipples made bumps in the cloth. The woman was crying, as was her husband, a skinny young man in red pajama bottoms with tufts of hair bursting from under his arms.

Juancito walked by on his way home from a concert at school. "What all this commotion? What you done now, girl?" He'd been acting insufferable since he'd gotten an A+ on his essay. He put down his clarinet and loosened his tie in the manner of a man who enjoys such a gesture. Then he noticed the woman. His eyes touched her breast, fled in disgust, wandered toward it again.

His mother said something in Spanish to the couple. They didn't seem to hear. Then she and my mother went home and came back with slippers and robes. The skinny young man was slight enough to fit into Juancito's bathrobe, the one with the trains running every which way.

Juancito said, "Mama! What you doing, that mine!"

His mother turned and slapped him.

He looked at her as though everything she'd taught him, except for that slap, was revealed as a lie. She'd extracted those promises about being good to keep him from harm, as she would have restrained him from dashing in the fire to save someone's life, all the while hoping that he'd break from her grasp and run inside anyway.

"You hit me!" he said. He picked up his clarinet and wandered down the sidewalk. He sat on a bench, stroking his cheek.

My mother wrapped the woman in her black-and-gold kimono. She repeated the phrase Anita had said—*Ven a mi casa*—and tugged on her arm, but the woman wouldn't budge.

"They don't want to come," my mother said, surprised that someone had declined to take her advice. A few minutes later the bristly priest, fussing with his collar, led them away.

"Well," my mother said, "if they think he can give them something I can't . . ."

I watched as a fireman carried out a body in a green plastic bag. Who was inside it? The girl I had glimpsed at the window that day? I tried to recall what was ugly about her, but the face I kept seeing was smeared with black tar.

We read in the paper that the building, by law, was required to have a fire escape, but the landlord hadn't bothered, and the fire inspector hadn't turned him in. I should have been angry. But already I had given up my black-and-white view of the world: rich vs. poor, wrong vs. right. I had begun to acquire a sense of aesthetics. I had come to believe that the image of a woman in a black-and-gold kimono, watching her nephews go up in flames, was a beautiful thing, more deserving of attention than a matter of law.

The building was leveled. The lot was paved over. I left home at eighteen and moved to New York, where I worked as a stylist for a slick magazine. Eventually I was able to help my mother rent a nicer apartment on the hill west of Main Street. While she was packing she came across an envelope.

"There were pictures of a building and a dead cat," she said. "They did not look special, so I threw them away."

After leaving Miss Stark, I put her film in my pocket and walked very slowly by the edge of the road. The colored leaves, the pigeons, even the cars seemed panting with life. When I got to the store I paused by the registers, blinking against the absence of sun. I watched as my mother tried on a necklace of very blue stones. She swiveled the mirror on the counter so it faced her, put her hand to her throat. Light from the ceiling flashed from the mirror, the necklace, the chrome of the counter, the glass, the fake charms and chains.

Mr. Gipps strolled by. He nodded his approval and gave her

some compliment, but he didn't say to keep it. As soon as he'd left, she unclasped the necklace and ruefully locked it back in its case.

I knew I was safe then. My mother wouldn't marry Solomon Gipps. What was the privilege of staying home and painting compared to the insult of living with a man who never gave you anything but secondhand gifts? And I knew something else. I knew, to my shame, that I wouldn't spend my life searching for evidence that the world was unfair, but for beautiful things to lay before my mother as an offering of love.

THE
FIFTH
SEASON

THE
FIFTH
SEASON

I work in chocolate, and the smell there's as pleasant as a nose full of Bosco. We wear white coats and caps, but that doesn't matter. Parts of the body you'd never expect get smeared with brown goo. By the end of a shift, a person would sell her soul for a shower, but the only thing we get is a room in the basement and a cart where we toss our sticky white coats.

I was heading there yesterday when somebody pulled me into a closet. He didn't turn on the light, but I knew who he was.

"John Drake, unhand me!"

John Drake is short, with a short brown mustache like a little smudge of chocolate under his nose. When he carries his boxes past the line where I work, his muscles bulge out like braids of string cheese. I hadn't enjoyed a man's arms in years, and if he had hugged me out in the open I might have been nicer. But closets and muscles . . . I'd learned to fear those from my ex-husband.

"Let me go," I said, "or I'll tell your boss you've been taking home cocoa butter."

When the light came back on, John Drake was grinning. "Go ahead," he said. "You'd just be killing the goose who wants to lay you a chocolate egg."

I let this go by me.

"Well, what about it?" John Drake has no patience. Coke machines quiver when they see him approach, they can't belch out their cans fast enough to keep from getting a kick.

163

"A person," I told him, "requires a question before she can answer."

John Drake stomped his foot, then grabbed an empty box of Swiss Dream from a shelf. "See this?" he asked. He was pointing to the words ELIRIA, ILLINOIS. "Who has the faintest idea where that is?"

"We do. We live here."

"But *they* don't! To them, it's just one of those places with too many vowels. All of these boxes get filled up with candy and shipped to L.A., or New York, or Miami. The people who buy a box of Swiss Dream haven't a clue about who makes their candy. And Jesus Christ," he said, "the chocolate is lousy." He whacked the box with his fist. "So, are you with me?"

I asked for more details. He stomped his foot again, but then he revealed how he'd cooked up a candy that put Swiss Dream to shame. John Drake owned a semi, and even though he'd lost his license to drive it (his fender bore traces of a toll booth he'd been too impatient to go through the regular way), he would soon get it back, and then he'd truck his candies all across the Midwest. JOHN DRAKE CHOCOLATES, he'd call them, with a photo of his face on the front of the box.

"John Drake," I said, "a person wouldn't buy dog food if it had your face on it."

"Aw, who needs you anyway."

"You do, it seems. For what purpose I don't know."

That loosened him up. "To cook the candies when I'm driving. To pick up the phone when I call home from the road. I'll set you free from this dump."

A man may say "freedom," but it's hard to believe him when he's already got you locked in a closet.

"Aw, maybe you're right. About my face, I mean. We'll put *you* on the box."

"No thanks," I told him.

"Okay, okay. If that's not enough, I'll let you be my wife."

That was just like him. He'd seen me, decided, and now we were married. By way of an answer, I took away his box and opened the lid. A chart showed each candy and explained what it was.

"John Drake," I said, "I've seen this chart so much, it shapes the world for me. When I meet a person, I can tell right off: This one's a nougat, all nutty and soft. That other person is solid fudge right through. But I can't tell what you are. And I have a bad feeling. . . . For all I know, you've got a hot pepper inside you."

John Drake was scornful. "Isn't any such thing as a hot pepper candy!" He reached in his pocket and took out a chocolate. "I'll show you what *I* know. Close your eyes, woman." But I wasn't about to. "All right then," he said. "Just go ahead and eat it."

"The last thing I want right now is a chocolate."

"Take your time," he said. "You've got 'til tomorrow." He tried to storm out, but the locked door wouldn't let him. He smacked open the bolt, kicked the door and left.

In the changing room I tossed his gift in the trash. But then I was sorry. Not even John Drake deserved to have his dream thrown in the trash. I would have retrieved it, but I didn't want the other girls to ask why.

I needn't have worried. They were too busy guessing the ending of some mini-series.

"*I* think he'll rape her."

"But Celie's a slave!"

"And *you* are a babe in this man's world, honey."

"Hey Bess, what do you think?"

I shrugged and kept quiet. I'd seen the first episode, but I hadn't enjoyed it. Too much was happening, and no one in charge. I'm not a fan of these soap-sudsy programs where everyone's trying to sleep with each other or steal away their money, or those comedies where an addle-brained wife is running out the back door while her husband, all bug-eyes, is running in the front. I like the news best, and game shows come second.

"If you keep dawdling, Bess, they'll make you work swing shift."

I wadded up my coat and chucked it in the hamper. "I'm coming," I said.

I waved to the others and got in my Chevy, checking the back seat in case John Drake was in it. When I saw it was empty, I felt sort of let down.

The City of Five Smells, that's what we call it. The drive through the chocolate to the heart of the corn chips takes twenty-five minutes in going-home traffic. At first the smell's pleasant, like a few kernels popping. Then the corn starts to burn. It scrapes your throat raw. Your stomach's on fire just from the smell, and even a woman of forty, like I am, can feel a big crop of pimples burst out on her chin.

In the fields beyond town, the odor of corn chips must rankle like neglect. The stalks grow there, patient, their roots in the earth, their reedy arms stretched up and holding a gift, a spindle of gold. If a person unwraps this corncob and boils it, dips it in butter and bites a sweet mouthful, she can't help but think with love of the stalk. But what of a person who munches a chip? Bag to mouth, bag to mouth. If a person's mind strays from the TV at all, it might get as far as the huge vats of pap. That's why a man like John Drake's so desperate to do something big and see his face on a box.

By five, I'm on the outskirts of Feed'N'Gro Fertilizer. I switch on the news, and even though it's usually just births, deaths and taxes, I fix my five senses on that announcer as if he were saying the A-bomb was coming. When I lose concentration, well, at least this stink's honest, it's just what it smells like.

The fourth smell is oats. It sneaks in your nostrils like the first hint of breakfast on a bright, frosty morning when you're warm in your bed and your mother is singing a hymn about Jesus in the kitchen below. Then it starts to smell musty, like somebody's left his breakfast untouched on the table so long it's got all full of weevils and the milk on it's spoiled.

I live in beer malt. Here the yeast bubbles with such foamy passion that it turns the air doughy. I usually shut off the radio now—thoughts of my sofa are company enough—but yesterday I heard the announcer say "hostage," and that caught my ear. Some words can do that. "Hostage," or "Bess." When I hear my name—"Bess!"—my heart starts to beat, even when I'm not the Bess being called.

The voice from the dashboard told me a story. I saw wealthy men lounging on a ship on the Nile, palm trees and camels, a sphinx here and there. Then pirates with knives clenched in their teeth rose over the rail. The announcer kept talking—this country, that king, Moslems, and Jews . . . and Mormons, I'm certain, though I might have heard wrong, my mind was so cluttered with boats made of paper, as graceful and weightless as God's boats to heaven, and ladies in robes, and servants with fans.

Then I heard "Illinois." It's usually New York that gets taken hostage, but this time it was us. It might have been Rachel, my cousin from Springfield, a woman who dances around the globe so fast you'd think that her shoes were filled with hot chestnuts. I imagined reporters crowding my driveway, Dan Rather on my steps, so near I could smell his leather suspenders. In a worried, gentle voice, Dan Rather said, "Bess, how do you feel that your poor cousin Rachel is lying in chains on a boat on the Nile?"

But the closest I came was some man from Decatur who sells Allstate insurance in the lobby of Sears—I shopped in that store once, and I passed by that booth on my way to buy socks. The captain of the boat, they said, was from Texas, and the mate was from Spain, but all eighteen passengers were from Illinois. This cruise on the Nile was some sort of reward for selling insurance, except for the wives, who'd just shown good sense when they'd married these men.

Then the announcer said that there might be a twenty-first hostage, no one was sure. Zap! I felt tingly. I *knew* that I knew him. I was shaking so bad I almost swerved off the road. But I had to get home. Something was waiting. If it wasn't Dan Rather, well, something else.

My street was deserted. The houses are small—they look like garages with the other rooms missing, except that they each have a window in front. In mine sat my mother. Even at eighty, she still is a woman whose face in a window looks like a portrait. Her delicate features haven't yet collapsed into slack, wrinkled flesh (my own face, once high-boned, sags under the weight of my worries for her, is lined with her wrinkles). Her white hair is high, as if it's still hopeful for better days ahead and just won't lie down. This fools the neighbors. If a face hasn't sagged yet, a mind can't have either. They wink and say, smiling, "I just saw your mother. My, she looks lovely!" But here's what they're thinking: "You're a very cruel daughter, keeping your mother locked in your house!"

My mother jumped up and clasped her hands to her breast. "I was worried," she said. "You should have been home from school at three-thirty."

"Mom," I said softly, and gave her a bag of cracked chocolate cherries. She sucks out the juice, then eats the dark shells. She can't get enough sweets. "How do you feel, Mom?" You have to say something.

Her white head was shaking. "It's no good to get old."

"Oh, Mom," I said, as if she'd just lied.

"You think I don't know." Her head was still shaking. "But what else can I do? I can't give myself poison." She licked the cherries from her fingers.

"Never mind poison," I told her, forced cheerful. "What'd you eat for lunch?" I have to keep checking, each day she's lighter.

"Oh, something," she said. "I can't recall what."

"Mom, we're not poor. You don't have to skip meals."

"I did eat! I know it. I remember chewing."

I went in to see if she'd even dipped a spoon in the Tupperware bowls I'd left in the fridge. These were full to the brim. But I did find potatoes in a pot on the stove, so mushy I knew they'd been boiling for hours.

"Dinner," she told me. "And all of that came from just one potato!"

She says that each time, proud as a wife who's stretched her few pennies to feed all her children. "Just one potato," though any fool can see a dozen ends at least.

"Mother," I scolded, "the stove's been on all day."

"I never can please you." She outlined a floor tile with the tip of her shoe.

If I hide the potatoes, when I get home she's crying. "No dinner," she tells me. "Not a single potato. Nothing to feed to the children tonight."

I live in the fear that she'll search for the farm where she begged for potatoes and beets as a girl; its scrubby fields now lie beneath the fried chicken and hamburger places out near the mall.

This fear that my mother will wander away isn't some bogey I've dreamed up in boredom. It is the terror, chilly and gripping, born of an instant when I looked in a window frame and saw that the portrait inside it had vanished. By the time I finally found her, just before sunset, she was talking to scarecrows six miles from town, where the burgers and nuggets haven't quite reached. In her thin hands she cradled a bunch of grapes bluer than any grapes I've seen for sale in a store. I felt I was Noah quizzing the dove: "Where'd you get *those?*" She held out a grape. I took it and ate it. Sweeter than jelly. We shared the last few, and I washed off the stains from her fingers and lips.

From then on she got worse, until I was frightened to go to the bathroom for fear I'd come out and find she was gone. I can't afford a sitter. And the county home is out. One day in those wards and even *her* curls would lose hope and lie down.

This is my mother, a woman who's been kind to many, many people. For thirty-two years she humored a husband whose moods were so bitter that he could do nothing except to wash bottles at the brewery next door. She raised five sons and daughters, all of whom left her. Only I came back. She didn't ask me questions—the answers were written in black and blue on my skin. She stood in the door, calming my husband with the same smiles she'd once used to placate my father.

"Never mind," I said. "We'll have mashed potatoes," the seventh time that week.

She smiled at me, grateful that I hadn't raised my voice. Sometimes I do. The same question ten times. Oh, tell me, who wouldn't. (John Drake would shake her like a pinball machine on tilt.) But still I feel awful when I curse my own mother, a woman whose only fault is that her brains are as soft as mashed potatoes.

"Mother," I said, "just let me take my shower. Then I'll make dinner."

Under the nozzle I always find peace. With my eyes shut I

conjured the twenty-first hostage on that boat on the Nile. A man about my age. Slender, a frail man, his hair like a wheat field with the sun coming up. His face was as lovely as a woman's, but stronger, and his eyes were a warning that he understood pain. Quiet, so quiet, a man who was used to nobody listening, and so he'd stopped talking—he didn't even like to give out his name, unless he was forced.

Then he saw I was there. His gaze made me feel so naked that I had to open my eyes. The shampoo got in and stung them until I started to cry, and then I was sorry, because my hostage was gone.

I toweled off and fried some liver for Mother, but I was so anxious for the six-thirty news that I served the meat raw. Not that it mattered. Liver, fish, pancakes, she rains salt upon them as fiercely as if she were Lord God Jehovah and her dinner plate Sodom. Her tea is the same—sugar, not salt. Spooning and spooning until I can't watch.

When she'd finished her tea, she asked, "Can I wash them? Now? Can I now?"

She thinks she's being useful. Some nights she washes without any hot water, and other nights, no soap. Her eyesight is milky with dreams of the future—I'm a young girl, and she is a widow with courage and faith that things will get better—so she doesn't see the dirt. The plates come out crusted and I have to wash them a second time after she's gone to sleep.

I turned on Dan Rather. "Good evening," he said.

That's the part I like best. I'm wrapped nice and warm in my terry-cloth robe and Dan Rather comes home. "How are you?" he says, patting my head. "You've done a good job." What job I don't know—it's not for Swiss Dream. "Don't worry," he says. "Keep up the good work and things will change soon." Dan has that power. It's like when he tells me: "This-and-that happened in this-or-that city," and it right away happens over his shoulder, quick as a genie granting a wish.

Last night I wished that he'd show me my hostage, and Dan got right to it. He said that the pirates had released all the women. I was happy for their sakes. But I knew I could never leave a husband of mine in the clutches of pirates. What if they shot him? Who'd stop his blood? Who'd throw her woman's body on his to keep off the blows?

My mother tiptoed in and sat on the sofa. "The dishes are clean now. The little ones are sleeping." She nestled against me and started to coo. I must have looked angry, because she drew back. "Oh, sweetheart, she said, "you have to cheer up. You've sat on that sofa every day this week. Go, call the fellas, go bowl or play poker. I'll mind the children. Go have a good time." I shook my head, shushed her: Dan Rather was saying that the pirates had made a sort of home movie to prove all their captives were healthy and safe.

And that's when I saw him. The twenty-first hostage. While the other men jostled to prove to their loved ones they hadn't been hurt, mine sat to one side, quiet and hunched. He didn't have a loved one. None, that is, but me.

"I'm here! I can see you!" I lifted my hand to stroke that soft cheek.

But just then a man with a stubbly face pushed forward and shouted: "Kill them all! Bomb them! Don't worry about us!" My hostage went sideways, and then he went blank.

"Well, I think I'll go to sleep now." My mother stood from the sofa, though it wasn't yet seven. I should have assured her that I didn't mind her presence. But I just kissed her forehead and she went to her room.

Soon the newscast was over, but I kept up my vigil through four painful hours of car chases, cowboys, and chimpanzees dressed up like college professors. I was losing my patience when Dan Rather came back, looking like a man whose wife has been screaming in labor all night. He said that the pirates were beating a hostage with the microphones on so the whole world could hear.

I heard a man moan. William, I said. That's what I called him. Oh, my sweet William. They'd lashed his thin wrists, as fragile and white as the necks of two swans, to the mast of the ship. Then they tore off his shirt and whipped his pale skin until it bloomed scarlet, whipping and whipping.

I must have dozed off, because when I woke up the cheery blonde who talks in the morning was saying: "We repeat our top story. One hostage is dead. We'll bring you more details at nine o'clock."

No, no, it couldn't be.

I couldn't stick around until nine to find out. I made sure that my mother had eaten her doughnut, then ran out the door.

Malt, oats, manure . . . I listened to EZ as if the music could have saved my life, and just at the border where the fertilizer turns into corn chips, the announcer interrupted. The hostage who'd been killed was the man who'd sold Allstate in the lobby of Sears.

My William wasn't dead! My old Chevy lifted its wheels from the pavement. We soared above the building where the corn chips are fried. We rose, dipped and darted, then glided to earth inside the steel fence where we park at Swiss Dream.

The other girls were kicking their bags in their lockers, pulling on their coats, adjusting their caps. I waltzed in the door.

"Listen who's happy."

"Only one thing makes *me* hum in the morning."

"Oh, not our Bess. She'd rather play solitaire with her mother."

They started to laugh.

"Don't be so sure." This came from Mill, who stands by me on the line. "John Drake in shipping sure has been trying."

When she mentioned that name, he threw open the door to my mind and roared in. All brash and brawn, he tossed William aside, then demanded my answer: Would I marry him or not?

"So *don't* tell us," Mill said. "Just because we share our deepest souls with you." Mill is my friend, and I wanted to tell her, but as soon as you mention a man or a mother, everyone pulls out a man or a mother and yours kind of gets lost. Mill gave a shrug and led us to the line, flouncing as if her sensitive feelings were in the bottoms of her feet.

We pulled on our gloves, which are made of white plastic that feels like dead skin. This is to keep our prints from the chocolates, but we all play a game whose object is to sign one candy each day with the whorl of a thumb. If Mrs. Sales sees this up in her booth, she doesn't let on. Mrs. Sales never scolds us, but she never praises either. A hostage, at least, can do or say something to earn a kind look.

The boxes flowed past me, marking the minutes. My hands knew their business and this left my mind free to think about William. Now and then I'd hear a BOOM and look up. Off in a corner, John Drake was stacking cartons of candies. When he'd start a new pile, he'd drop his big box from as high as he could. I'd look up and see him mouthing his questions, and just for an instant I'd want to nod "yes," but then I'd see William and I'd put my head down.

My job is to finish the last row of caramels, and quick, shut the lid. The cardboard flaps fight back—they'll slice through your gloves—and some girls have smashed their boxes in anger. But I never could smash the picture on top. It's one of the Alps, with snow on its slopes and a hut with a chimney and grass on the roof and lambs in the yard. If we lived in that cottage, I could nurse William's wounds until he was healed. Whenever my mother cried for potatoes, he would take her arm gently and lead her to find them. "Please, William, come home." I must have said it out loud, because the other girls heard.

"She's talking in her sleep!"

And Bea started singing "Bill Bailey, Won't You Please Come Home."

"Come on, Bess," Mill said. "Who is this William?"

I almost said, "He's my hostage." But then I saw William stretched on the belt, and all my friends touching him as though he were chocolate. So I didn't say a word. The boxes kept coming, and each candy that I set in its brown paper doily seemed like a gift I was wrapping for him.

When the buzzer went off I raced for my Chevy, not even pausing to pull off my coat—we only had forty minutes for lunch. I knew a store at the mall where a row of TVs played in the window all day and night. It usually made me nervous to see so many people saying and doing the same thing at once, but that's where I went. A lady in sequins was telling her husband that she'd just killed their son. I didn't care about that, but I had a premonition . . . and, sure enough, the lady in sequins got choked off mid-sentence, and Dan Rather came on, happy as a father whose child's born at last. A few people gathered. I heard Dan say "frogmen," and I lost a few seconds thinking about a story I'd read as a girl. A beautiful princess small as my thumb was set on a lily pad to float to her death. A slimy old frog jumped on the lily and croaked that he'd save her—if she'd marry his son. Had she married the frog, or drowned in the weeds? I tried to recall.

Then I heard clapping. "Three cheers!" someone said. The crowd pushed from behind. I laid my cheek to the glass and said, "William, come home."

I got back to Swiss Dream with just enough time to rip off the paper from the radio I'd bought. I hid it in a pocket inside my coat, then stuffed the earphones under my cap. The girls might have poked fun; if they did, I couldn't hear. My William was free! Over and over the voice in my ears said, "The hostages are free!" but it never revealed when to meet them, or where.

Still, I was happy. Music was playing. It was only a song from the Chamber of Commerce, but it made my hands fly. The song said Eliria had been blessed with five seasons. The first one was spring, a time to plant seeds (how my hands flew!). Summer was second, a time to hoe weeds. In autumn we reaped (coming home, coming), and in winter, chopped wood (each box held my love). I just couldn't imagine what the fifth season might be, but then they explained. The fifth season, they said, was the time Nature gave us to enjoy the first four.

That's when I'd be with my William, I thought. That's when he'd come. I imagined us washing the heat from our skin in a clear, sparkling stream. Crunching through leaves. Licking off snow from each other's warm lips. We'd walk through a field that was newly turned up, such a rich brown, so moist . . . A month or two later, that field would be green, so fresh and inviting that we had to lie down.

A hand pinched my bottom. I jerked, and a flap on the box slashed my hand. A thin red line opened across my white glove. I turned and saw John Drake standing behind me. I slapped him, and left my blood on his cheek. I saw violence on his face. I watched his fist rise.

Mrs. Sales stopped him. I was sure we'd be fired. But she only sent him back to his corner by the boxes.

"Bess," she said. "Bess!"

I turned off my Sony.

"Bess, they just called."

My first thought was William. Someone had finally called to inform me where the airplane would land.

"Your mother," she said. "They called from the diner. You'd better go get her."

The diner is five or six miles from our house, on a highway that's frantic with cars full of people who've run out for fast food and are trying to get home before their French fries turn cold. How had she made it without getting hit? And *why*, I said, pounding the dashboard. Oh, why had she made it at all.

No, I didn't mean that. But what could I do? How could I safeguard a woman who strolled down a highway and thought she was wandering through a field of potatoes?

And that's when it hit me. How bad could she be? How bad, if she'd told them whom to call, where I worked? She couldn't swallow poison, but she sure could run off and live on wild grapes instead of forced kindness. She'd found the door un-locked—I must have forgotten in my hurry that morning—and set off for the hills. Only much later, when she crossed that big highway and gave up in despair of finding that field, when she knew she'd be shipped to the county home and treated as a nameless old hobo, only then did my mother say who she was.

She sat at the counter, wearing a dress, beads and a hat, handsome as ever, hardly mussed at all. They'd given her tea. She was pouring some sugar into her cup, pouring and pouring. I went over and kissed her. She seemed pleased I was there.

"This is my daughter," she said to the Greek who managed the place. She patted my hand. "She does *such* a good job."

The Greek had a little color TV propped by the stove. It showed a jet landing at some New York airport. The heavy door swung open and a soldier sprang out. Then came a hostage— the man who'd yelled, "Bomb us!" Waving a "V" sign, he walked down the stairs. Another man came out. His wife. Another couple. Each in turn waved. A brass band was playing.

"Come on, Mom. Let's go." I knew who'd be next, and I couldn't bear to watch as he stepped through that door, searching the faces of the crowd on the tarmac until it sunk in that his Bess wasn't there.

HOW CAN
YOU
TELL ME

HOW CAN
YOU
TELL ME

They are cracking my mother's breastbone. Stripping the veins from her shaved thighs.

My father sits, sleeping. He cannot exist now. For three days, since we brought his wife to the hospital, his trembling hands have been slopping coffee over his neglected sandwiches. "My intestines are churning," he'll tell me, and we barely have time to get back to the motel before he needs to use the toilet.

Each morning we arrive here long before visiting hours. He wanders past the nurses' station with an assumed air of ignorance. On what grounds could he ask dispensation? Because he loves his wife more than other husbands love their wives? But no one stops him. The white cardboard boxes that once held his bribes lie empty on the counter among charts, tiny cups and oscilloscope screens. Three times a day—once for each shift—he brings cakes and cookies for the nurses, attendants, interns and orderlies who care for his wife. Because they've been kind. So they'll run twice as fast if she cries out in pain.

Yesterday, the cardiologist showed us a poster on which someone had drawn with red and blue markers the ventricles and atria of a crude human heart. With yellowed lengths of tubing and thumbtacks he showed us how the surgeon will graft segments of veins here and there to circumvent my mother's choked arteries and feed the starved muscle in the middle of her chest. As he went on describing the procedure they would use to drain the blood from her lungs, my father removed a

179

plaid handkerchief from his pocket. He dabbed at his face, which was gray as his hair, slumped forward and finally slid to the floor.

"It was hot," he said later. "The windows wouldn't open. I barely could breathe."

This morning, when they came to wheel her away, he couldn't even speak.

"They took a razor to me," she said. "I'm just an old woman. My privates hang like a turkey's wattle." Then the interns marched in. More needles and tubes. Piercing and piercing. "No sense, no feeling," she said to us, twice.

My father touched the crucifix over her bed.

"Someone should dust Him," my mother muttered, drowsy. "I meant to tell the nuns. Don't forget to tell them after I'm gone."

The magazines in the waiting lounge proclaim the death of a Russian dictator five years superseded, analyze the popularity of a game show long cancelled. My father angles his head so the crown of his olive-green rain hat is crushed against the wall behind him. He closes his eyes and huddles inside his padded jacket, as if he expects a beating while he sleeps. Interlacing his fingers, he works his thumbs into the crease below his belly and suspends his hands palms-down to shelter his groin.

I take a sheet of graph paper from my bag, spread it flat on the table. Residents in the houses represented by these squares will receive flyers and pamphlets, and in those houses, visits from a gubernatorial candidate they'll mistake for an actor. A field organizer conducting the last weeks of a campaign *in absentia* is grossly abnegating her duties, but not so grossly as a daughter avoiding her mother's triple bypass.

"You *must* nurse your mother," the candidate said in his long Boston accent, imagining, no doubt, that I'd sit by the bed of a weak, gasping woman with soft, grateful features and puffy white hair, reading her the Bible or *Wuthering Heights*.

My mother has red hair, cropped in harsh lines. Her face is a blade from the center of her brow along her nose to her chin. While she recovers, she'll sit straight up in bed, clipping coupons from the paper and drawing up lists. "Don't forget Kaopec-tate," she'll tell me, "for your father. And iron his boxers. I know that I spoil him, but it's too late to stop now." Then, when she's better: "I hate to be babied. I still don't see why you missed your campaign. I didn't need you, really."

I leave my father napping and pace the square path around the halls of the ward. As I start my tenth circuit, I hear the surgeon's clogs announcing his progress from the O.R. to the lounge. His paper gown and mask are white against his skin. He wears a thick mustache, and his shiny black hair is pulled back in a band. If my father didn't see this man as a savior, he would say he resembled a pretty-boy gambler. We've argued all week as to whether his accent is Italian (my father) or Puerto Rican.

I rush to the lounge, thinking to spare my father the embar-rassment of being caught napping. "Father, get up." I might as well have jabbed a knife in his ear. He jerks his head forward. His hat drops behind the chair. His hands are still clasped; when he jumps to his feet, he loses his balance and falls toward the door. The surgeon grabs his arm and steadies my father under the guise of shaking his hand.

Even before the surgeon has said, "It's over. Your wife, she went very well," my father has hugged him.

"Thank you," he says. He's afraid to impose on the surgeon's good will, but he makes himself ask: "Was it hard on her, Doc?"

"This operation," the surgeon says with forced patience, "you know, I have told you, it has no more danger than for the appendix."

"It's a heart operation," I protest. "You drained the blood from her lungs and pumped it through a machine. You tore veins from her legs and changed the path to her heart."

But my father has been talking at the same time as I have, and the surgeon hears only: "My wife's a tough bird, isn't she, Doc? Me, I'm a coward, but my wife's a tough bird."

The surgeon nods and squeezes my father's arm again, smiles once and exits, his wood clogs applauding as he walks down the hall.

"Your mother may be tough," my father says, blotting his eyes with his handkerchief, "but no man could love any woman more than I love your mother."

Yes, I think, yes, she's a tough bird, and you're a soft chick, and it's not inconceivable that you and my mother should have lived with each other for so many years. But how can you tell me that no man on Earth loves a woman more deeply, with more passion and faith than you love your wife. You, with that crushed green hat on your head, your churning intestines and wrinkled plaid handkerchief. My mother, with her coupons and blade of a face.

"It's impossible," he says, "just impossible how attached a man can become during thirty-six years."

Habit, I think. Mostly habit, that's all.

"Excuse me," he says, "but my stomach is churning," and he leaves for the men's room.

I use the phone in the lounge to call Creighton in Boston. "She's all right, she came through. But how can I stay here another three weeks? I can't stay. I need you."

"Honey, I miss you. But why the big rush? We're under control."

"You want me to stay. You're making love to one of the envelope lickers. Don't deny it. It's true."

"Honey, they're chubby. They wear pink Izod sweaters. I'm fifty years old. They're adolescent groupies. And what about that P.R. surgeon of yours?"

Creighton is six years younger than my father. He's been married three times. I've never been married. It's never been my idea of a romance, a marriage. Oh, maybe at first. But then the new lover I'd thought so romantic would reveal himself to be a man who'd doze off in a plush hotel lobby with his mouth slightly open or use a kitchen knife to scrape the corns from his feet. It's never stayed perfect. Not until now.

"I know I'm being silly," I tell Creighton, offhand, "but I'm afraid you'll run off with the circus."

"The circus? What circus?"

My father comes back.

"Promise!" I order. My voice is so level he can't tell I'm crying. "Promise you won't run off with the circus."

No, he won't promise. He says I'm being silly. Like his first wife, he says.

My father complains that his stomach is empty.

"Please, Creighton, promise that you won't fall asleep with your mouth hanging open. You won't trim your corns."

"If this doesn't kill me . . . ," my father is saying. "Let's go get some lunch. A sandwich, that's all. Nothing fancy. I'm empty."

"Nothing fancy," I whisper into the phone. "His wife is alive, and he just wants a sandwich." I can't hide my sobs, though I know he dislikes women who cry. "Let's get married, okay? Nothing fancy. Just promise you'll never run off."

THE
VALUE OF
DIAMONDS

THE VALUE OF DIAMONDS

Her mother was dust, so when her friends berated their mothers Ava didn't join them. She twisted her ring and let her mind caress the two images of what she had loved most in Hannah.

There had, first of all, been the potato chips. Her mother had spent her mornings comparing the prices and styles of jackets and nightgowns, spatulas and placemats, coasters to keep the sofa legs from denting the carpet, potions to keep her elbows from flaking. Each day at noon she stopped for lunch at Horn & Hardart's—turkey club, kosher dill, and a small mound of chips. These last she didn't eat, but wrapped in a napkin which she tucked in her purse. Three hours later, when she picked up Ava from school, she produced this white packet, translucent with grease now, to sustain the child for a second assault on the stores, where Ava must choose among her mother's favorite knife racks or scarves.

Ava hated the malls, the same plaid wool jumper repeated ten times in ten sizes in each of ten stores, the cookware and loungeware mirrored in succession until Ava felt sick, her world cheap as mud. Standing in stores by her mother's side, she saw other girls by their mothers' sides, each adult holding up a cowl-neck sweater, each girl looking thoughtful, hands deep in the pockets of a red winter coat with a fuzzy black collar.

"Which one is me?" she would ask half-aloud. And a voice would cry out: "Here I am! Ava's here!" But the voice was composed of thousands of voices, thousands of Avas in unison crying, "I'm here, Ava's here," all of them her, and so none of them, she had ceased to exist, like one grain of sugar in a cube with its sisters. Desperate to escape, she would praise the first garment or trinket she was shown, inventing unspoken curses like "bee-brained babbler" and "stupid silly shopper" if her mother insisted that she inspect the rest of the choices anyway. And yet, the tenderness with which her mother unfolded the napkin, holding the cracked chips outstretched in her palm as if offering sugar to a disdainful pony, lured Ava each day, this packet of greasy crumbs, and the showers.

Twice every week, Hannah would beckon Ava into the pink-and-white stall of the shower, position her under the racks of rose water, loofah, pumice and balsam, then step in herself, so the spray pattered gaily against the mushroom-shaped cap protecting her hair. Off came the caked beige foundation, off came the powder, until Hannah's cheeks glowed, warm and pure. Two ridges of bone pointed down from her throat to a pure polished plane of white marble, bare now of jewelry. Her small, uptipped breasts sent lovely cascades in arcs from the nipples. Her belly, a thin slice of pear, glimmered with moisture, and droplets nested below it in hair the hue of a peach, as soft and as neat. Ava's eyes followed the white wisps of soap as they ran down her mother's backbone to pool in the cleft of an ankle or a knee.

Ava's own scaly body remained dry and unscrubbed. *Her* legs were scabby, arms chubby, chest flat. She crouched by the wall, small and inert, ten minutes, twenty, until her mother reached out and groped across the tiles, as if in search of a new bar of soap, and Ava submitted herself to the hot, rough ceremony of having her hair washed.

A few moments later, mother and daughter stood naked on the bathmat, Hannah combing the snarls from Ava's hair, one palm held tight to the scalp so the tangles wouldn't smart, though a large diamond ring on Hannah's finger kept plucking strands from Ava's head until her eyes watered in pain. Then Hannah wrapped Ava in a pink terry-cloth towel and whispered, "I love you."

But Ava didn't answer. In a minute or two, her mother would

ask what she had learned at school that day, then stand there, befuddled, as Ava tried to reveal the mysteries of bean growth or equations for solving "less than" and "more than."

If only her father would ask what she had learned! But he never was home. He worked days and nights at the Erasmus Vocational Technical College, of which he was president. The campus lay across the parkway from the largest mall in the suburb. As a young child, Ava often had confused the two buildings, though she knew that her father's office, deep in the college, had dark wooden walls and a forest-green carpet, reminding her of an owl's nest in the trunk of an old tree.

Once, in fourth grade, instead of meeting her mother in the lot near her school, Ava had slipped onto a public bus and gotten off at the college. A girl in her class had called her conceited. "It's a sin from the Devil to think that you're special," this girl had explained. For the rest of the day, Ava heard the Devil hiss in her head: "But you *are* special, Ava. *Sssspecial.* You're *ssssspecial.*" Only her father would know how to make the Devil shut up.

Lost in the intricate halls of the college, Ava was jostled by bantering boys in denim jackets and jeans and girls in spike heels. Just as she thought that the hiss of the Devil would burst open her head, she saw her father's name on the door of an office and rushed in, ignoring the men who stood around his desk, waving their arms and arguing loudly.

"Ava," he said, "this isn't the time."

"But Father. I hear a voice in my head. I think it's the Devil. Please make him stop."

And while the men waited, her father placed his hands over her ears and said very slowly, "Hush, Ava, hush. The Devil is only a concept. If we tell him to go, he must leave you alone."

The Devil's voice died. He fled Ava's head.

But suddenly, she missed him. "Father?" she asked. "Is the Devil ever right?"

He looked, not at her, but a man with black eyebrows that pointed toward the ceiling and a shock of black hair that pointed toward his nose; under his arm was a black leather book that said LEDGER in red. "Oh, yes indeed," said Ava's father as he stared at this man. "He often is right. And eloquent besides. That's why he can be so hard to resist."

A few minutes later, as she left her father's office to wait for her mother, she heard shouting again, and her father's voice, level, soothing these men as he just had soothed her. So *that's* what he did. People brought him their troubles, and he calmed them down. If only, she thought, her problems were worse, he would spend more time with her.

What she couldn't understand was why a man like her father, a man who could make the Devil shut up, would have married a woman as senseless as her mother. True, her mother was prettier than a man of her father's stoutness and baldness might otherwise have attracted. She kept his house neat and cooked all his meals. ("My dear Mister President," she liked to announce, "your dinner is served!") But surely he hated his wife's prattling as much as Ava herself did.

Her father spent only Sundays with his family. Taking a seat at his organ, he would open his big, plastic-bound edition of *The Songs We Love Best*, adjust the knobs and levers for vibraphone, flute and marimba percussion, then start to play. His large hands commanded the chords on three keyboards, fingers fanned wide. His black patent shoes pumped the pedals with vigor. On ballads, his chest bowed low to the keyboard; on show-stopper dance tunes his bottom bounced along the gold velour cushion. Sometimes a smile would slowly spread across his soft, sweating face, thrilling his daughter, who peered over his shoulder, turning the pages, awaiting these smiles, glad that her mother remained on the couch, though she wished she wouldn't sing.

How childish she sounded, with that airy, lilting voice! She got the lyrics wrong, then apologized, giggling, when corrected by Ava, but blithely continued. Her favorite song was "A-Tisket A-Tasket," which Ava despised. She was sure that her father felt as demeaned playing it as she felt merely turning the pages, and she led him away the moment he finished its closing refrain.

After the songfest, the Gouldens would stroll past two-story duplexes with gray shingle siding, white scalloped canopies over the porches and inflatable pools in yards too small for trees, past Two Guys and Shoe Shak and Ali Baba's Carpet Bazaar. These outings would end with an early dinner at the Jersey Pagoda, where her father would order Shrimp Sweet and Sour, then toy with his chopsticks and seem to forget that his family was there. By dessert, his wife would feel compelled to distract him by holding the tiny pink parasol from her ice cream above one ear and lisping "Three Little Maids From School Are We," though the only words she knew were the words in the title.

This final annoyance always caused her father to call for the check. Back in the house, her mother would retire to the bedroom to flip through old *House and Gardens* and burble misquoted snatches from the day's songs.

"I think I'll get a jump on the coming week's quandaries," her father would sigh. Then he would leave for his office, and Ava would wish that she could tell her mother that she had to get a jump on *her* quandaries, so she and her father could spend Sunday nights together, huddled in his office, reading a book.

Only as a treat on her thirteenth birthday was Ava allowed to enjoy several hours alone with her father, missing school to attend a Careers Fair at his college. He led her down aisles between posterboard photos of white-cloaked technicians drawing bright blood, Hotel Management graduates conducting awed chefs through cavernous kitchens, dental hygienists, commercial artists and beauticians. Here was every profession to which a girl might aspire. But none suited Ava. She wanted a job so essential, tailored so snugly to her talents, that it would make her irreplaceable to humankind. Gazing at the blank side of a poster, she tried to envision herself performing some task that no one but her could do nearly as well. But every sort of job that Ava could think of brought with it the picture of someone who had done it before her. As her self-portrait faded, Ava did too. She tugged her father's arm, but he didn't seem to feel her, she was weak as a ghost. She might have disappeared completely if the man to whom her father was speaking had not stooped to ask what she wanted to be when she grew up.

"There's nothing," she said, and ran from the gym.

Her father, gasping harshly, caught up with her at the side of the parkway. "Don't worry," he said, and held her to his vest.

Ava kept sobbing, afraid to tell him that she would remain unemployed all her life while the children of strangers, with degrees from his college, would find satisfaction in the jobs at the fair.

"It's all right," he said. "I'll always love you, even if you become nothing at all. Your mother has no career, and I love her, don't I?"

Appalled that her father would place her in the same category as her mother, Ava couldn't answer. How could he love a woman who only that morning had endlessly chattered about the drawbacks and virtues of various models of garlic presses?

She sat in silence, puzzled, as he drove them both home and pulled into the carport. The house was unlit. Usually, Hannah returned from the stores by five to cook dinner. By seven o'clock she hadn't appeared. Ava's father murmured something about going out for fried chicken, then phoned his wife's friends to ask if they had seen her. Ava climbed a chair and began rummaging through a high cupboard.

"Be careful," he said, poking his head into the kitchen between calls. The phone rang. "Yes, yes, I'm coming," she heard him tell whoever was on the other end. Then: "Ava, stay here, I'll be back in a while."

The front door banged shut, leaving her half-in, half-out of the cereal shelf. Maybe her mother had taken to shoplifting and, unlike Ava's more clever peers, gotten caught. She pulled down a box of cinnamon Pop-Tarts and ate two for dinner.

Her father returned at nine-thirty. Her mother never did. Hannah had been driving home from Korvette's when the truck she was tailing bounced through a pothole. Its rear doors flew open, crates crashed to the pavement. Swerving, she sideswiped a van, initiating a chain of collisions that left eleven cars in nose-to-tail jumbles, the parkway strewn with toaster ovens, vacuum cleaners and mannequins, and Hannah herself, stretched as though napping across the front seat, sprinkled with glass.

The morning after the accident, Ava lay on the floor of the living room, her fingers clenched to the shag, afraid she would float unanchored forever unless she could see her mother again.

Her father pried her hands from the carpet and rolled her over.

Would the coffin be open? she asked.

"No, honey," he said, brushing lint from her face. "Jews think it's too tempting to worship the dead." Through bloodless lips he went on. "You wouldn't have wanted to have seen her anyway. Her body was bruised. So bruised and broken. She was beautiful once, wasn't she, Ava? When she was living?" He stood with great effort and hurried from the room.

Ava tried to picture her mother, but great cuts and bruises distorted her features. Later, at the side of the grave, she stared at the coffin lid so hard, wishing for one final look at her mother, that the boards turned transparent, revealing her mother as she had looked in the shower. Ava gasped. She always had known that her mother was pretty, that their times in the shower were full of wonder, but she hadn't suspected that her mother was perfect. Not until now.

Hannah lifted one arm. In her hand was a napkin full of crushed chips. Feeling no terror, Ava reached down to take it. But just then her father let out a groan, and Ava looked up, certain he was seeing the same vision she was. But her father was cradling his eyes in his hands, and when she looked down again her mother was gone, the coffin opaque.

Her father sprinkled a spoonful of dirt on the lid. Ava did likewise, without protest, because she knew that the mother who lay in the coffin was not the same mother she had seen in her vision.

That evening, Ava carried to her bedroom the two shopping bags the police had found on the seat next to Hannah. She unwrapped them gently, fondled the blue skirt and blouse for a while, then put them on. The blouse drooped from her chest. The A-line wouldn't button because her waist was too thick.

"Awful," she said, then hung them in her closet, so that every day when she dressed for school she would have to recall her mother's perfection and how she had ignored it while Hannah was alive.

The two Gouldens still spent their Sundays at the keyboard, the mood somber now, Ava's father omitting the dance tunes in favor of torch songs, which would have sounded like dirges if not for the bossa nova accompaniment he added from habit. She hoped that her father would also stay home one or two evenings during the week. When he didn't, the stillness in the house, unbroken by her mother's aimless humming, drove her mad. The pink-and-white shower stall yawned like a crypt. The torn sheets and the glasses with cracks in their rims seemed a reproach to the girl who couldn't replace them.

One night, as her father was clearing the remains of a fish-and-chips dinner from the table—white cardboard boats for the fillets, whale-shaped containers for the French fries, forks like harpoons—desperation welled inside Ava until she blurted: "If you stay home this evening, I'll try not to bore you."

Arms full of cardboard, her father sank back into his seat. "I guess I can tell you." His expression was troubled. "You're so like your mother. . . . I'm sure you'll understand."

Would her father stay home and tell her a secret?

"I wasn't ready," he said. "I was called on to become president before I was ripe." His predecessor, he said, had resigned in the sixties after a student occupation of his office. Soon after this, the vice president was indicted in a shopping mall scam. The Regents appointed her father to guide the college until they could find a more qualified candidate, but in the confusion of that decade, they forgot to look for one. Ashamed to request a demotion, he struggled to quell strikes over racism, sexism and drug busts on campus, endured ugly debates over discipline, tenure and whether to expand the industrial arts department at the expense of the cooking school, or vice versa.

"The battle was constant," he told Ava now. "Only your mother helped keep me calm."

Aided by little more than a strong sense of balance between debits and credits and an unshakeable faith in the merits of decision theory, he had plotted a course through eight years of turmoil.

"It's quieter now." He swept salt from the table; Ava could hear the particles grate against the Formica. He started to fidget.

Fearful that her father would leave for the college, she frantically sought a question with which to detain him. "I'd like to know more about decision theory," she said. "If you don't mind."

He brightened. Uncapping a pen, he drew elaborate diagrams on the white paper bags: rectangles, rhombi, parallelepipeds, trapezoids, squares, octagons, triangles. He connected these figures with thick, branching lines.

"It's a tree," he told Ava. "You start here, at the base, with all possible choices, then say yes or no at each juncture until you've narrowed your problem and reached your solution, here, at the point."

To demonstrate, he said, he would use the tree to find a job she might like.

Holding her breath, she waited until her calling would shine in brilliant inevitability from the star at the top. But her excitement diminished at each branch as he said, "You could study such-and-such, like so-and-so's daughter," or, "You might go into a field not far removed from the one that your cousin in Baltimore pursued."

When he reached the tree's apex, her father said, "There! If we followed this logic, we would therefore discover that you're cut out to be a buyer for a store. A big one, like Macy's."

Ava felt as if she were no more than a tinfoil decoration tacked atop one of the millions of trees at the Christmas Warehouse on the Jersey Turnpike. "Father, I'm special," she wanted to say, but since he hadn't noticed, maybe she wasn't. Hope congealed within Ava like the dull drops of grease on the cardboard before her.

"Ava," he said, "aren't you well? Is that why you asked me to stay home? Do you want to play a game?"

"A game?"

"One for adults. Like honeymoon bridge. Or checkers, or Scrabble."

"Scrabble? You want to play Scrabble?"

"Why not? I've seen the box somewhere."

She hated the game. Her mother had been such a poor player that Ava, upon turning ten, had refused to accept further challenges from her. Anyone else who could convince her to play consistently beat her, however, because Ava would let her opponent make words worth five or ten points while she kept saying "pass," preferring to wait until she could draw an "x" or a "j" to fill the missing letter in a rarely seen word, but falling so far behind that she never caught up.

In this game her father plodded along with "sum," "try" and "goals," while Ava laid "unique" on a triple-word score, even though she was sorry that she couldn't use her seventh letter, which was "r." To Ava's surprise, she won the first game. Jumping ahead in the second game with "zygote," a word she had learned that very same day, she studied her father to see if he might be letting her win. But his armholes were wet and his face very moist. He rubbed his palms across his scalp as if wiping away cobwebs, then blinked several times like some big nocturnal bird who'd been caught in the light—not wise, but ruffled.

She started to cry.

"What's the matter, honey?" And when she couldn't tell him, he looked so bewildered that she only sobbed harder. "I'll give you a prize," he told her at last. He ran from the room, then returned a moment later with a small purple box. "It's your mother's ring," he said, "from our engagement. I think we should keep it at the bank until you're older, but you can wear it tonight, if you're careful."

She examined the ring, half-expecting to see a clump of her hair still wrapped around the setting. There was only the diamond, an oversized teardrop flat as a penny and framed in white gold. She imagined the undertaker working the ring over a knuckle of her mother's limp hand.

"Don't you like it?" he said.

She nodded, but with such weak conviction that he felt called upon to explain the value of diamonds: their carats and colors, their feathers and fractures and the placement of their planes.

Then he went on to teach her about supply and demand. Diamonds were made of carbon, he said, like charcoal or pencils, but in a form scarcely found and very hard to mine. "This diamond is large, but the cut is quite shallow. It's not near as costly as you'd think by its size."

Ava said nothing.

"I don't mean it's worthless. The pear shape, in fact, is the same as the great Cullinan diamond which is displayed with the royal family's jewels in the Tower of London."

"The shape," Ava echoed. "It's shaped like a pear." She tried not to start crying again.

"I just remembered," he said, "I have to go back to school after all, to pick up some papers. Maybe tomorrow I'll try to fix dinner. Spaghetti, perhaps. Then you'll have to give me a rematch at Scrabble."

She thought of her father draining spaghetti, steam from the noodles fogging his glasses. She relived the silence that had dragged on between them, imagined herself beating him a third time at Scrabble, then startled herself by wishing that he wouldn't come home that night, or the next, until she was asleep.

After he had gone, she climbed to the bathroom and stoppered the tub. She sprinkled some powder under the faucet and let in the water. A mountain of bubbles grew in the tub. Breathing and shifting, these prisms of color dissolving in air seemed exquisite compared to the stone on her hand. Water, so common that Ava had never really seen it before, now struck her as precious. She ran her hands through the bubbles like a pirate scooping pearls from a chest of stolen jewels.

She stepped in the tub and slid beneath the foam. Eyes closed, she floated. She was one with the bath, and the rivers and lakes from which it had come, and the ocean, all oceans, the rain and the clouds. Only a need to breathe again brought her back to the air. She burst up, exultant, and stood from the water. Bubbles popped on her skin, tickling so much that she giggled out loud.

Then she saw her body, as lumpish as ever. What was it worth, this body of hers? Nothing, she thought. Her flesh, blood and bones were in constant supply and little demand. If one tiny speck or crack in a diamond could render it worthless, what of the scrapes and cuts on her knees, the bruise on her shin, the mole on her cheek, the pimples, the lack of a bosom and a waist? What was she worth with so many flaws? Not a cent, she thought, and pulled out the plug.

She toweled off glumly and retreated to her room. She went to the window in the hope that her diamond might seem more enchanting in the moonlight; it didn't. In the driveway below, her father backed awkwardly out of his car. The skin on his head caught a gleam from a street lamp. As he shut the car door, his papers slipped from his arms. A breeze wafted them just beyond his reach, then across the sidewalk, then into the road.

She turned from the window and lay on her bed. Her bathrobe fell open, exposing her naked belly and chest. People who believed in supply and demand, Ava decided, were as silly as the boy she had known in first grade who had refused to eat hamburgers, pizza and ice cream because he was obsessed with a food he never had eaten, only heard mentioned once by an aunt. Caveyard eggs, he said, I won't eat a thing except caveyard eggs. For days he went hungry, his parents refusing to pay for this food, until desperation sent them to buy a tin of black eggs, which he gobbled, then spit out. The eggs were so salty and slimy, he said, he'd almost thrown up.

Value, she thought, had nothing to do with supply and demand. But what *was* its measure? Unable to think of an answer, she sank into a world as formless as pudding. Why seek to be different? That just brought frustration. It was easier to merge with the sameness completely.

But then, whether as a curse or a boon she couldn't decide, she was shocked to discover that she did have a calling, an assignment so special that she couldn't turn it down.

Ava would be a value assessor, like whoever assigned values to the letters in Scrabble. Someone must do this; letters didn't come with predetermined points. But why should a "z" or "q" be worth ten, while an "e" or an "o" was worth only one?

Vowels abounded, but these were essential in ways that "q's" weren't.

"Too," she said softly, "soon, spoon, moon, croon." Why not reward a person for making such comforting sounds? Clearly, the system was open to tinkering. It only seemed settled until you looked closely.

Not that she wanted to devote her whole life to assessing a game. This example just proved that her field did exist. She thought of the man who had visited their house to figure the taxes her father had to pay. That was more like it. She would go door-to-door, talk to the people and figure the worth of the objects they owned, then leave them a chart to tack on their wall: This is our worth. This is the order of things we hold dear.

When they cleaned out their attics, they would call for her service. "Should we keep these?" they would ask. "Are such things worth saving?" Cracked vases, blurred photos, burned dinners, strayed turtles—which to mourn? For how long? Which replace? Which forget? Which culprits to punish, and which to forgive? She would teach little children methods by which to divide an allowance: Movies or paint sets? Gumdrops or goldfish? She would help older kids decide what they wanted to be when they grew up. She would advise all her clients to eat the good food they had in their cupboards and not hunger vainly for hard-to-find caveyard eggs; tell them when to spend time, and when they should horde it; suggest whom to value and whom not, and not on the basis of whether a person rarely came home, or stayed there so much that she seemed like a fixture, no more worthy of love than a bulb or a pan.

Her business would prosper, Ava was sure. Most people knew only one useless system by which to judge value—supply and demand. She would have to invent some other accounting. What kind she didn't know, but she rested content with the prospect that she had found her life's work at last.

She took off her ring and set it between the puffs of her breasts. Flat, harsh and sharp, the stone made her nipples seem rounded and soft. She moved the ring to her navel, and suddenly her belly seemed like a cushion on which a crown jewel might rest. She imagined a row of girls like herself, stretched flat on their backs, arrayed behind a glass in the Tower of London, a beautiful jewel in the navel of each, a long line of tourists straining to see.

A chord from the organ sounded below. Her father's voice joined it, so stately and rich that she needed a moment to recognize the words.

"A-tis . . . ket . . . , a-tas . . . ket . . . , a brown and . . . yellow . . . bas-ket . . ."

Hadn't she always hated this song? Then why did each syllable now seem to be carved out of gold?

He picked up the tempo. "I sent a let-ter . . . to my moth-er . . . and on the way I . . . drop-ped it. . . ."

She started to cry—deep, choking sobs. She wanted to hide beneath her blankets and cry for her mother forever, but some stronger feeling urged her from bed.

"I drop-ped it . . . , I drop-ped it. . . . Yes, on my way . . . I drop-ped it. . . ."

She wiped her nose on her sleeve and retied her robe.

"And if I do not . . . get it back . . . I think that I will die."

She set the ring on her nightstand and went down the stairs to sit by his side on the gold velour cushion, her head on his shoulder as he played it once more.

THE HOLE
IN EMPTY
POND

THE HOLE
IN EMPTY
POND

I.

The cops had found a hole in Empty Pond. That's all her editor had told her. Go up, look around, he would hold final deadline until twelve-fifteen. The publisher owned a summer cottage on the pond; she could call in from there. Her editor threw a gold key ring at her.

As she tried to follow the branching dirt roads to the pond, she hoped she would be able to locate the hole once she got there, and, if she could do this, recognize its significance. Maybe the story was like a parcel and all she had to do was pick it up and deliver it back to the newsroom.

The driveway of the cottage was choked by a battered brown truck and three State Police cars. A stocky man in a navy blue parka—she guessed him to be the chief of the local police, Marty Auclair—stood at the far end of the yard, talking to a slight man in a shiny black uniform. Six troopers formed a tight circle in front of the pickup, their black patent belts cutting stripes through the gray air. Crowded on the dock were four teenage boys and a middle-aged woman with a kerchief around her head. A skinny blonde in a canvas coat sat on a boulder to the left of the dock, her long back held rigid. Something about the woman forbade easy approach, so the reporter joined the boys on the dock. One boy handed her a pair of binoculars.

"See that orange speck out there?" he said. "That's the guy's hat. I heard the cops talking about a wallet, too, but you can't make that out from this angle."

"I've got to leave," said the woman in the kerchief, her face blank as a gourd. "I'm going to be late for the lunch shift, but I had to stop by. My dad and Henri's, they grew up together on neighboring farms. So when I heard about Henri being under the lake—I listen to the police radio like it was a disease with me—I thought I should stop by. Funny, you know, what you feel you owe someone."

The reporter left the dock and approached the chief.

"Must have been tough over in Nam," he was saying to the small man in black. "Awful hard keeping track of people that small, wearing black, even if you've got a chopper to look from."

"What's wrong with being small and wearing black?" said the pilot.

"Excuse me," she said. "I'm from the paper. I'd like to find out—"

"New, aren't we?"

She reached for the press badge in her handbag.

"Little close to our deadline, aren't we?"

"The man," she said. "Are you sure he's under the ice?"

"Sure? No, I'm not sure. He *could* be on the moon. He *could* be sunning himself in Miami."

She thought of forcing Auclair to tell her the facts right away. But that seemed simpleminded. There had to be something more, though she didn't know what. "Why isn't anyone trying to pull him out of the water?" she said. "Why the delay?"

"We've got to wait until the Fish and Game men get here with their diving gear," he said primly. "It's cold down there."

She asked how much longer before they arrived.

Auclair shrugged. The men had to drive to Bridgefield to get their equipment.

"Shouldn't they keep it in the truck?"

He shrugged again. "It's a small truck."

"Okay," she said. "Why don't you just give me the facts. I'd like his name, and his age, and I'd like to know exactly what happened."

"You want the facts? These are the facts. This dumbshit woodchuck was so scared of doctors he went and got himself killed. You put that in your first sentence. You say: 'Henri Germaine was so scared of getting killed, he got killed.' That's called something, isn't it?"

"Called something?"

"Some sort of special English thing."

The helicopter pilot snorted. "Never mind your special English things. I'll tell you what it's called in plain English. It's called plain stupid."

"I wasn't asking you," Auclair said. "It's something a girl like her would know."

"I don't know anything," she said, "because you won't tell me." She feigned departure. Auclair grabbed her handbag.

"I'll take you there," he said, "over to the other side of the lake, to the hole. And I'll tell you everything that happened to Henri Germaine."

Her watch said noon.

"Miss? Are you coming?"

Not knowing what she hoped to find on the far side of the pond, she followed.

The road snaked up the hill, then banged its head on a stone wall.

"Can you make it?" he asked.

She hiked up her skirt and climbed over. Her shoes sank in the mud. She crossed the misty pasture several paces ahead of Auclair. The ground smelled as if a woolly mammoth were entombed beneath it, thawing, decaying. Odd, she thought, that spring should bring decay. She looked down at her shoes and was glad for their mud; she wanted to cover herself in wet soil.

She kept walking. The ground sloped down to the pond. At its edge, two policemen balanced on their haunches above the rocky shore. When they saw their boss and a woman, they rose awkwardly.

"Hasn't moved yet, has he?" Auclair said.

The men laughed, too loudly, and for the first time she saw

the hole, two or three times the size of an ashcan lid, separated from safety by a thin band of honeycombed ice. One of the cops pulled a brown paper bag from his jacket, took out a sandwich and offered half to Auclair, who accepted.

12:15. She was on the wrong side of the pond, and she didn't know enough about Henri Germaine to compose a decent obit for him. She wouldn't be able to stay and watch the rescue. It wouldn't even be a rescue, really. Just a removal.

"You haven't told me anything," she said.

"Isn't much to tell. You know his name, don't you. Know he's down the hole."

"What about his age?"

Auclair bit his half of the sandwich. "Gus, you took the report, from the girlfriend. How old was the guy?"

"Old? Thirty-eight, I think. Same as my brother."

"And there was a girlfriend?"

"Some would call her different." Auclair winked. "Heels with hinges."

"Hinges?"

"You see that blonde thing at the cottage? Linda Looie. Seduced half the town before she was sixteen. And the mouth on that woman!" He rolled his eyes heavenward. "She was the one who brought him to the hospital last night. Said he cut his hand sawing wood. Gus can tell you the rest."

"Not much else to tell," the officer said. "Guy found out he was at the hospital and lit out."

"Didn't anyone try to find him last night?"

"Lots of anyones," Auclair said. "Best part of my goddamn force, if you'll pardon my language. And a dog. But it rained all night, in case you were inside. Awfully hard to track a man in the rain."

"But you looked all night?"

"Looked until twelve, one in the morning. Then the chopper came in and sighted the hole. Ice was so thin the rotors churned it to slush. You'd think a native like Germaine would know how thin the ice can get in March. Dumb woodchucks haven't the sense God gave them at birth." He unzipped his jacket and scratched his chest. "You might give the pilot credit. He is a vet, you know."

"But your men stopped searching at midnight, didn't they. And the pilot didn't start until morning."

Auclair cleared the last bite of sandwich from his throat. "What the hell are you driving at? You going to write about him, or about us? If you've got a gripe, spit it out and I'll answer."

She looked again at the hole and imagined a man sitting beneath the ice, as if he were hiding beneath the floorboards of an old cellar. She wanted to tell the cops to leave so he could come out. Instead, she turned and walked up the hill, reciting to herself: Cold Spring farmer, age thirty-eight, sawed off his hand and was found by Linda Looey, or maybe it was Louie, girlfriend of the deceased. . . .

She heard someone puffing. Auclair trotted to her side. "Aren't planning on . . . walking, are you? Won't make it before . . . deadline. I'll drive you."

She walked no slower, though his puffing worsened. They got back in his car, and all the way to the cottage she scribbled on her notepad, Auclair breaking into her thoughts only once, to ask if she'd ever seen a corpse. She shook her head no.

"It's a shame you'll miss seeing this one. Disappointed?"

Before she could catch herself, she'd nodded her head yes.

As soon as the car stopped, she jumped out. Linda Looie still sat on her rock, facing the far shore. The reporter decided that she didn't dare waste time interviewing the victim's girlfriend. At best, she would say that Henri Germaine was the finest man who'd ever lived. More likely, she would tell her to mind her own fucking business.

She fished the gold key ring from her handbag and opened the door. Seeing the white fleece rug she took off her shoes, but the wet dye of her stockings left faint prints anyway, a dotted black line that curved between white-shrouded couches and lacquered oriental chairs. Camphor and varnish embalmed everything. If she were to remain here too long, her memories would turn to parchment, preserved forever, just as her story would soon be preserved in the morgue at the paper.

On her knees beside a white marble table, she phoned her editor.

"Don't waste time explaining," he told her. "We're holding page one."

"He fell through the ice. He hurt his hand and fell through a hole in the ice."

"What kind of a lead is that, for Chrissake, 'He fell through the ice'?"

"Lead? You want me to write the lead—in my head?"

"I want you to write the whole fucking story in your head."

She thought for a moment. "Okay. This is my lead: 'He was afraid of doctors, and his fear killed him.' That's my lead." Then she gave him the facts, strung them together with prepositions and articles until they cohered in a semblance of sense. *"Henry Germane, 38, a Cold Spring farmer, died early this morning after misjudging the thickness of the ice on Empty Pond and drowning approximately fifteen yards from the shore."*

II.

The misfortunes that had dogged Henri Germaine's family since the mid-1940s still kept their neighbors from going to doctors. Henri's mother, Yvonne, had delivered her first two children at home with no complications, two healthy girls. But bearing the third child she'd gotten the jitters, couldn't see right, puffed up like a mushroom. One night, serving dinner, she had a fit, which scared her so badly she went to Doc Grant, who said that her blood pressure was high enough to turn a mill-wheel and checked her into the hospital for some bed rest, even though it was only her thirty-third week. Her pressure kept rising.

"Either I induce labor right now," the doctor told Yvonne's husband, "or your wife is going to lapse into coma."

Omer nodded and left the room. Seven hours later, the doctor told him he had a son.

"And Yvonne?" Omer asked.

"She's doing fine, but she'll have to sleep some." Then Dr. Grant put in a good word for hospital deliveries, hoping that

Omer would spread the gospel back in the hills. "She started bleeding quite badly. She's lucky that we had her here so we could pump more in. Wonderful development, these modern transfusions."

She died two days later. Omer took her home in the back of his pickup, holding the infant Henri on his lap as he drove. "Yvie went in with blood so strong it 'bout popped open her veins," Omer told the folks who came to pay their respects. "The doctors slowed her blood to ice, froze it down solid and killed her."

Omer did not speak to another doctor for seventeen years, not until the truck he was fixing slipped off its blocks and mangled his leg. He told his son Henri to sew up the leg. Henri went in for a needle and thread, but kept getting sick all over the barn, so Omer finally said to call Vernon Grant. The doctor came out to the barn, but refused to perform surgery in a pile of hay and manure.

"No hospital," Omer said.

"You'll get gangrene," Doc Grant told him.

"Then saw it off here."

The doctor shrugged, rolled up his shirt-sleeves and ordered Henri to bring him a saw. The boy threw up again. Omer gave in and let himself be loaded into Doc Grant's black Chrysler.

Henri stayed home from school the next day to do his father's chores, then walked the eighteen miles on the backroads to the hospital. The doctor intercepted him on his way out of Omer's room, led Henri into a small office and said in a kind but unyielding voice that Omer Germaine would be dead within a month—routine testing had shown him to have a highly advanced but as yet asymptomatic case of leukemia.

Henri made the trip to the hospital only once more before his father died, the funeral coming five days after Omer's accident with the pickup. Henri never returned to school. He took over the mortgage on the farm and worked his father's land as his own, never blaming Doc Grant for killing his father, not outright, in words. He only knew this: Omer Germaine had gone into Mercy with a busted leg, and he'd come out dead.

For more than ten years, Henri kept his distance from the

town, spoke as little as possible to the clerks in the seed store
and the other farmers at the Grange. The only women he saw
were the cooks to whom he delivered vegetables at the infir-
mary, the jail and the foster home. He hated those places, felt
wrong bringing food there. He only did it for the company, and
finally gave it up when Linda Looie came to live in his house.

She came in December, and by March his way of living had
changed greatly. In ten winters alone, he'd never let his cord-
wood get low, and now it was nearly gone. True, February had
been a cold month, but Linda liked a fire when it wasn't needed,
liked to lie naked in front of the fireplace until late at night,
naked on the hearth, lean and white, like a birch, white against
the reds and blues of the rag rug, white against the browns and
blacks on the floor. The fire would die down and Henri would
lift another log on the irons so he could watch as her ribs turned
amber in the flaring light. And all those long nights sent Henri
into the forest late one afternoon to cut more wood.

It wasn't winter and it wasn't spring, just March, chilly and
drizzling. Threads of mist drifted up the sides of the valley and
wove themselves into a fabric as dense as the mattress ticking
that once had been turned out by the town's mills. Henri swung
his chain saw. Its buzzing tore through the fog that blanketed
his land, let everyone know to whom it belonged. He thought
of Linda, washing herself in the bathtub where he'd left her,
soap on her stomach, blond hair dripping down her back, and
he knew that she could hear the buzzing, hear it and understand
this was his way of laying claim to her too. He rubbed his beard
and pushed his hair out of his eyes, under his cap. Gripping his
chain saw with both hands, he lifted it above his head to cut at
a thick branch hanging from a tall, dying tree.

If Henri had seen a less experienced cutter attempting to do
this, he would have told him to stop and sharply explained the
dangers of sawing a limb above eye level. But he was cocky
with the confidence of a man who'd grown up with a saw
vibrating in his arms, exuberant with his love for a woman
whose very existence seemed a miracle. He didn't even notice

the second dead branch dangling from the trunk so it rested its weight on the branch he was cutting.

His saw freed the first branch, it dropped to the ground, and at the same moment the hidden limb crashed on his head. It caught his left ear and thumped on his shoulder. He reeled. His arms flew around in front of his face like a wild bird. The saw twisted back and sliced through his hand, carving the meat and the bone so his right thumb and the flesh of his palm hung like a strap of leather. He threw the chain saw. Its blade screamed against a rock. The handle cracked, the buzzing stopped. He dropped to his knees. The hill flowed away, unprotected now that his saw no longer buzzed, and Henri Germaine slumped forward onto his land.

When he came to, he felt himself moving, leaning against a wall . . . a door . . . a window . . . his head so full he had to keep his eyes shut because if he took in one more thing it would burst. He reached up to touch his head and found that his hand was wrapped in a thick wad of cloth. Opening his eyes just a slit, he saw a windshield, a blurry dusk and two Lindas grasping two steering wheels. He rattled his head, but nothing helped. Linda's old flannel bathrobe swaddled his two right hands.

"Where we going?" he said.

"Three guesses."

"Can't guess. Hate guessing. Linda, I'm going to puke."

She stopped the truck, stretched over and wound down his window. "Puke then," she said. He leaned out and did, then fell back against the seat and closed his eyes. "Can't stand looking at me?" she said. "Can't stand looking at the woman who worried herself witless because you were too wooden-brained and selfish to take care with that buzz saw?"

"Where are we going, I say?"

Linda just drove.

"Where are you taking me?"

"Well, open your eyes and find out, we're there." She slid her leg and one arm out the door, pumped her horn and began waving. The horn made Henri's head pound and pound. Next thing he knew, the door on his side of the truck opened and some snotty kid in a white suit made a grab for his arm.

"Take it easy, mister," the kid said. "If you think you can't make it, I'll go get a wheelchair."

Henri looked around and saw he was in an empty parking lot. At one end he saw a big gray building with two sliding doors and a sign in red that said EMERGENCY. He pushed the orderly out of his way and got out of the truck. He lifted his good fist. "God damn it, Linda. You *knew*." He loped off across the parking lot, the orderly trotting after him, though Henri had a full head of height over the boy and a much stronger motive for moving quickly.

III.

Linda watched Henri vanish into the woods across from the hospital. Best not to follow when he thought she'd betrayed him. Let him ravage his anger on willows and wrens, waste it and spend it on his long walk home. When he found her again in the farmhouse, he wouldn't try to hurt her, just crook both elbows around her and say, "I know you did right," and lead her to bed.

So she stood and rubbed her hand on her forehead, watching as he ran from the hospital. The orderly went back into the emergency room and told the doctor on call what had happened. A squad car pulled up. One cop talked to the orderly while the other questioned Linda, asking for Henri's full name and address, age, occupation and relationship to her.

"I live with him," she said, and the cop wrote down "girlfriend." He asked her part in the accident. "I dragged him down from the woods," she said.

"Hasn't anyone ever told you not to move a man who's been hit on the head? How come you didn't call for an ambulance?"

She shrugged.

"So why'd he bolt? You fight or something, in the truck?"

"He's got some strange ideas is all, about hospitals."

"What sorts of ideas?"

"He doesn't like them."

The cop asked if Henri Germaine was a violent man.

She wanted to say that despite his temper, Henri Germaine was the gentlest man who'd ever touched her. Even the reverend up at the foster home where she used to work liked to get rough, feeling her up in the kitchen at night when no one was around and she might be too tired to fend him off. Well, she was never too tired to keep men like him from having their way, but Henri could have torn her apart like a chicken if he'd wanted, and yet the roughest he ever got was when he spread his fingers around her ribs and squeezed. He could feel her strength that way, he said; she looked so fragile, but he could feel her strength, and it drove him crazy.

"I'm asking you, ma'am. Is he violent?"

"No. No, he's not. But if you try and take him to a hospital, he'll fight you."

"What for, ma'am?" the cop said, writing "combative" on his pad. "What the hell for?"

She looked at the woods. It was getting late. "He don't like doctors," she said. "He . . . thinks they killed his dad. Now, aren't you going to look for him before he kills himself?"

She paced around the parking lot while five policemen, the whole force on duty, organized a line search of the land across from the hospital. Heavy fog filled the spaces between the trees; a steady cold rain wore at the snow until it washed away Henri's trail and his scent. The police refused to let Linda join in the search, so she took a flashlight and compass out of the truck's glove compartment and walked into the woods on her own.

She had left the farmhouse earlier that evening still wet from her bath, wearing nothing but a T-shirt, sneakers and jeans. After an hour in the rain, her feet and her arms went numb. She looked at the compass one last time, shook her head and sat on a stump. She heard a dog yapping.

"This way," a voice shouted through the fog. "He's over here."

"No," Linda said to the sergeant who shined his light in her eyes. "No, it's not him, only me. We must smell the same." She tried to convince the sergeant to let her help in the search, but again he refused.

"You'd get as lost as him, and we don't need the extra work of finding you both."

"Like hell I'd get lost. I got a compass."

"Look, lady, we're going to give up soon ourselves, just for the night. There's no sense of it in this weather. Can't pick up a trail."

"Maybe *you* can't, but I know where to look."

"He'll be all right. I've seen your boyfriend. He's a hearty fella. He'll make out fine. He's probably home in your bed right now."

She struggled to free herself from his grip. "You don't own the woods. Can't stop me from looking."

"City owns these woods. Means I could arrest you if I saw fit. I understand how upset you must be, but unless you let Officer Craw here take you on home . . ."

"I'll go," she said, and walked back the way she had come, Officer Craw close behind, following her in his car all the way to the farm.

When Linda got home, she changed into warm clothes and spent the night searching alone. At dawn, having found nothing but a deer and a mongrel, she returned home to attend to the milkings and feedings and muckings. At eight-thirty, she drove to the store down the road and called the police. Auclair informed her that his men had resumed their search, but couldn't find the trail. Two hours later, when the pilot spotted the hole, no one drove out to the farm to tell Linda; she only found out because she returned to the store at eleven and called the station again.

IV.

The troopers had vanished. Only Linda Looie remained on the shore, huddled now, a mottled egg.

"I didn't want to disturb you before," the reporter told her. "I only came over now to offer my condolences."

Linda kept staring across the lake. "They told you he was stupid, didn't they. Stupid, and crazy. And you'll write that, because you didn't have the guts to ask me. Afraid you'd catch some disease? He tell you I was a slut? Afraid you'd catch crabs?"

"I didn't want to—"

"Wasn't throwing no fit, was I? Speak English, can't I? Aw, forget it. Now you'll just say I didn't care none about him because I'm not crying." She got up and walked toward the road.

The reporter followed. "I could write another story. About what kind of man he was."

Linda turned around. "I'll tell you what kind of man he was. You take a map of this city, and you draw a line on that map. You draw a line between Mercy Hospital and Henri Germaine's farm, and you know what you'll get? You'll get fifteen miles of woods and hills, and you'll get Empty Pond, right on that line between Mercy and home. That's how stupid Henri Germaine was. A man gets his head knocked silly and his fingers sliced up, a man takes off into a night as black and slippery as the insides of a cow, nothing to guide him but his addled head, and he makes a straight line through the woods to his home. You think you could do that, smart lady? You think your fat-boy police chief could do that?"

"But shouldn't he have known about the ice being so thin?"

"He almost made it, didn't he? Only mistake Henri made was thinking he could swim those last fifteen yards with his hand torn to shreds and his head fit to explode. If it had been one shock, just cold water . . . It was the two shocks he misfigured."

"I'm sorry. I got it all wrong. I said Henri drowned just a few yards from shore. I mean, the side he started out from."

"Look, it wasn't you that killed him. He's dead now and I don't care two farts what anybody says about him. Only thing I care about is telling those cops they're dirty shits because they could have kept him from getting killed and they didn't."

"But they searched—"

"Weren't any real search, lady. Not 'til this morning. Last night they just said, 'Hell, we ain't staying out in weather like this for no farm boy. We're going to have us some coffee and go home to our wives.' "

"They couldn't see. There was no moon."

"Enough moon for Henri to see by, and he didn't have any big flashlights like those police boys. They killed him, not you."

"Maybe no one killed him. Maybe his fear of doctors was what killed him."

"Is that what you said? In the paper? You said his being afraid of doctors killed him? Like it was some sort of . . . jokey thing, like you read in a Ripley's? You think a man can die from a Ripley's?"

"If I could find out why he was afraid—"

"This isn't any Ripley's, and it isn't any Sherlock Holmes either. There ain't one clue you got to find out so you'll understand. It wasn't one thing made him afraid. It was lots of things in his life, all tied together. You'd have to know his life to understand, and I'm sure not going to freeze my tits off in this fucking cold telling you his life."

The reporter kept pleading. Linda shook her head. "You'd get it wrong. And even if you got it right, you tell me who'd care. Who'd want to read about a dirty farm boy with shit on his shoes and the slutty woman he took up with?"

She put out her hand. "They'd print it."

Linda backed away. "Maybe they would, but like I said, you wouldn't get it right." She climbed into the truck, leaned her head against the wheel for an instant, sat up. "And who'd care anyway," she said, and drove off.

The reporter thought of going back to the newsroom to write a second story. She didn't have all the facts, but maybe she had enough.

No, she didn't know a thing, really. Instead, she drove to the far side of the lake, then retraced her route across the field, a confusion of new tracks obscuring the old. She descended only far enough to view the shore. Auclair's men had been joined by two divers, who were still struggling into their wet suits. She looked across the choppy ice. The orange hunting cap still hung from the rim of the hole. A man is under the ice, she thought, and none of us can get him out.

NEVERSINK

NEVERSINK

The reservoir was low. Waiting in the bushes for Jack Noble's car, I searched the water's skin for the steeple of the church that lay drowned beneath. My father had explained how the village of Neversink had stood here until the late 1940s, when the river was dammed and the valley became a giant cup of water for thirsty New Yorkers a hundred miles south. He tried to convey his awe for this feat, but I wasn't impressed. New York was downhill. How hard could it be?

For me the magic lay in the name of the town. As a child, I had imagined God sending a flood to punish the boastful people who lived there. Sometimes I saw them swept up in a wave and tumbled about like clothes in a washer. At other times the water oozed from the ground; the people kept on with their everyday lives, silent as fish. If they ever repented their vanity and changed the name of their town, the flood would recede. I still searched for the steeple whenever I passed, maybe from habit, or maybe from a wish that forgiveness was possible, no matter the sin.

Jack's big green Ford swerved from the road. I left my bike hidden under a hedge and emerged, picking twigs from my hair. As I spit on my hand and rubbed the scratch on my arm, I felt like a child, but with every step I aged. By the time I reached the car and slid in the front, legs drawn in last, I was graceful and poised. I eased my dress down my thighs, faced Jack, then smiled a tiny, wry smile. Where had I learned such gestures as these? It was almost as if by reading Jack's mind I was able to learn how a woman should behave.

"You came," I said softly.

"What did you think, I'd let a woman stand in the middle of nowhere and just not show up?"

He had never been sarcastic. And he had always sped away as soon as I'd climbed into the car. Today he just sat there with the Ford's big engine idling, his muscular arms slung over the steering wheel, hands dangling as though he had broken his wrists.

"It's just that . . . I only . . ." The telepathy by which I sometimes was able to guess what to say had suddenly gone dead. Whenever this happened I tried to keep my mouth shut in the hope he would think me wise, enigmatic.

"Did you think I'd forget?" he asked. "You'd just slip my mind?"

How could I describe what it felt like to wait on a brilliant summer's day for a man who was nearly three times my age, my teacher at school, handsome, experienced. "Do you know when you're driving on a hot day like this and you see a mirage? A pool of water on the road?"

"Yeah?" he said. "I'm listening."

"Well, imagine you're thirsty. Very, very thirsty. And just when you get there, the water evaporates."

"Thirsty?" he said. "Is that how you feel?" He stopped scowling. But still the car sat there for anyone to see—my parents, his wife, someone from school or Colonial Conn.

"The fact is," he said, "I just stopped off to tell you that you'd better not come. It's not that I'm . . . How could I be tired of you? This has nothing to do with you."

Why didn't it, I thought. So many things that mattered in his life had nothing to do with me.

"I'm in a rotten mood, Dianne. Not many laughs today."

Should I really get out? I studied his face. He coached football at school and he had the stony features of a man used to hiding his strategy. With no clue from him, I simply said what I felt.

"I'd still like to come."

He nodded as though this confirmed some fine truth he had suspected about me. This happened all the time, which was one thing I loved about being with Jack.

"All right then," he said. He put the car in drive and finally pulled out. "But don't say I didn't warn you. This case we're on today, it isn't going to be any picnic."

Besides teaching history, Jack worked part-time for a firm that insured camps and resorts across the Northeast. With his "pull," as he called it, I had gotten a summer job at this company. Five days a week I sat by the switchboard with a pad of blank forms. Every few minutes the telephone rang, bringing reports of broken bones, cuts, and sometimes much worse. From Bar Harbor, Maine, to Cape May, New Jersey, middle-aged men like too-heavy pears were dropping from trees, Girl Scouts were taunting each other to taste bright orange toadstools. When I looked out the window next to my desk, I was startled to see that anyone made it down Main Street unscathed.

Something about insurance intrigued me. But I didn't want to sit in that office and get as spooked as the women who worked there all year. To hear them talk, booby traps lay beneath every pine cone and rock. They spent their vacations weeding their yards and would just as soon allow their children to play with poison and knives as to send them to camp.

The men who went out to investigate the accidents scoffed at such fears. They always found someone or something to blame, and this made them cocky, like soldiers who wrote home from the front: Don't worry, Mom, only the stupid fellows get killed.

So I jumped at Jack's offer to take me "out in the field" on my Saturdays off. What a wonderful game—sniffing out risks, judging who was at fault. I had to find out: What kind of man was Zachary Blunt to order his wife up on the roof of Finkelstein's Inn at three in the morning? And did Harriet Schliesser of Flushing, New York, really see a hand reach in her shower and turn off the cold water, and, if she did, why would this villain want to scald a naked old woman in her nineties?

"You'll make a hell of an adjustor," Jack told me. "I'll teach you everything I know, and Eicher will have to give you the job."

Mo Eicher, our boss, refused to let women out in the field. They were too soft, he said. They'd feel sorry for the claimants and pay them too much. Like Mo, Jack considered women a species apart. But the code that Jack followed said that a man had to be fair. And it surely wasn't fair that a "girl with my talents" shouldn't be allowed to be an adjustor.

"People tend to badmouth the profession," he said on our first trip together. "But that's a load of horseshit. The root of the word 'adjustor' is 'just.' Why is it wrong to go out, look around, get the truth down on paper and prove our insured isn't to blame before some shyster lawyer tries to palm off some lies? Now, if someone gets hurt and it *isn't* his fault, the company pays. I give him a check. I even kick in a little something extra for his suffering and pain."

This "little something extra" had gotten Jack in trouble with Mo. If a kid broke his leg, it was one thing to pay to have the leg set. But you couldn't measure suffering, Mo scolded Jack, so what in the world would you write on the check?

"He's just being cheap," Jack explained to me. "I mean, maybe I'm off by a dollar or two, but I usually can guess what their suffering is worth. And sometimes it's not the money at all. What I give to most claimants doesn't cost Mo a thing."

I didn't like when Jack called Mo Eicher cheap. Mo and I were both Jews. But Mo *did* find it hard to part with a dime. The switchboard was old and its wires so frayed that it cut people off and I had to apologize. And Jack's view of life, whether Catholic or not, had its appeal. Someone was liable for every mistake, and that someone paid. Whoever got hurt received compensation.

And so, on our trips, Jack catechized me in this doctrine of risk, cause and effect, suffering and pain. He had reached middle age and he feared he would die without having taught someone everything he knew. I was willing to learn. The autumn before, when I'd been in his class, he had taken us to Gettysburg. We could barely keep up as he scrambled over fences and up and down hills describing how the soldiers— boys our own age—had run here and there, blinded by smoke, as frightened and confused as we would have been, stumbling over friends who cried out for help. It was even more exciting to be alone with Jack, to hear him describe not a long-ago battle but the world I could see from his car as we drove. I didn't have a vision—things always seemed to go by in a blur—and Jack gave me his. The name of a town or a marker by the road, the sign for a camp where he had handled a case would set off a story about some evil person who wreaked terrible harm, and then, in a chain of cause and effect, brought his own demise. ("Take Nixon," he said as we listened to the hearings. "He's like some old lady who's too vain to wear sensible shoes. She falls on her ass, and she blames the hotel instead of the three-inch spikes on her heels.")

But today Jack was silent all the way across western New York. Finally, when we passed the sign that said WELCOME TO PENNSYL-VANIA, he peered in both mirrors and blew out a sigh.

"If you want the report for today's case," he said, "it's back there, in my bag. Tell me when you're finished," as though he would quiz me on what I had read.

I found his heavy briefcase between two smaller bookbags in green and blue plaid, the kind that kids carry at parochial school. His wife's umbrella lay across the rear shelf. Just a few days before this I had seen Helen Noble struggling up the hill from the store to their house, clutching groceries to her chest and holding aloft this very umbrella, which showed cats and dogs tumbling through a cloudy pink sky. It hadn't rained for weeks, and even when I realized that she must have been shielding her skin from the sun, her face was so grim and her hair so unkempt that she seemed half-insane. Not only was Jack's wife too broad in the rear, she also was cracked! I was relieved, as though this could absolve me for wishing her dead.

I leafed through Jack's bag and pulled out a sheet labeled ACCIDENT REPORT. Under each heading someone had noted the facts of the case in a big childish script; even the f's and l's were so round that I expected to see a smiley face in each.

DATE OF OCCURRENCE: July 21, 1973, 4:05 p.m.
LOCATION OF OCCURRENCE: on the rifel range of Camp Fratrnity, in Pocono, P.A.
DESCRIPTION OF CLAIMANT: Sebastien Soole, mail, aged elven . . .

It must have been Bunny who had taken the report. Not only wouldn't Bunny look up a word, if an accident bored her she made up details ("Tatoo of Elvis on left butock" she had written of an elderly man who had slipped in the tub). When *I* wrote reports, I thought of myself as a biblical scribe. I treated an outbreak of diarrhea caused by a spoiled batch of liver as solemnly as a plague wrought by God. An old Jewish man who owned a hotel would say on the phone: "Just a minor haxident, a bruise and a cut." And, with a flourish, I would inscribe on my pad: "The claimant fell and suffered hematomas, abrasions, contusions and lacerations to the right knee."

I wished I could use a fountain pen, a quill, but that wouldn't have worked. Whatever I wrote had to echo itself on the sheet underneath, and the sheet under that, fainter each time, in lavender ink (ALL NEW MAGIC CARBON, it said on the form). I would clip the original sheet to the file, then give the yellow copy to the adjustor who would handle the case. No one had told me what the third sheets were for. I stashed them in my desk, hoping to someday put them to use, compile the best accidents in a chronicle to rival Exodus or Job.

I picked up the yellow sheet from my lap.

MANNER OF OCCURRENCE: Claimant was particpating in weekly lessen on rifelry. Claimant was laying on blanket on rifelry field, trying to hit targit. Claimant called over counslor and said his gun didn't work, it was stuck. Counslor picked up gun by handel. Rifel went off, hitting claimant in groin regin.
NATURE OF INJURIES: Bullit entered public area, travling thru claimant's penis and testies . . .

Jack punched the button for the lighter on the dash. "Eleven-year-old kid with his manhood shot off. And we're totally liable! Not much I can do except pick up the pieces."

I pictured Jack on his knees on the "rifel range," searching for the boy's missing piece. If somebody found it, would the doctors be able to sew it back on? If not, could they make Sebastien a new one, of rubber, with a winch to make it stand up? The thought made me laugh.

I expected Jack to say, "Perhaps you can share the joke with the class," but he was absorbed in plucking a Pall Mall from its pack with his lips. The lighter popped out of the dashboard. When Jack touched it to his cigarette, it made a dry hiss. My parents didn't smoke, so whenever someone used the lighter in his car he seemed to possess some secret power that my family didn't have, as Jack had the power to feel this boy's pain and I was left cold. (Not that his face showed what he felt. But inside, I could tell, Jack's passions glowed like those hidden red coils.)

Maybe if I'd had a penis myself, I could have understood what it would mean to have it shot off. Hadn't the girls, less squeamish for once, laughed at the boys who writhed in their seats when the rabbi described the way Abraham had sealed his covenant with God? Then again, as Mo said, girls were supposed to be softer than boys. Never mind a penis, what I lacked was some organ of sympathy that other girls had. Or maybe I had one, but, like the lighter in my parents' Pontiac, it had never been used. If I wanted to be an adjustor like Jack, I would have to learn to measure suffering and pain.

I gave it a try. I envisioned a boy who stood weeping in the showers as his classmates pranced around him, naked as imps, and tried to snatch the towel he clutched to his waist.

The only emotions this scene made me feel were a mild titillation and an urge to snatch away that towel myself. Ashamed, I tried harder. He was older, a man now, staring out a window at a woman, at *me*. His nails scraped the glass. He would never make love (this gave me a pang, but for my loss, not his). He would never have children. How did that feel? I was tired of hearing thirdhand reports. Who was this boy with his manhood shot off? I had to find out. Would I ever get to meet him? And, if I did, was it better to remain objective, as Mo seemed to think, or sympathetic, like Jack?

"I'll tell you," Jack said, his thumb and index finger rubbing his eyes against the sun's glare, or maybe the smoke from his cigarette, "when that mother's phone rang, and she picked it up and heard, 'I'm calling from camp. It's your son. He's been shot,' you know what she felt? Here's what she felt. She was standing on a railroad track and she saw a train coming. It was moving so slow that she wasn't afraid. She'd step out of the way long before it got to her. But she couldn't move her legs. And then the train hit."

It was hopeless, I thought. I could never compete with Jack. Not only could he feel the boy's suffering, he felt the parents' as well; he had three sons himself, twins a year older than Sebastien Soole, and a boy in ninth grade. (He also had three daughters. In what organ did their "womanhood" abide?)

He leaned so far back that he seemed to be driving with his eyes on the roof. "I warned you I'd be lousy company today."

If only I could cross the distance between us on that hot plastic seat . . . But how could I comfort someone like Jack? He gave and I took. All I could offer was my blankness, my youth.

We turned off the highway at the exit for the Poconos. I held my arm out the window. The maple trees came right to the road; their leaves slapped my palm. An insect smacked my wrist and fell like a stone. I took a deep breath: melting tar, dry grass, hot vinyl, smoke, the detergent Helen used to launder Jack's shirt. On Saturdays, with Jack, each sight, sound and smell seemed like a letter in a language that I had only started to learn.

He stubbed out his cigarette in the tray beneath the radio. I had to avert my eyes from his hands. Not a boy's hands, as smooth as a bar of wet soap. Rough, callused hands. If they touched you, they would leave a mark on your skin. I imagined how they'd feel on my neck, on my breasts. I was almost content with all Jack had taught me about insurance and history, but I hoped he would someday throw in a lesson on how to make love.

"Hold onto your horses!" He laughed like a man who knows that he's been gloomy too long. The car dove in a creek and ploughed through the water. "It's been five years, at least, since that bridge washed away. I keep telling the people who own the camp that they ought to put up a new one. Engine gets wet and Colonial Conn has to pay for a car."

They hadn't even bothered to fix the arch across the entrance—most of the sticks that had spelled the camp's name were broken or missing; the ones that remained formed a pattern as mysterious as runes on a stone.

We parked on a patch of dirt ringed by logs and walked through the camp. "Okay then," Jack said, "tell me what you see," a game he had invented called "Spotting the Risk."

What did I see? A cluster of tents made of dirty, torn canvas. A wooden pole with no flag. We seemed to have stumbled on the encampment of some defeated army. Most of the soldiers already had fled. Half-deflated kickballs, broken bows and bats lay strewn on the ground. A boy dragged a duffel bag out of his tent; from the way he hung his head and tugged at the cord, it seemed to contain all the bad dreams he and his tentmates had dreamed for a month. Another boy was throwing darts at a bird.

"Shouldn't someone be watching the kids who are left?"

At long last Jack smiled. "People wonder why accidents happen in twos and threes, but now you see why. When one kid gets hurt they forget about the rest."

He led me to a cabin a little way off from the main part of camp. Its mottled walls blended so well with the leaves it could barely be seen. Inside, it was furnished with a cot and two chairs. An elderly couple sat on the chairs, so desperately sad they gave the room the feel of a cell on death row. Even in July they huddled inside misshapen sweaters that hung to their knees. The sweaters had frayed, and the old people seemed to have unravelled as well.

"Adelaide. Paul." I waited for Jack to reproach our insureds. Their neglect was so clear! Instead, he patted the hump on the old woman's back. "Don't worry," he told her. "You won't lose the place. We'll pay the boy's bills. We'll defend you in court, if it comes to that."

"Who cares for the court." She had some sort of accent, maybe German, or French. "It is better they should lock us away. It is better they should line us up on the wall and shoot with the gun."

"The whole life," Paul moaned. "To think the whole life should come to this end."

"Now Addy. Now Paul." He cradled Paul's hands in one of his own. "That isn't God's way. It's not like a race, where only the end matters. He knows what you've been through. He'll weigh the good with the bad."

Paul moaned again, then pressed his face to Jack's knuckles and cried.

I turned away, as though the old people's torment were an unpleasant smell. Lining the walls were every sort of artifact a camper could make from shells, macaroni, clay, acorns, leaves and popsicle sticks. A few objects had decayed so completely they had left a thin layer of loam on the shelf. I lifted an ashtray modeled in the shape of a small hand. TO ADDY AND PAUL LOVE PATTI '49 was inscribed on the bottom.

"It is our fault, our fault." Addy yanked at her tufts of gray hair. "Put *that* on your paper!"

Jack was trying to take a statement from Paul. "All the court will want to know is whether you saw the accident or not, how you found out, what you did then. Just keep to the facts—when you bought the rifles, when they were last cleaned and repaired. Save the guilt part for me."

Paul bowed his head and murmured an answer to whatever Jack asked. Then his wife did the same. Jack slid their statements into his briefcase as tenderly as though he were handling their wills. When we left they were calm, hands on their laps and chins on their chests.

He didn't show me their statements, as he usually did, pointing out some phrase that wasn't quite a lie but would help our attorneys defend our insureds. As we walked across the camp we no longer bothered playing our game. What was the point? The risks were as obvious as the shiny red ivy leaves choking our path.

The rifle range was just a bumpy field in which big paper bull's-eyes kept watch over a row of moth-eaten blankets. While Jack took some photos to document that nothing about the range was amiss—the problem was that it existed at all—I knelt by a square of flattened grass and searched for spatters of blood, hoping these would remind me that Sebastien Soule was the one who had been hurt, not Addy or Paul. They were old and pathetic, but how did that excuse them for ruining a life? I would have asked Jack, but I didn't see him anywhere, and this made me nervous.

I found him at last outside the latrines. The stench there was foul. He went in to use one, and when he came out he was shaking his head.

"What's the matter?" I asked. "Don't tell me you found another risk in there."

He worked the handle of a pump, cupped water in his palms and buried his face.

"Didn't you hear what I said, Jack?" Okay, he had warned me not to come on this trip, but I couldn't have imagined he would be so distraught over someone else's troubles. Not for so long.

He wiped his face on his shirttail, then tucked it back in. He seemed surprised I was there. "Oh," he said, "it's nothing. It's just I was thinking . . . Years ago, in its time, this camp wasn't bad. They had a way with kids. But then they got old. They couldn't keep it up. And a rifle range! In this day and age of liability! If I told them once I told them fifty times they were asking for trouble. But after all they'd been through, over there, in Europe . . . Addy thought that children ought to be able to defend themselves, in case it happened again."

He was trying to confuse me. If this had been a trial, the judge would have ruled this story inadmissible. Like any good juror I should stop up my ears. "Shouldn't we talk to the counselor? They said he would be leaving pretty soon."

Jack looked at me and nodded. "You're right," he said. "We'd better."

We found him in his tent, slouched on his cot. He was already packed, except for some photos. He was only a year or two older than I was, with pale yellow hair and a face round and blank as the top of a corn muffin. He told Jack what had happened in an agitated way, confessing as quickly and completely as possible to show he was innocent, not of the crime, but of evil intent.

"I'm really just in charge of nature," he said. He only had agreed to supervise the range as a favor to his bunkmate. "I shot a boy. I shot him!" He pounded the mattress. Little flakes of rust snowed to the floor. "I wanted to do something worthwhile with my life, but with *this* in my files . . ."

What files did he mean? Did this muffin-faced boy think God

would keep a file on a life such as his? If He *did* keep such files, I hoped that He kept them in real metal drawers instead of old shoe boxes such as Mo brought to the office; I imagined the boxes in heaven collapsing, as ours often did, and folders raining down, everyone scrambling to find his or her file and read what God had written there over the years.

By now the boy was crying. "I mean, never mind I shot him, what kind of person would stand there and watch while a little kid bled?" He picked up a photo. I could see a family posed by a barbecue pit. "You know what my mother told me before I came up here? She said, 'Scottie, you're my life. You're the reason I've lived. Be careful, because if anything were to happen to you, I don't know what I would do.' "

He flung himself face down on his cot, crushing the photos. He was begging for comfort, as obvious as a five-year-old child.

Jack sat on the cot, which squeaked beneath his weight. "Listen," he said, "did you do it on purpose?"

"On purpose?" The counselor twisted his head. "Of course I didn't!"

"So what caused it?"

"What caused what?"

"You did a favor for a friend, right? This friend of yours shouldn't have left you in charge of those guns."

The boy slowly sat up.

"And what else?" Jack asked. "You were standing there, right, and the kid called you over? Why'd he call you over?"

"He said his gun was stuck."

"Well, was it?"

"I don't think so. He was kind of, well, clumsy. On this nature hike we took, he tried to carve a slingshot like this other kid had. He couldn't get it to work. He threw down the knife and it sliced his shin. I was like that once. I hated to watch how unhappy he'd make himself. I thought, with this gun, I could fix it before he got frustrated, hurt himself."

"So the accident happened because you did a friend a favor. And you felt sorry for the kid."

"I was careless!" he said. "What kind of jerk picks up a gun by the handle!"

"All right, you were careless. You were a jerk. You did a terrible thing. Did you think you were going to lead a perfect life? What are you going to do now, kill yourself because you've made a big mistake? Is that going to help the world? Will that help your mother, if you waste the rest of your life because you made one bad mistake? You're the reason she's lived. You want to waste *her* life?"

The kid wiped his nose. He sighed and took a breath. "You're right," he said. "I know. I just had to hear someone tell me the truth."

Jack pulled out his pad. "Okay then," he said, "tell me what happened—what you did, what you saw."

Did he really believe what he had said to this boy? Or was he just trying to keep the boy's guilt from leaking all over the statement, which was meant to help our insureds? What gave Jack the right to comfort this boy? He wasn't the one who had been hurt.

The counselor stood from the cot. He was taller than Jack, who was over six feet. "Thank you," he said, pumping Jack's hand. He held it so long I thought he would kiss the fingers, as Paul had. It was his fault, I thought. But then, Jack hadn't said it wasn't.

On our way to the car we stopped to see the nurse. She was Jack's age, very black, though she'd dyed her hair red. In her stretchy white uniform she was shaped like a backwards S. She stood before a cabinet sorting through a jumble of Band-Aids and gauze, tongue depressors, gum and Tootsie Roll Pops. Jack sat on a trunk, his ankle on his knee, and took down what she said. He didn't need to first absolve her of guilt. This was a woman who had never blamed herself for anything for which she wasn't to blame.

"Good thing *somebody* kept a head on her shoulders." Her tongue, which was pink as a stick of Dentyne, tsk-ed against her teeth. "Lord, when something like this happens, people seem to have nothing better to do than stand around and argue! I wouldn't have been surprised if all three of them—Addy and Paul, and that boy who did the shooting—had started fighting for that gun, who had the most right to shoot themselves. 'It was my fault.' 'No, *my* fault.' And there I am, on my knees, shouting for an ambulance and trying my best to keep that poor boy from bleeding to death."

Jack said, "Maureen, you don't think they'd do it? Addy and Paul?"

She locked up the cabinet. "Nah. They're too dead to kill themselves. 'Cept they don't eat. I'll watch out they eat."

He patted her back, just above the bottom curve of the S. She slapped away his hand. Then she turned and saw me by the door of the cabin. "What's the matter?" she asked. She held out a Band-Aid. "Tell Maureen where it hurts."

Jack clicked shut his pen and put away his pad. "Her?" he said. "Dianne. My assistant, Dianne."

"Your *assistant*?" She laughed. "Girl, whatever you're *assisting* this man with, watch out."

Before this, I had wanted people to assume I was sleeping with Jack, even though we weren't. But now I wasn't sure. I couldn't meet her eyes.

"Ooh, girl, I can see it. You're gonna get your heart broke. Better take one of these." She waved the Band-Aid in my face. I didn't want to accept it. Until now I had never admitted that I cared if Jack loved me or not, cared that he was married and wouldn't leave his wife for a girl of sixteen. The risk was so clear! Why not stop now, before I got hurt?

I looked over at Jack. I willed him to say, "Don't be crazy, Maureen. I'm teaching her about insurance, that's all." But he didn't say a word. He fiddled with his pen. He uncrossed his legs, then crossed them again the opposite way. How could she have said such things in his presence! I wanted to run.

"Come here, girl," she said. She took a step closer. "Maureen was just kidding." She put her arms around me. She smelled of clean nylon, iodine and salves. If Jack hadn't been there, I would have tried to stay in her arms for a month. And I understood then there are two kinds of people: the kind who need comfort and the kind who need to give it, and I wasn't sure yet which I wanted to be.

The grass around the hospital was so high that it hid the pedestal and feet of the statue of St. Joseph. I wondered how Catholics decided which saint to name a hospital after. It wasn't as though a particular saint had donated money. Did the priests take a vote? Did this or that saint specialize in curing certain diseases but refuse to treat others?

No one sat behind the information desk, but Jack said we could find Sebastien's room simply by reading the names on the doors. We didn't see a doctor, only a nun in a habit so gray that she almost was invisible against the gray walls.

"Should we be here?" I asked.

Jack took this to be a question of ethics. "I'm not fooling myself that we'll settle the case. But if we talk to the parents, maybe they won't think we're such ogres. And maybe, if they let me talk to the boy, I might get a statement that's close to the truth before some lawyer in the city slants things his way."

We came to a room in which a woman sat knitting, and a man in Bermudas and a wrinkled madras shirt was eating a sandwich, a messy submarine whose sausagey smell permeated the room. In the bed lay a boy, covered from his ankles to his neck by a sheet. A squadron of paper airplanes lay on the floor in a ring around his bed. The boy looked like one himself, delicate but gawky, a plane that wouldn't glide. He was so very young! It struck me that he probably didn't understand any better than I did what a wound like his meant.

Jack knocked on the door frame. The woman dropped her needles.

"I'm Jack Noble," he said. "I know this is hard. I won't stay too long."

"Who are you, the priest or something?" asked the father. "You the chaplain at this lousy excuse for a hospital?"

Jack seemed to regret that he had to say no. "I'm the adjustor from Colonial Connecticut. We insure the camp. I just want—"

The man jumped from his chair. Still holding his sandwich, he danced around the room, trampling planes underfoot. "I know what you want! How dare you come here! You ambulance chaser, you!"

The boy cringed. He pulled his sheet to his eyes. "Dad!" he said. "Oh, *Dad*."

Jack moved toward the boy. He held out his hand.

The man slapped it away—not in jest, like Maureen, but as hard as he could. "Get out of here! Don't go near my boy! You want us to sign something that says it was all Sebby's fault! You think I'm an idiot? You think I haven't already gotten the best lawyer I could afford? Maybe those two senile old wrecks can't make good what we lost, but I sure as hell can get some money from your company!"

When Jack finally spoke, his restraint made his words worse than a shout. "*You* didn't lose anything. You know how lucky you are? All right, it's pretty bad for your kid. I admit that, I'm sorry. But I'd trade in a minute. In a minute, you hear? Take your lawsuit and lawyer—" Jack's fist flew up, but he turned and stalked away before it could strike.

By the time I reached the car, Jack was already gunning the gas. I scrambled in beside him. He sped past the stop sign and took the next curve in the on-coming lane. By then, the world seemed so full of dangers that it was almost a relief to know how I would die, in a crash in Jack's Ford. We were nowhere near anything. He was arguing with someone, moving his lips, and I couldn't interrupt to ask why he had been so kind to the people to blame for the shooting and so harsh with the father of the boy who had been shot.

"Damn," he said finally. He lit his cigarette, shook the lighter as though to put out a match, then threw the lighter out the window. It hit the pavement and bounced. He saw what he had done, slammed on the brakes, flung the door open and began kicking through the grass.

I got out to help and found it in a minute. I gave it to Jack. He slumped on a rock and rolled the dented lighter between his palms.

"It doesn't matter if Mo fires me," he said. "I couldn't let it go. 'What *we* lost!' The jerk! He sent away his son. I'll bet he didn't even check out the place first. He picked it from a magazine. And he *is* goddamn lucky. All right, so the kid lost his prick and his balls. He can have operations. He won't die from losing his prick and his balls."

That's when he told me that his eldest son, Hugh, had gone for his physical to play football that fall for the junior-varsity team. What are all those bruises? the doctor had asked. (*Contusions*, I thought.) Are you tired a lot?

Oh yeah, but it's nothing, Hugh told the man. It's just I've been running some plays with my brothers. They hit pretty hard for little kids. And I'm not in great shape, so I can't catch my breath.

But the doctor was suspicious. He ordered some blood tests, and, as it turned out, Hugh was pretty far gone.

Earlier that summer, I had overheard Jack tell another adjustor how much he looked forward to coaching his son in another year or two, when he made the varsity team. Hugh was a born wingback, he said. How magical that had sounded, as though Hugh had the power to lift himself over the other boys' heads. Now, as Jack spoke, I imagined a very pale, shrunken Hugh going out for a pass. He couldn't lift his arms and the ball smacked his chest. A magnificent bruise bloomed on his skin.

"It doesn't make sense," Jack said to me now, crouching on that rock. "Why would God punish Hugh for *my* sins?"

Something was wrong with his logic, I was sure. But I had come to regard him as an expert in matters of cause and effect, so I let him go on.

"The others didn't count. They weren't whores exactly, but they knew what they were doing. And I did it for Helen. She sure didn't need any more kids. But a girl like you . . . How can I fool myself? You're for my sake, not hers."

Was he saying it was *my* fault that his son had leukemia? "But you never even kissed me!"

"In my *mind* . . . in my *thoughts* . . ."

So he had felt what I'd felt. He hadn't just asked me along for the ride. What had we done in his mind? Was it sinful enough to cause his son's death? It was frightening that our thoughts, let alone our actions, could matter so much. But it would have been even more frightening if they hadn't mattered at all, if death could strike anyone. That I could inflict suffering on such a grand scale made me godlike myself.

"Maybe I should go. I can find a way home. I can hitch. Or find a bus."

"I told you before, this has nothing to do with you. I'll take you home, of course. But not right away. Helen's there, in the kitchen. It's her fault, she says, cancer runs in her family. And she should have noticed sooner, about the bruises. I can't face that right now. And Hugh. And the other kids . . . I don't have it in me. Not yet, at any rate." He stood from the rock. He wobbled a bit. "I need to clear my head. I'll go for a walk. Then I'll be fine. I'll drive you home." He climbed a broken wire fence and walked across the pasture.

A sheet of inky clouds, thin as a blotter, covered the field. In the heat the crickets sang like tropical birds straining toward speech. And I finally understood this language of the senses, the meaning of these sights, odors and sounds. They meant that I was alive to see, smell and hear them. After Hugh died, he wouldn't see or feel.

I came upon Jack lying face-down in the grass, his head on his arms.

"Oh God, oh Christ."

He was asking for pity. He was glad I was there, watching this show.

"If thy right hand offend thee, cut it off. . . ." His voice was so muffled that I barely could make out the words. "For it is profitable that one of thy members should perish, and not that thy whole body should be cast into hell."

Hadn't Jack told me that if you had faith, you would receive compensation for your suffering and pain? According to Jack, God had sent Christ out in the field to learn to adjust the claims of the soul. Well, it didn't seem to work. I wanted Jesus Christ to appear in this field and make Jack feel better, as Jack himself had done for Addy and Paul and the counselor who had shot Sebastien.

"It's my fault. My fault."

So what if it was? Should he cut off his hand? (Or his

manhood, I thought.) Even if Jack had caused his own grief, did that give me the right to walk away and leave him?

I knelt by his side. I smoothed his ruffled hair, ran my hand along his shoulders, then down his spine. He started to shake. I bent over and pressed my face to his neck. And, as I did so, I could feel what he was feeling, hear what he was thinking: *A few months from now, my son will be rotting in a box in the ground. My sins caused his death.* And some horror much worse that I couldn't put in words.

I had never known anything like it before. Had I had this capacity all the time and not used it? Or had it come now, in a moment of grace?

I felt Helen's grief too, as though love were the ink on a sheet of Magic Carbon, transmitting copy after copy, weak but still faithful, of other people's pain. She sat in her kitchen, her son very sick and her husband out somewhere, maybe at work, or maybe with a whore, or with one of his students. She trudged up that hill with food for her children and soap for Jack's shirts, braving a storm that no one else saw. But even at the moment that I felt Helen's pain, I also understood that I had to ease Jack's.

The grass that we lay on was dry from the drought, but comfort seemed to flow from my hands like a stream that seeped up from somewhere deep underground.

All through that summer I comforted Jack. After Hugh died, Helen wouldn't leave her room. What I did wasn't right. But I like to think that Jack was able to hold his family together because I consoled him.

On the ride home that evening I sat very close to Jack. I didn't want to let him think his own thoughts, but I dropped off to sleep. I awoke with his arm draped around my shoulders, my head on his neck.

"Thanks for coming," he said. "I'm glad you decided to come."

He looked at me the way he did when I asked a question in class, shaking his head because even though he knew the answer, it would be too hard to explain. He ran a knuckle down my cheek. Then he kissed me good-bye. And he kissed me again, with gratitude, and love, and finally with desire, which also gripped me.

"See you Monday," he said. He leaned across my lap and opened my door.

I watched as his tail lights traced a red line over the dam, then I pushed through the hedge to look for my bike. There was no moon that night, and I couldn't even catch a glint from the frame. I started to panic, until my legs brushed the handlebars.

I pedaled towards home, rehearsing the excuse I would make to my parents. The road across the spillway was so narrow and dark that I stopped in the middle, straddling my bike.

The dam had to have a valve. What if I turned it? The steeple of the church would reappear first, then the roofs of the houses. The people of Neversink, repentant or not, would arise the next morning, dry themselves off and try to make up for the long years they had missed.

I worked my way through college as an adjustor for a much larger company than Colonial Conn; the boss wouldn't allow any adjustor, female or male, to offer claimants money for their suffering and pain, but, as Jack had told me, what most of them wanted had little to do with the figure on a check.

After graduation, I got a job teaching history in a town outside Reading. Every fall I took my class on a trip to the battlefield at Gettysburg, as Jack had once done. I knew he lived in Pittsburgh, and I knew he loved the park, so I wasn't surprised when I saw him there finally. The place, after all, is a monument to ghosts.

What surprised me about seeing Jack in the lot as we filed off the bus was how guilty I felt. I had to remind myself that I hadn't killed Hugh. I had hurt Helen, not Jack.

We couldn't really talk. I'm doing well, he said. The family is fine.

"This is Jack Noble," I said to my class. "He was *my* teacher," I told them, as though being links in a chain would make them more important than they were in themselves.

They must have guessed that Jack had been more than my

teacher—kids always can sense something like that. I still thought him handsome, though gaunt and distracted. His hands no longer seemed large enough to spread across the shoulders of a big high school lineman.

He had given up teaching sixteen years earlier. He looked at my class so wistfully that, on an impulse, I asked him to lead our tour of the park.

At first he seemed wary. Then he roused himself and said that he would be glad to. He gained more and more vigor as he strode around the park, describing this or that skirmish or flanking maneuver.

He tried to make certain that my students understood what had caused the deaths of so many boys. "Those who cannot remember the past are condemned to repeat it," he said, as every history teacher does.

He had taught this same lesson when I had been here the first time. Because I had loved Jack even then, I had believed him.

But now I wasn't sure. Was it really so vital to know whom to blame for the thousands who died? It's the virtue of the human mind that it tries to judge who's at fault. But it's the virtue of the heart that it sometimes forgets.

After the battle, thousands of wounded Confederate soldiers were left to the mercy of the people of Gettysburg. What if I'd been a farm wife, I wondered, with all those wounded Rebels moaning for water not far from my house? They had brought it on themselves, fighting for a cause that couldn't be more wrong. They had killed other men.

But as Jack went on talking, describing the charge up Cemetery Ridge, I saw myself kneeling next to some dying soldier, his face sometimes Hugh's, sometimes the face of a boy in my class. He strained to sit up, as my own son strains forward when he is eager to nurse, and I leaned down to offer what comfort I could.

ABOUT THE AUTHOR

Eileen Pollack grew up in Liberty, New York. She has received fellowships from the Michener Foundation and the MacDowell Colony, and her stories have appeared in such magazines as *Ploughshares, Prairie Schooner, The Literary Review, The Agni Review, Playgirl, Sojourner* and *North Dakota Quarterly*, as well as in *The New Generation*, an anthology of fiction. She lives in Belmont, Massachusetts, and teaches at Tufts University.